Z IS FOR ZOMBIE

OTHER BOOKS IN THE ARGOSY LIBRARY:

Kingdom Come

BY MARTIN MCCALL

Henry Rides the Danger Trail: The Complete Tales of Sheriff Henry, Volume 3

BY W.C. TUTTLE

The Bait and the Trap: The Complete Adventures of Tizzo, Volume 2

BY MAX BRAND

Minions of Mars

BY WILLIAM GRAY BEYER

Swords in Exile: The Rakehelly Adventures of Cleve and d'Entreville, Volume 2

BY MURRAY R. MONTGOMERY

Men With No Master: The Complete Adventures of Robin the Bombardier

BY ROY DE S. HORN

The Torch

BY JACK BECHDOLT

King of Chaos and Other Adventures: The Johnston McCulley Omnibus

BY JOHNSTON MCCULLEY

The Blind Spot

BY AUSTIN HALL & HOMER EON FLINT

Z IS FOR ZOMBIE

THEODORE ROSCOE

ILLUSTRATED BY

V.E. PYLES

STEEGER BOOKS • 2019

PUBLISHING HISTORY

"Z is for Zombie" originally appeared in the February 6, 13, 20, 27, March 6, and 13, 1937 issues of *Argosy* magazine (Vol. 270, No. 5–Vol. 271, No. 4).

Visit steegerbooks.com for more books like this.

CHAPTER I

THE TAFFY-HAIRED MAN

THE TAFFY-HAIRED MAN said, "Get out of here! *'Raus mit!*" His voice was slow, husky, a male imitation of Garbo's.

Ranier stood up to return the stare. There seemed to be four taffy-haired men, four faces spread fan-wise like a handful of playing cards. The doorway behind them was a blur; and the four faces scowled, then swam together, came into focus as a single face, a German countenance—taffy shoebrush hair, granular yellow eyelashes and little camera-lens eyes in a face as white as a plaster cast.

Ranier didn't like it, but he hiccoughed hospitably, "Y'want me t'shove off? Why? 'Sa big world."

The camera-lens eyes seemed to take his picture. The voice from the plaster-cast face said thickly, "I said for you to get out. Now! *Macht schnell!*"

Ranier looked around in indignant astonishment to see if anyone else could be hearing this. But the café was otherwise unpopulated; Hyacinth Lucien, Haitian proprietor of the place, had gone out back to milk a goat. Ranier had been keeping his own council; drinking, here, in solitude. He turned to give the man who had interrupted him from the doorway a challenging, "Says you!" but the pale German never gave him a chance.

It was over before Ranier could re-focus his glare. A cruel blow glancing off the side of his jaw. A hand snatching him by the lapel, yanking him off balance, propelling him in a body-twist through the door. Shoved, he went stumbling across a dark

"Dead!" she cried. "Dead for fourteen years!"

verandah, caromed off a post, floundered backwards into night, and turned his lame foot on loose gravel.

THE SPRAWL must have knocked him out. He wondered afterwards if his head had struck a knuckle of coral, for he came to wandering lamely in wet fog around the side of the ramshackle building. He felt as if he'd been walking in his sleep. What with liquor and that blow and this wool-thick mist in night, it was hard to chart his bearings.... This was the Blue Kitty Café. A goat's bleat came from somewhere in the rear, and a Negroid voice scolding in thick-lipped syllables. That would be Hyacinth.

Lamplight, pumpkin-yellow, flowed from an open window

near by; Ranier saw his sea cap was lying in mud under the sill. When he stooped to retrieve it he saw the German sitting at table within, back to the window. The man was scribbling on an envelope. Ranier puzzled a moment at the shoebrush head, then remembered!

"Slugged me, by heaven! Now he's drinking my drinks! *My* drinks!"

In his haste to reach the front door and return to the fray, he fell again. It didn't sober him any. Fury always blinded him, and he had to lie flat for a couple of minutes, waiting for his head to clear. Scraping mud from his knees, he ground his teeth together, outraged. The gall of that Dutchman! The damned gall! Hitting you before you could ask the reason why! Wanted the whole café to himself, did he? Only one remedy for that sort of swine. A crack on the jaw!

Ranier recrossed the verandah and stood, fists clenched, in the doorway, glaring savagely at the usurper. Flies swooped through the torpid lamplight of the room; there was no sound but that. The taffy-haired man seemed unaware of Ranier's return. Slumped at table in midroom, shoulders sluggish against the back of his chair, stomach half-under the table, left hand in pocket, right hand on table fixed around a glass, his chin on chest and his eyes three quarters closed, the pale man stared down his nose in reverie and did not so much as give Ranier a glance.

Ranier scowled darkly.

Fellow must think he could toss people around, take a comfortable posture and forget about it. Well, Ranier would refresh his memory. He snorted; stepped forward.

Still the figure at table refused to move. The bottle at his elbow was half-emptied during the few minutes Ranier had been outside; an inch of oily white liquid was in the clutched glass. Huh! A punch in the nose would rouse him lively enough. Ranier hiccoughed a warning of hostilities to begin again; he limped into the room another step, fixing his man with a fighting glare.

Was something wrong with the bird? Walked in here to start trouble, then passed out? The man's features were dull with that expression of blond Teutonic pokerishness; they had hardened into a stupid blank. White as chalk. Like the face of a statue with real hair and glass eyes.

Ranier stalled near the threshold to consider this phenomenon, angrily balked—you couldn't hit a man who refused to look at you!—then was conscious of familiarity in that face. He knew he'd seen that extraordinary pallor before. This Dutchman was one of the cruise passengers from the ship. All right, that would make another reason for pasting him in the jaw.

Ranier's lips thinned back. He'd wanted for a long time to take a sock at one of these bulldozing tourists. One of these small-timers who had three drinks and thought themselves Napoleon. Nobody could give Ranier a bum's rush and get away with it. Ready or not, the Dutchman had it coming. The man must be drunk—

Drunk.

Thought stayed Ranier's intended onslaught; held him at sudden standstill. Something in his spirit sank like a stone while slow flush crawled up his throat and cheekbones. When the flush reached his forehead resentment against the taffy-haired man had turned to resentment against himself. He, himself, was drunk. Going to make a spectacle of himself, stage a loutish row because some lout had tapped him on the chin. Violating the only rule he had left not to violate—to hold his liquor like a gentleman.

A sickening weariness came over him, a headache, and a pucker of quince in his mouth. He spat dryly, walked across the room, and limped into an alcove off the bar, looking across his shoulder at the German in disgust. Something was abnormal about that Kraut. Queer.

In the alcove by himself, his drinks restored by the black Hyacinth who had reappeared with goat's milk and diplomacy only after the crisis was dispersed, Ranier found himself watching the taffy-haired man without wanting to, nor quite knowing why he watched.

FROM THE alcove where he sat, he could watch the whole room in the back-bar mirror without himself being seen. He shifted his chair to watch the man better. It wasn't the man's slumped attitude of reverie, or the bleak whiteness of his face. The fellow had, so much as Ranier could now remember him, never been particularly animated on shipboard; Ranier had decided that the man's healthless pallor was functional. But the eyes looked bad. Glassy. Why should he walk in here and throw out the first person he saw? Ranier choked on a swallow of *aguardiente*.

Probably that Dutch pugnacity had come from liquor. Ranier

fingered soreness under his cap, wondering how long he'd been unconscious and how many drinks his assailant had had to fold up during the interim. The room was stifling, and the German had put down a lot of that *aguardiente,* by the looks. Half a bottle. Enough to make anybody glassy-eyed if you weren't used to the stuff.

Ranier, who'd been putting down a lot of that *aguardiente* himself, poured himself another drink. Now his anger had faded; he felt only curiosity at his antagonist's conduct. The shabby adobe-walled room was airless in the hot yellow light of oil lamps; it smelled like everything else in Haiti, first cousin to a chicken coop. No breeze from the beach. A lazy sluffing of surf outside; inside a somnolent mosquito drone. Ranier turned his interest from the face in the mirror to the tide going down in his liquor glass.

"I'm drunk," he decided, lowering the tide. This Caribbean mouthwash did things to a fellow. Made a man stare the way that pale bird at the table was staring. Made another man's nerves think something was wrong. Ranier gulped half a glass, still watching the back-bar mirror. Trouble was, instead of deadening his sensibilities, alcohol always sharpened them. His mind could shut off, but the nerve-ends under his skin couldn't. They felt things. Way they were feeling queer atmosphere, right now.

John Ranier muttered, "To hell with it," and drained his glass.

He meant the taffy-haired man who had thrown him out of the door, then gone into a trance. He meant the Blue Kitty Café, the island of Haiti, tropical cruises, the ship out in the bay waiting to sail, the fact he was ship's doctor sitting here in this waterside hole, imagining something uncanny was the matter with that fool across the room.

He pushed the smudged white sea cap back on his rumpled dark head; ran slim brown fingers over his jaw, and regarded the surgeon's stripe on the unlaundered cuff of his uniform.

"To hell with it all."

HE MEANT the M.D. certificate in his cramped ship's quarters; the five years he'd spent between New York harbor and Caribbean ports with this down-at-the-helm steamship line, dispensing seasick pills to nauseated ladies, adhesive tape to the crew, tomato juice to soused tourists who wanted to see the world through the bottom of a gin glass.

And what's Dr. Ranier doing now? Dispensing seasick pills and tomato juice! Don't tell me! Not the Dr. Ranier who was going to be the greatest surgeon of his day! Not the young, brisk, clever Dr. Ranier who ran that big glass and chromium office on Park Avenue, and did all those positively-miraculous-my-dear operations on pinguid millionaires? Not Dr. *John* Ranier who was wounded with the Rainbow Division when he was sixteen, "came back and made good," social position, stock market, elegant practice, engaged to Helen Goddard of Goddard Steel and Coal—not *the* Dr. Ranier.

John Ranier put down a dry glass. "To hell with everything."

He meant *the* Dr. Ranier. The stripling who'd gone out to fight the war to end war, and came back decorated with a limp. Who'd fought through medical school to save the world from cancer and ended up doing wonderful operations on wonderful millionaires. Who'd been listed in the best stocks and at the oldest clubs and doffed his shiny tophat to shiny Helen Goddard who's accepted his shiny ring. "Oh, John, I love you so." At least until the Depression. "But you couldn't expect me to go to that five-room house in Newark, John."—"I'll have to do seven million tonsillectomies and ten million trepannings before we can afford anything better."—"Honestly, John! Be the wife of a small town doctor?"

"And nuts to you, too," said John Ranier to John Ranier, grinning expressionlessly at the bottom of his glass. Four more of these *aguardientes* and his head would be pleasantly like the fog. He'd forget *the* Dr. Ranier who'd lost everything in a market crash and learned the price of everything and the value of nothing. Four more *aguardientes* and he'd even forget he'd been marked down low enough to consider brawling in a bar room with a taffy-haired Dutchman who—

Ranier drowsed.

Later, when it was important, he could not remember just what it was that jolted his attention back to the taffy-haired man. When it was important, he could not remember at just what moment the tourist party from the ship entered the café to join the Dutchman at his table and start ordering drinks. He was certain everything was all right with the taffy-haired man when those people from the cruise walked in; he could have sworn he heard the man grunt *"Ja"* and *"Jawohl"* in the opening conversation.

But later he couldn't remember. He'd paid little notice to the incoming crowd, except to mark them as tourists from the ship and hope they'd clear out soon with their ugly-natured friend.

Then, all at once, he was watching that white face in the mirror, again. He was aware that the man had not spoken for the past quarter hour. The taffy-haired man had not altered his posture or expression—chin on chest, glass in fist—his table companions were engaged in commonplace discussion among themselves—but some instinct, some galvanic tension in the atmosphere told Ranier there had been a change.

Were the others aware of it, too? Did those people now sitting at that table know something was queer? Cords tightened in Ranier's neck-nape. Something *was* the matter with that taffy-haired man!

He sat so still.

He looked so white.

He seemed dead—but wasn't.

CHAPTER II

A BLADE IN THE BACK

THERE WERE EIGHT at the table, counting the man in question, and John Ranier was destined to remember them—the café as the stage, his encounter with the taffy-haired man as prologue. The table was almost centered in the room, endwise to the bar and broadside to the door. It was long and rectangular, imitation Mission oak, outcast of some white planter's dining room; its company of chairs as chance-assorted as the tourists sitting in them.

The taffy-haired man slumped at the far end of the table, looking down its length toward the bar, which stretched across Ranier's end of the room. His back was toward the open window that admitted clammy tatters of fog, as if white curtains tacked to the outside kept blowing in over the sill.

At the Dutchman's left was the tourist named Mr. Brown. There was always a Mr. Brown on these $100 cruises. This Mr. Brown wore plus fours, golf jacket and camera case on a loaf-of-bread figure; the face of a damp but genial pie; eyes like blue huckleberries behind horn-rimmed spectacles; chuckly mouth. His name was Al, and at moment's introduction he would call you "Fella." Composograph figure of all the fraternal orders in Ohio. As Ranier observed him first he was kissing a cigar almost as plump as himself and chuckling smoke at the slat-thin Roman-nosed individual at his side.

The man with the Cæsar nose was a Professor Philemon Schlitz, narrow and nervous with a face four inches wide and pince-nez glasses which flaunted a prissy black ribbon. He wore a Ph.D. on his name and a sun helmet somebody'd told him to buy in Cape Haitian, the effect being that of an old maid school teacher playing Frank Buck. Not only an entomologist he was a walking glossary of limericks; liable to veer from a discussion on dragon flies to come up giggling with, "Did you hear the one, 'There was a young lady from Sweden—'" or " 'There was an old man from Siam—'" Everybody on the cruise liked him.

Nobody liked the man next to him—Angelo Carpetsi, swarthy New York Italian youth who'd been seasick on the way down and remained sour ever since. Coat on arm, he displayed a pink silk shirt, high-waisted trousers, trick suspenders. His eyes were feline, sleek, and he wore a Dance Palace haircut with sideburns. Ranier had found him taciturn and disagreeable, but had been amused at his cabin-mate who now bulked large beside him—Mr. Coolidge.

The name didn't fit a Brooklyn truck driver sweating in gaudy tourist attire. Mr. Joseph Coolidge, beetle-browed, grinning, cropped and cauliflowered, resembled a Tanganyika gorilla on a holiday. First night at sea he'd gone trampling and swinging his arms after every woman on the boat, and failing there, he'd resorted to bellowing rum-battles in all the Haitian ports of call. Both Coolidge and Carpetsi were more the Havana-cruise calibre, and Ranier had wondered what brought them on this Haiti excursion anyway.

ON THE other side of the board, at the right of the taffy-haired man and across from Mr. Brown, was the woman called Daisy. Ranier had often wondered what became of those Baby Peggy prodigies when they grew too old for Hollywood; this blonde was the answer. Eyes big as black-eyed susans, the petals wide, as if they observed the world in a transport of childish wonder from under the floppy brim of a picture hat. Peroxide hair. Much powder, more paint, flabby cheeks, hard mouth, and that Kiddy Koop stare. Ten to one she'd roll those bulgy eyes (did they come from exophthalmic goiter?) and mew, "Itsy bitsy" and "Ooo, it's cute." The type that ought to be in a pasture, Ranier thought. Five years old from the neck up; from the neck down, all bosom and behind.

She was traveling with the man who sat beside her and across from the oily Carpetsi—an Irishman named Kavanaugh. A man who looked to be successful in his line and in taking care of himself. Jaw lean, nose sharp, eyes that could pick winners at Belmont. Women went for the dash of gray at the temples, the belted waterproof coat and snapped hat brim, the quality of hard confidence. There was intolerance in the way he addressed a remark, cocking his thumb and pointing his finger at a listener, as if to say, "This means you!" But why did these smart operators who knew their way around always travel with some blond pin-cushion who blubbered baby-talk? A dozen times he'd ordered the woman to shut up—aiming his pistol-barrel finger in exasperation—to let them hear what the Haitian gentleman, who was with them, had to say.

Monsieur Marcelline, this was; and unlike his countryman behind the bar, Marcelline was as smartly tailored as any of his white superiors at table, and nearly as condescending. His tone was suave, his manner urbane. He'd boarded the cruise ship, Ranier recalled, at Cape Haiti with a second class ticket for passage around the island to Jacmel. Second class because his complexion was only a little darker than Spanish, maple-walnut with a few lavender pimples, known in the Haitian spectrum as *griffone.*

Languidly fanning himself with a new Panama, Marcelline was speaking good English with a Haitian-French accent, advising the white tourists in their plans.

"Everything I believe is ready, *monsieur,*" to Kavanaugh. "There is a new coastal highway from here to our capital, and once we are on it we may travel at high speed. *Mais oui.*"

"A night drive ought to be interesting." Kavanaugh spoke in a flat-keyed voice with just a fine shade of boredom. "If we're delayed too long I suppose we can stop at some inn along the way. I'd like to make it by midnight; at all events we've got to be in Port-au-Prince by tomorrow morning. That's flat. You're sure there won't be any hitch."

"The starting time is at your discretion, *monsieur.*"

"And I hope, monsoor has some idea of where he's going," the Daisy woman gave her Irish escort a look, surprising Ranier with a voice that sounded like a lumberjack talking through a doll. "I don't like this night air."

John Ranier deduced the party had decided to abandon the cruise boat and motor along the coast to Port-au-Prince where they could spend time buying souvenirs made in New Jersey in the quaint marts of the Haitian capital, and pick up the ship when it came along. Mr. Kavanaugh was engineering the shore excursion, and Monsieur Marcelline had been recruited to do the arranging, hire the car, go as guide.

It was the taffy-haired man who was curious. His quarter-open eyes trained down the table in that glassy stare. Like camera lenses under motionless lids. As if the eyeballs were taking a long-exposure photograph. But his table companions didn't seem to notice anything. Only John Ranier, watching the face in the mirror, felt his neck-hairs stiffening.

YET NOTHING had happened at that table since the tourist party came in. Ten minutes ago Marcelline had left the café on an errand, returning shortly to announce the car was outside waiting, and if they delayed a little longer the fog might lift. There was some concern about driving over mountain roads in fog.

Dense vapor which had rolled along the peninsular coast at early evening had thickened, burying the Gulf of Gonaives in blowing cotton. Coastline, headlands, bay and immediate foreshore were obscured in night-white blanketing, formless and opaque. A big German liner heading down the gulf for Port-au-Prince had vanished with the horizon, leaving in its wake a far, faint echo, like the moo of a lost cow groping its way through invisibility. Out in the bay the cruise steamer riding at anchor was a cluster of yellow gangway lights, pinpricks afloat in mist; and down beach the town was smothered. Mud streets, shanties, clay walls and palm-tops snared in drifting cobwebs. Outlines dissolved. Thinning, streaming, straggling, churning, the fog eddied around Hyacinth Lucien's Blue Kitty Café, curling up to the door, blowing in white curtains through the window at the taffy-haired man's back.

And something was wrong with that man!

Glaring at that face reflected in the bar mirror, Ranier gripped the edge of his alcove table, made as if to rise, shook his head, sat back with a frown. Anything was wrong, the man's tourist companions would know it, wouldn't they? Ranier tried to shrug off a feeling of undercurrents in the room. Hyacinth Lucien, behind the bar, swatting cockroaches with a chimpanzee hand. Bugs humming around the lamps. Somewhere out in the fog-hung town a gramophone was playing a Caribbean rumba, a tropical minor-key chant, the smoky snake-hipped rhythm quickened by the sifty time-beat of the *ouira* and the monotone *toky-tok-tok* of mahogany sticks.

For the last ten minutes not a flicker had crossed the taffy-haired man's face.

His table companions seemed to have forgotten him, their faces turned to the Haitian, Marcelline. Watching, listening, Ranier had a distinct impression that unseen wires had tightened in the room; a nervous emendation from that table, as if clocks inside those people had been wound up faster. Plump Mr. Brown was smoking vigorously. The boy, Carpetsi, kept turning his head to look out of the door at the fog. The blonde was fiddling with a powder puff as if it were a hot cake. Everybody was talking faster, louder. He stiffened in his chair, catching the words "dead man."

"Is it true the natives believe a dead man can be brought back to life?" Professor Philemon Schlitz was asking in a high-pitched voice. "I mean to say, this fantastic nonsense the guides were telling us in Cape Haitian about witch doctors who dig up bodies and reanimate them with magic so they walk about and—what do you call the things—?"

Marcelline throated an alto laugh. "*Monsieur* speaks of our Voodoo? *Alors,* there are mysteries, or, perhaps one should say, superstitions. Haiti, you comprehend, is not quite the United States. Especially in the mountains and coastal districts like this where the natives are, I am unhappy to say, the somewhat primitive. *Par example,* the matter of bullfrogs. Few Haitians are not afraid of the frog, *monsieur.* Toads are agents of the Devil. Bullfrogs? Demons, *monsieur.* I give you my word, if you dropped a live bullfrog through the skylight of the government buildings—pouf!—every soldier in the place, including Monsieur the President, would jump out the windows."

A TIME was coming, although he didn't know it then, when John Ranier was to remember that speech. A time was coming when he was to remember every detail of that scene. The professor's piping query; Marcelline's alto laugh and answer. The professor adjusted his pince-nez nervously, leaning up the table towards his informant.

"But what about these dead people flitting about and all that? Those creatures you read about in books—eh?—gombies?"

"Z, *monsieur,*" the Haitian corrected suavely. "Z as in *zombie.* Corpses resurrected, brought to life for magical purposes. One hears the rites are performed by that band of outlawed sorcerers known as the *Culte des morts.* The Society of the Dead, you would say. There are stories, then. Rumors of dead men who leave their graves to walk the jungles on silent feet—"

"Dave," the woman named Daisy snapped at Kavanaugh, "do we have to sit and listen to this? Frogs and live dead people—!"

"Madam will perhaps also hear the drums on the mountain," Marcelline went on blandly, "the *Rada* drums calling the people to some midnight dance, some *bamboche* to ward off evil. You see," he apologized with his shoulders, "we are Africans, we Haitians, after all. In the fog the drums will be beating, for the village people fear the white mists. It is said that on nights like this the dead walk best, and it might interest you to know there will be few Haitians lurking around the local cemeteries on such a—"

"Dave," the woman named Daisy said decisively, "I'll be so nervous tonight I could scream."

Kavanaugh's hard flat voice said critically, "You wanted to come, didn't you? You wanted to come on this shore party? And it won't hurt you, anyhow, if these shines believe all this hocus-pocus. So what?"

"Well, I could take less of it, myself," the guttural belonged to Angelo Carpetsi. "This place is givin' me goose pimples."

"*You* got goose pimples?" from Coolidge. "I got hen's eggs. Whaddya say, Kavanaugh, let's get under way. I'm a mass of nerves."

"We got to wait for the fog," suggested the plump Mr. Brown.

"The fog won't hurt," Kavanaugh said, "and I wish to God you people would quit stewing. It's quarter of eight, now. Okay with Marcelline, and everything's set, we can start at eight."

"Everything," Marcelline said in his darkey alto, "is ready."

John Ranier set down his glass with a little bang, tugged his cap down over one eye, slammed back his chair, limped out of the alcove and pointed a finger at the taffy-haired man.

"That man is dying!"

In the hot, close room he might have touched off a bombshell. He had a glimpse of everything happening at once; chairs going back, people leaping up. Mr. Brown's shellrim spectacles big as moons behind the smoke of his cigar. The professor standing in astonishment, his left hand somehow in a beer glass. Carpetsi in a half crouch backing slowly from the table; Mr. Coolidge standing on spread legs, elbows bent, hands open like a wrestler's; the woman with her powder puff mashed to her lips. Kavanaugh twisted to face him, jaw pointed, hands jammed deep in the pockets of his trench coat. Marcelline bent and half turned, as if from a blow.

Out in the night the gramophone's haunting monody, and

behind the bar a crash as Hyacinth Lucien lost control of a pan of bottles. Only the taffy-haired man at table's head hadn't moved.

Kavanaugh's flat voice started, "What the devil's—" when the googoo-eyed woman dropped the powder puff and screamed, her words running together in one long soprano screech.

"Ohmygoditsblood!"

John Ranier saw she was staring at a sticky dark liquor that had crept from under the taffy-haired man's chair to touch the toes of her big-bowed shoes. Everyone piled around the table to see. Everyone but the Dutchman who slumped in reverie with quarter-open eyes, hand fixed to a wine glass, shoulders glued to the back of his chair. Glued, Ranier saw, by a thin inch-small slit where a knife had gone through the cane chair-back into flesh. Blood wiggled in a syrup-like stream down the chair-back; dripped in Chinese torture-drops to the floor. But the knife was not there.

John Ranier moved his eyes in disbelief. Fog floated in silent curtains through the window ten feet away, but a thrown knife would have struck with a whack, and stuck. John Ranier knew the technique of knives. John Ranier knew cold steel had gone through that chair in one quick, expert stab; been yanked out deftly and with no more commotion than a butcher-blade through butter. John Ranier could recognize craftmanship with a blade. That knife-wielder had touched the right vertebra to paralyze his man.

BUT WHAT wizardish operator had done the thing? He'd been watching this room in the mirror for at least half an hour. That incision through chair and spine looked less than twenty minutes old. Yet for the past half hour not a soul in the room had walked behind the stabbed man's chair.

You could hear the stabbed man's faint, paralytic breathing.

You could hear the faint, paralytic breathing of everyone in the room.

It was Kavanaugh, breaking from amazement with an oath,

who caught the sitter by the armpits, swung him up from the red-backed chair. The taffy head lolled and the man's shoes scraped the floor.

The Irishman's voice began to crash, "Don't stand around pop-eyed, you fools! Haarman's been badly hurt; we can't wait to find out now. We've got to get him to a doctor!"

John Ranier moved forward. "I'm a doctor."

Supporting the limp body, Kavanaugh looked over its shoulder with a hard-eyed stare. "Get out of the way," he told Ranier in a brittle voice. "You're drunk."

Anger hazed across Ranier's vision. "The words may be right, but I don't like your tone. I've had something to drink. Not enough to keep me from seeing that man will die if his bleeding isn't stopped."

He blocked Kavanaugh's way to the door. A quick impression the others were crowding up on three sides; Brown's pie-face gone to crust; Carpetsi's Italian eyes unpredictable; Coolidge lumbering close with the expression of a menacing airedale.

Ranier directed, "I'll pack that wound, and someone better call the police. He was stabbed right here at your table. One of you must have the knife. One of you must have done it!"

Kavanaugh's lips were a pair of scissors, shearing out: "One of *us* must have done it? For all we know, you may have done it, yourself."

Ranier stared.

Marcelline's face swayed forward, glistening in lamplight, complexion gone from maple-walnut to vanilla. Under the rim of his Panama his eyes were circles of terror. He was pointing a finger at the window. His mouth flew wide and went, "Waaaaaaaah!"

CHAPTER III

CALL FOR DR. EBERHARDT!

HYACINTH LUCIEN'S BLUE KITTY CAFÉ was no glittering emporium at the corner of any Broadway and Forty-second Street, but a lamplit thatch-roofed obstruction on a fan of beach some distance from a fog-drowned Haitian village. Small Haitian villages are not lighted at night; the pedestrian walks the mud lanes armed with a small flashlight, a winkering beam against pitfalls of geography and the spirit; the sailor who knows his way about would never go venturing ashore without his pocket torch. Ranier's flashlight was in his hand before he crossed the doorsill.

Fog foamed up against the building's front, noiseless, turgid, heavy with the breath of tropic vegetation, the dead fish smell of a warm-water beach. Seaward the vapors had packed like cotton wadding, and conch shells were blowing. Inland, the night was blind as a cataracted eye. Ranier's mind, raw with that Haitian's scream in its nerve centers, calculated the distance to the wharf and the time it would take to row out to the anchored steamer, while his eyes followed the flashlight beam into mist. A searchlight couldn't have penetrated the whiteness, whatever Marcelline had seen would be evaporated.

"A face!" the Haitian was bleating. "It looked dead—straight at me through the window—eyes—eyes like the shark—waaaaaah—!"

Ranier plunged out across the verandah; started around the corner of the building. Voices clamored after him. Oaths. Shouting. The blond woman had fainted, plopped to the floor. Kavanaugh, trying to catch her, had dropped the Dutchman's body, *thump!* Ranier was relieved to discover no man among the party had followed him out of the café. His shins collided with an unseen bench, and he sidejumped, dancing, the pain clearing his head. He thought, "Great Lord, I couldn't have—!" then sprang back from a looming shadow, swerving the startled flashlight.

Angles of polished metal reflected through the mist—a big black sedan parked under a tree. Must be the car Marcelline had hired for the shore party; a gawky, antiquated seven-passenger Winton, high-roofed as a hearse, with a squeeze-bulb horn at the driver's seat and pre-Prohibition brass-rimmed headlamps.

Ranier stepped to the car; switched on the lamps. Cones of weak light spread out in the billowing steam, illuminating a scant area of ground at the side of the building. Hurriedly Ranier scouted the approach to that yellow-lit side window. Tracks! He swore under his breath. His own tracks straying past the window where he'd limped in somnambulistic daze. And—he scanned them in excitement—the tracks of someone who had walked around the big sedan and stood facing that side window, looking in, stationed almost where Ranier was standing now. He could see the prints clearly in the soggy earth. Too clearly!

For that second set of prints had gone no farther; had come to a stop within six feet of the sill. Then whoever had stood there had retraced his steps around the car, skirted the tree and entered the café by the front door. These tracks had been made, then, by Marcelline when he'd fetched the car a while ago.

Ranier made a frantic and swift inspection with his flashlight. The soft loam near the window would have recorded the prints of a cat. And there were no other prints. Marcelline's had stopped six feet from the sill; and, as he'd feared, his own tracks were glaringly under the window that had been open at the stabbed man's back. And the only ones there!

For five seconds John Ranier stood tense in the fog, listening. Voices babbled in the café; he could see into the lighted room, but, screened in vapor as he was, those inside could not see him. If Marcelline, looking out, had spied something, then it must have been nearer the window. What could the Haitian have seen? No prints to show what it might have been. Nothing.

WHEELING, RANIER sent his light in fast looping circles about the sideyard. Toward the building's rear a chicken run, a mass of glistening green banana plantain, the dripping boles of cocoanut palms. Stink-weed and ilex. Nothing had disturbed this boscage. In the steamy heaviness not a leaf stirred.

Hedging the yard, a dense thicket of tall, pole-straight bamboo, too closely wedged for a snake to worm through. From previous visits he could remember sheer limestone embankment walling up behind the bamboo, steep mountainside beyond. Anything might fade off undetected in this fog but there'd certainly be tracks. Only approach to the café was the donkey road along the beach, and the only tracks there were those imprinted earlier in the evening and by the Winton.

Ranier explored the chicken run; hurried to the rear yard. Goat-pens and garbage. Nothing there. He groped his way along the waterfront side of the building, fumbling through a smell of dead fish toward the verandah. His *own* tracks under that window! If he could only remember! If he could only remember what he'd been doing in that blank interval between the time the German threw him off the verandah and he struck his head, and the moment his mind cleared there in that side yard. Out on his feet, of course. Wandering semi-conscious. Blotto from that head-crack and alcohol. And he couldn't have—

He thought, "Or could I—?" Then pulled himself up, snarling aloud, "Don't be a fool, you left that sailor's-knife in your cabin aboardship, and the man was talking when that tourist crowd came in!" One of them did it. One of that crowd yelling in there did it, but the police—ten to one!—would try to fasten it on him. Steered, of course, by the guilty party.

Inside the café the voices were exploding like a package of firecrackers. "Give him air!"—"I tell you, messieurs, I saw a face!"—"Sit down! Sit down!"—"Look here, Brown, you was sitting at his left!"—"I tell you, I never left my chair for a—!"—"I'm goin' back to the ship and tell the—!"—"Right through his back! Right through his doggone back!"—"It was a dead face at the window, *messieurs! Ah, Sacré Nom de Dieu!* A dead face—!"

"The devil it was," Ranier had to say, stepping through the door. "Nothing out there in the soup. If Marcelline saw anything, I'm afraid he imagined it."

His glance scorned the bulgy woman reviving with dramatic energy in a corner; fixed coldly on the body on the floor. Mr. Kavanaugh, Mr. Brown and Mr. Coolidge were kneeling over the wounded man, struggling to remove his coat. Carpetsi cowered near the door, his sable eyes glowing fear in his olive face. In the background, Monsieur Marcelline mopped almost Aryan features with an unsanitary handkerchief, gasping incoherencies. The thin professor of entomology walked as if caged, wringing womanish hands.

John Ranier snapped, "Hyacinth! Bring water!" at the goggle-eyed Negro behind the bar; crossed the floor, shucking his white coat. He was thinking as he rolled up his sleeves, "The Dutchman hasn't a chance in hell. Lost about three quarts of blood. Whoever nailed him with this bunch at table, then sat tight while he was bleeding to death, is a cool customer." It made his neck ache. He was aware of Carpetsi's scared black eyes on his face.

"What you gonna do about it, Doc?"

"Try to stop that hemorrhage." He was about to add, "And you go call the police!" but his lips made a dry, thin line instead. After all, it was none of his business. If one of this bunch wanted to knock off a fellow-tourist in a mosquito-port in Haiti, what was that to John Ranier? Let the ship's captain worry, or the Secretary of State, or whoever it was had jurisdiction over crazy American tourists on foreign soil. The *Garde d'Haiti* would come soon enough. Stick to his own racket—doctor. Seasick pills and tomato juice for nauseated tourists.

But the man on the floor wanted something more than pills and tomato juice. John Ranier observed coolly, looking down, "He'll have to have a transfusion!" and he didn't care much, remembering that clip on the chin. Maybe the bird had clipped somebody else on this trip; got what was coming to him.

He said in a professional tone, "He'll have to go to some local doctor and go fast. Too far to row him out to the ship, and personally I'm not prepared."

"That's what I told you in the first place." Kavanaugh's tone was flat, metallic, authoritative. The Irishman regarded Ranier steadily with cold blue eyes that disliked Ranier's face and told him so. The stare implied Ranier was in need of a shave and clean linen; implied Ranier was a small time ship's doctor unable to manage a practice ashore, probably an alcoholic incompetent. The cold eyes scanned the shoddy sea cap, the soiled uniform; settled on John Ranier's foot. "That's what I said in the first place. He'll have to go to a doctor. You're too lurching drunk to be of—"

Quick crimson flamed in Ranier's cheek. "Lurching, am I? It just happens, mister, that instep was shot out by a Boche machine gun in '18. And by saying I wasn't prepared, I meant I hadn't come ashore prepared to give a transfusion to a man stabbed in the back by a murderer!"

Breath made a sucking noise through the Irishman's teeth. There was a sputter from the blonde; a bitten-off oath from Mr. Coolidge. John Ranier met a battery of angry glares with a shrug. They didn't like that word "murderer," it seemed. He'd pay this smart harp, too, for mentioning his bad foot.

BUT THE flush cooled from his face as his temper relaxed. What did it matter if they thought him an incompetent pill-disher relegated to a ship? Nothing mattered when nothing was worth doing because nothing was worth anything. If anything was worth the trouble, right now, it was getting rid of this knifing affair before the police lost the point in a game of questions and answers.

He said to Kavanaugh with professional brusqueness, "This hardly seems the time to bicker, does it? If you wouldn't mind lending me a clean handkerchief, and I'll donate my shirt. All of you gentlemen. You there, Professor, if you'll rescue that basin from Hyacinth before he slops it all. Mr. Brown, will you lift his head? We can lay him on the table—"

The wound proved interesting.

Ranier managed a compress with skilled hands while his mind revolved on the puzzle of how a man could have been stabbed like this at a crowded table. Powerful blow to drive a blade so deep; knife double-edged, razor-honed, and must have been buried to the hilt. Short-circuited a vertebra to cut off the brain telegraph, ossifying the body to stone.

Slumped there full of *aguardiente,* the Dutchman mightn't have made a sound, anyway, and this toadstabber had gone in like a bullet, paralyzed him stiffer than *rigor mortis.* By the looks, it wouldn't be long before *rigor mortis,* either.

"He'll be with the angels by midnight," Ranier observed with forced geniality, looking up at the blond woman as he tied a bandage. "I don't suppose you're carrying any iodine or mercurochrome in your handbag?"

Lips compressed, she shook her head. He wondered what she was carrying in that bead bag gripped in her hands. Her hands, he noticed were a lot older than her face. Looked, somehow, like her lips—compressed, defensive. It would take a lot to open her lips or that bag if she didn't want them opened. But a bloody knife would have leaked a stain through the bead-mesh; and even if she had been sitting at the Dutchman's end of the table, a little nearer than Brown who'd been at his other side, she couldn't have done it. No woman could reach around behind a man's chair and drive in a knife like that. Or could one?

But her build looked flabby as the mumps, and that blade had been powered with muscle.

"No antiseptics among you?" Ranier's dried smile traveled to Brown—that moon face sweating like icebox butter. He'd seen men sweat like that before. From strain. And anybody was entitled to go yellowish when the man at his elbow has just been quietly stabbed.

Or had Brown put that glad hand of his around behind this Dutchman's chair? Then thrown the knife out of the window? Ten feet to the sill, though, and certainly such a toss would have been seen. No knife out there in the mud.

"Great Maker!" the fat man blurted. "He was sitting right next to me. Right there at the head of the table. It might've been me. *Me—!*"

"I'd like something to pour on this stab wound," Ranier interrupted the outcry. "You wouldn't have some American whisky in your coat, Mr. Brown. Any of you? Then I'm afraid I'll have to use this impure Haitian stuff. God knows what's in it."

Kavanaugh moved around the table. "God knows there's plenty of it in *you!*" he snapped at Ranier. "You realize if the man dies from this delay you'll be held responsible?"

"You mean one of *you* will be held responsible. Fellow's almost certain to die of tetanus in this country, even if he does survive hemorrhage." Turning his back on the Irishman's showy belligerence, he put an ear to the wounded man's chest. Not much blood left in that faint-tapping pump. He studied the Dutchman's white, unconscious face. "Transfusion or not, I don't think he'll live out the night. We can move him as soon as the bleeding stops." He looked around curiously. "He was going with you on a motor tour, wasn't he?"

"At my invitation," Kavanaugh said harshly. "Or, rather, he asked if he could join us. Professor Schlitz wanted to come, and since Haarman was sharing the professor's stateroom—"

The thin man's mouth opened in a high-pitched outburst that dislodged the pince-nez from his nose. "I didn't do it. He was my cabin-mate, but I didn't do! No, no, no! I hardly conversed with the man at any time on the cruise. I never saw him before until the first night on board. Why did I beg to come on this shore excursion? I'm an insectologist—yes!—my first vacation in years—from Upsala College—I don't know him—I didn't do it—" Sinking to the edge of a chair, he mopped his narrow face, staring wildly. "You don't think I did it, do you?"

"I didn't ask who did," Ranier reminded coolly.

Brown panted out, "None of us knew him before this cruise. In fact, I never seen any of these people until the cruise, myself. I—we—" He swallowed, looked about apprehensively.

RANIER TOOK a bottle of rum from the table, shook his head doubtfully; shifted the wounded man's position, poured the liquor into the crimson-soaked bandage. From the corner of his eye he noticed an interesting expression on the face of Mr. Coolidge. Doorknob ears, gold-plated teeth, squinty eyes, the face followed Ranier's every move with the brute concentration of a mastiff watching a cat that might jump. The squinty eyes caught Ranier's surveillance. The big man sidled up, and put a hand the size of a ballplayer's mitt gently on John Ranier's shoulder.

"You don't think one of *us* knifed this guy in hot blood, do you, pal? You wouldn't be thinkin' nothin' like that? It would get on my nerves."

"Certainly not, Mr. Coolidge." Ranier didn't look around. "You can see for yourself; Mr. Haarman tried to commit suicide."

The fingers on his shoulder tightened viciously. "Don't get funny, Sawbones. This dinge Marcelline says he seen a face out there in the fog. A face, get it? There's th' mug who dunked a knife in Haarman. Pitched it through the window at him, see?"

"And it jumped back out of the window, Mr. Coolidge."

Ranier was whirled to face the man's brilliant teeth. "Listen, quack! If you're gonna start a story that one of my friends here was playin' mumbledy-peg with Haarman, I'll slap your damn—"

Kavanaugh shouted, "Shut up, Coolidge!" catching the big man's elbow, jerking his aside. "We'll talk to the right authorities when we see them."

"Authorities will never catch he who used knife." It was Marcelline's voice, mediumistic in his blue-shadowed throat. The

Creole was crystal-gazing at the door where the fog creamed, his features gray as stale fudge. "It was a dead face I saw, *messieurs. Mort de bon Dieu!* A face all streaming hair—sightless eyes—"

John Ranier pointed the empty rum bottle angrily. "Rot! There wasn't anybody out there nor anywhere near the café. The knife that stabbed Mr. Haarman must be somewhere right here in this room!"

SOMEWHERE RIGHT here in the room, perhaps nestling under somebody's sport coat or cuddling up a sleeve, waiting, watching, biding its time, measuring the distance to John Ranier's own spinal cord. He didn't fancy that. It didn't mix with *aguardiente,* and his digestion was beginning to feel it. He suppressed a hiccup, shifting his position so that his back was toward nobody in the vicinity, and found himself confronted by Mr. Kavanaugh who was facing him combatively, feet apart, eyes directed from under slanted hat brim levelling that finger at Ranier in the manner of a "You Buy Liberty Bonds" poster.

Mr. Kavanaugh did not say, "Buy Liberty Bonds." He said flatly, "The knife ought to be around, Dr. Ranier, but it seems that it isn't. While you were outside just now, we made a search. Mr. Brown, Mr. Coolidge and Mr. Carpetsi permitted me to go through their apparel; and Professor Schlitz allowed us to search him. Since Marcelline was sitting at the far end of the table, he is obviously eliminated. I'll stand personally responsible for Miss May, here; she's quite unarmed. And since we're all going to be under suspicion in this mess, I allowed my friends to frisk me. Is that right, Brown?"

The plump tourist gulped, "That's a fact. There ain't so much as a penknife on any of us."

Kavanaugh aimed his finger at John Ranier's chin. "No, we didn't find any knives. What we did find out may interest you. Our friend the bartender there," he tossed his chin obliquely to indicate the bar, "our friend the bartender crashed through with the information that *you* were in the café here when Mr. Haarman first came in. The bartender says he was out in back, but he heard you havin' a quarrel. That was half hour or so before the rest of us got here. The bartender says you went outside in front for a while, and then you came back in and sneaked into that alcove, there, where nobody could see you. Interested?"

"No," Ranier said. "Hyacinth was partly right. Mr. Haarman swaggered in here like a boiled owl and took a pass at me. Matter of fact, got pretty ugly. Shoved me out on the verandah. I didn't sneak back into that alcove, but walked there to avoid further annoyance and mind my own business. Haarman sat right here where he was sitting when you came in. He was all right when you met him here, wasn't he?"

Kavanaugh said in a hard voice, "He looked bad when we got here."

"He looked a hell of a lot worse after you'd been here a while," Ranier countered evenly. "And he looks rotten, now. But I'm not interested. It's none of my affair which one of you stabbed Mr. Haarman. As ship's doctor, I'm responsible to you people only when you're aboard; but I'll be called as a witness and expected to make a report on this case, and I'm going to make one."

He didn't tell the tall man his stomach felt gone because he'd hunted through the wounded man's clothing under pretense of physical examination, and the knife wasn't concealed on Haarman, either. It made his diaphragm contract when he turned his back on Kavanaugh; bent over the table to inspect the bandaging. When he rounded on the Irishman again, he was holding two rumpled envelopes in his hand. One of the envelopes was smeared as if by red ink.

"These letters were in Haarman's hip pocket. He doesn't seem to have a wallet, but there's fifty *gourds* change in his trousers. I'll turn these letters over for Haarman's identification when I go aboard ship."

LIFTING THE stained envelope toward the light, he read the typewritten address, postmarked ten days before in New York—*Leo Haarman—Murray Hill Hotel.* He was about to tuck the letter in his pocket when his eye caught a name scrawled in pencil across one blood-stained corner, some jotted figures. The pencilled name was "Eberhardt"; and the jotted figures looked like stock market quotations—"4,000,000 m.—1,000,000 $." Hastily, and without reading these cryptic jottings to his audience, he stowed the letters in his tunic.

"You'll witness my taking them. I'll turn them over to the captain when I go aboard. Meantime," he told Kavanaugh, "I've done all I can for Mr. Haarman. One who did this job can rest assured the assassination's a success. He won't survive this phlebotomy, if you know what I mean."

The blond woman said hoarsely, "Ohmygod—ohmygod—!" closing her goitrous eyes as if she knew what he meant; and John Ranier turned for a last inspection of the Dutchman's pulse. Packing had stopped the hemorrhage, but the man was probably bleeding internally. Ranier picked up the almost lifeless hand. Dangerous to move him with the count that slow. Almost out. He stooped over the dying man's wrist, suddenly curious about a scar, brown and faded, on the man's damp palm.

Cut by a knife a long time ago, the scar looked like a brand. As if someone had branded that palm with the letter Z. Ranier moved stony eyes to the Dutchman's death-mask face. Violence in the past had marked his palm; had that deadly pallor of Haarman's—no whiter now than it had been on shipboard—come from fear or tuberculosis?

He pinched the man's index finger between his own thumb and forefinger. You could sometimes detect tuberculosis by a splayed condition of the finger-tips.

He said, without looking up, "I think this man was a con—" meaning to say "a consumptive"; but the sentence was rudely short-circuited by a hand collaring his neck-nape; wrenching him about-face from the table.

It was Kavanaugh's hand, and the Irishman behind it looked mad. Slanted hat brim and outthrust jaw; eyelids almost closed, and the pupils glinting like nail-heads centered in the iris.

"What do you care what he was? Don't you think you've

stalled around here long enough? Trying to let the man die? We're getting him out of here now—right now!" the tall man gritted out, releasing his hold on Ranier to flash a hand into his waterproof, extract a wallet, snap out a card.

"My name and address if you happen to think you want to bring any charges. David C. Kavanaugh, Caribbean-American Sugar Company, New York. Get this, Ranier. I'm due on important business in Port-au-Prince tomorrow. I'd arranged to drive overland tonight and these tourists—Haarman included—were going with me for the ride. You can check all this with the purser on the ship, but you're not going to muff this murder affair any longer."

He jabbed his finger at the doorway. "If you're smart you'll hike out of here and report what's happened to the ship's captain. You can also report you were in here stewed when this happened and in no condition to handle an emergency case. If you don't report at all—I guess we'll know who did this job. If you do go back, tell your skipper I took charge. I'll see these people are under proper surveillance, and we'll all go together to the police; but first I'm takin' Haarman to a hospital, and the whole crowd's going with me."

He trained his finger at Marcelline. "*You!* Go out an' start that car! You—" at the black man saucer-eyed behind the bar—"where's the nearest hospital in this mud hole? The nearest doctor?"

"Hôpital Médecin?" Hyacinth Lucien ogled the body on the table; groaned. The man's black face shone like a dancing shoe while his fingers dabbled prayerfully with a little cloth packet of castor-beans, hair, rooster feathers and toenail parings—an *ouanga* charm suspended under his throat. "But there is one hospital, *monsieur,* five miles on the road that runs north from the village. Half way up the *morne.* The doctor, a white man, has been there many years. The name is Dr. Eberhardt."

Kavanaugh started for the door. "Brown—Carpetsi—Coolidge! For God's sake, don't just stand! Let's get Haarman under way! Daisy, go out and get into that car. Professor, you go with her!" Over the shoulder at Ranier, "Are you going, or not? Somebody ought to row out to that barge and bring back the captain. She was posted to sail at nine, and you won't have much time, either. We'll be waiting at this hospital—Dr. Eberhardt's. Get it?"

John Ranier nodded calmly. He was thinking: "Eberhardt? Eberhardt? Eberhardt?" wondering where he'd heard the name before. There was a commotion at the table as Brown struggled with Haarman's inert shoulders, and Coolidge and Carpetsi wrestled with the Dutch man's soggy legs.

Then Kavanaugh was shouting again. "I told you to start the car, Marcelline! What in hell are you waiting for?"

Ranier looked up to discover that something had happened to the well-dressed Haitian's urbanity. Posed in the doorway, Monsieur Marcelline was peering out at the night, his lower lip hanging, body bowed forward, one hand cupped behind an ear. The sclerotics of his eyes were yellow butterplates beneath the brim of his Panama; his voice a ventriloquial squeak from the pit of his stomach.

"Listen—!"

FAR OUT in night, echoes muffled in fog, a pulse had started beating. A pulse almost as faint as the heart-beat of the man who was dying on that café table. When the wind stirred the fog to cloudy churning, the sound loudened; when the breeze petered out and the fog hung in the torpor of yeast, there was scarcely more than a tremor in the night.

Tumpy-bum-bum—Tumpy-bum-bum—

"Drums!" Marcelline whispered. "Drums of Damballa! Drums to ward off the un-dead dead who walk the jungles on silent feet! Drums to ward off *zombies—!*"

"Dave," the woman called Daisy screamed, "I'm going to scream!"

"You fool!" Kavanaugh's palm went stiffarmed into Marcelline's shoulder, catapulting the Haitian across the doorsill. "Get out there and drive that car! Come on, the rest of you! We're taking Haarman to the hospital!"

A floundering rush as Carpetsi, Coolidge and Brown, hats awry, faces sweat-oiled, hustled Haarman's sagging body out of the door. Kavanaugh's sharp commands rapping out through the mist. Doors banging on the Winton. Cough of an engine breaking into a rhythmic chugging. With that uproar outside, the café seemed empty as a hall.

In quick stealth Ranier dropped to one knee, sped a glance under the long table. The knife he had expected to find jabbed into the underside of the table, tucked under one of the chairs, somewhere on the floor, wasn't there. A last hurried scrutiny of the room; blank adobe walls, two lizards on the ceiling, Hyacinth Lucien rooted like a black cigar-store Indian behind the bar, the room's mirrored picture in that dim back-bar looking glass. No place for a knife to hide. Nothing.

He swerved; went swiftly to the door.

Out on the fog-smothered road the clumsy sedan was backing to turn around. Gears clashing. Saffron eyes wheeling in mist. A glimpse of scared faces crowded behind glass. Daisy's voice falsetto, demanding, "Dave Kavanaugh, if you're jamming me into this car with a murderer—!" A window cranking down, and Kavanaugh's face glaring out at Ranier.

"I advise you to bring back that captain! Don't forget! Dr. Eberhardt's—"

Eberhardt!

Something clicked in the foreground of John Ranier's memory. That was the name jotted on the envelope from Haarman's hip pocket. Along with that notation—four million m, one million dollar-sign. Had Haarman, himself scribbled that cryptogram? An untutored German might write a million dollars like that. A million dollars! Eberhardt! Name too unusual for coincidence—

Sea-ward the fog gave echo to a deep-throated, funneling *rhoooooom!* The call hung trembling in the waterlogged air. Half hour to sailing time! John Ranier cried to Kavanaugh, "I'll get to the ship! See you later!"

The Winton lunged by his vision, going into second with a clashy roar. Mud spouted in brown streaks from the wheels. Kavanaugh jerked in his head. A clot of mire spatted Ranier across the mouth as the Winton's rear end rocked by, sending him back in a recoil. Then he flung himself forward as if launched from a springboard. Head lowered, arms stretched; threw himself through flying mud at the ruby tail light of the sedan, catching with sure hands the spare-tire frame.

Not for nothing had John Ranier spent a boyhood on the streets of a city clogged with taxicabs. As the Winton spurted into high, he was sitting in the spare tire, back wedged as if in a life preserver, neck bent, arms hooked around the rim, knees pulled up, heels skimming the road. Fog whirled in the car's wake, and the doorway of Hyacinth Lucien's Blue Kitty Café was a banana-yellow adrift in mist, diminishing down the beach.

Nobody in the car was looking back, so John Ranier was the only one to see Hyacinth Lucien's shadow flick out of the café door and go racing off toward jungle and invisibility.

CHAPTER IV

THE GIRL AT EBERHARDT'S

HAITIAN ROADS WERE never surfaced for joy-riding. This one following the beach was little better than a wagon track, deep water-filled ruts and unexpected potholes threatening any minute to overturn the skidding sedan. On one side, banks of foliage and sharp palmetto lashed at the fenders; on the other, the beach sloped down-grade into blackness and combing surf. The headlights gave glimpses of phosphorescent water slopping along the sand under the fog. Decaying marine life smelled dank green.

John Ranier, clinging to the spare tire of a 1919 Winton—a sedan occupied by a dying man and his murderer—told himself he was a fool. *Aguardiente* and that hieroglyphic notation had gotten him into this—the name Eberhardt plus the one million, dollar-sign. That fatal suggestion of money! A million dollars! Anybody ought to know by this time there wasn't that much money in the world, and those figures pencilled on that envelope probably meant no more than the jotted name. Haarman, before coming ashore tonight, had doubtless asked the ship's captain the name of the local doctor; written it down. As for the figures, people were always scribbling. As for the *aguardiente*—that was bad. Bad.

If he could only see through that blind-spot where he'd been wandering while outside that open window. Hyacinth might tell the police that quarrel story; Kavanaugh certainly would. That settled it, right there. He'd have to stick with this surprise party to clear himself, as much for his own peace of mind as anything. Not that he could've stabbed Haarman, but—you could do strange things while you were unconscious.

But a minute later he was regretting the decision, cursing himself for a fool. He spat a mouthful of wet sand as the Winton took a curve, and clung to his scanty perch with numb arms. Puddle water, gravel, dead fish, seashells all blew up between his knees, and his troublesome foot throbbed. Why the devil had he obeyed an impulse to grab this car? Footprints under a window weren't circumstantial evidence to anything. Thing to do was drop off in the village and go straight to the *Gendarmerie.*

The superstitious Haitian at the wheel was driving like a maniac....

If big money was behind this fandango Ranier figured was a double sucker for sticking in his oar. Whoever had poked that knife into Mr. Haarman, then vanished the blade under the noses of his table companions back there in that café, was not only a magician but a chap who meant business. A killer familiar with his stuff. Someone in this sedan was laughing with a knife up his sleeve, while his other sleeve was probably supporting his victim.

It was as good a theory as any other possible one.

Ranier cranked his bent neck to look up at the sedan's rear window. Curtain was down. He could visualize the jam in there; Haarman doubled up on the rear cushions; the others crouching together, shoulders colliding as the car bounced over the ruts, eyes glaring at each other. He could hear nothing but the streaming wind, the spinning whine of the tires above the roar of the exhaust. Clutching his sea cap, he waited hopefully for a chance to drop off—the hell with this. But the Winton wasn't slowing down.

He could see nothing of the Gulf of Gonaives, and he wondered if the bay was still there. No sign of the cruise ship's gangway lights. Either the vessel had wheeled in the tide, or she was already standing out to sea. The Old Man wasn't the skipper to hold up sailing for late arrivals. He couldn't have made the ship, anyway, with a mile's row to her anchorage, but he might have had sense enough to keep clear of this sedan.

So he hung on. Weaving like an ark in a storm, the clumsy car swerved on a break-neck curve, wheeled through a cloud of mud, hit a stretch of gravel, roared across the loose planks of a bridge.

THE VILLAGE was gone before John Ranier realized they were beyond it. Crooked windows yellow with misty candlelight; pale adobe walls leaning at crazy angles; thatched roofs. Loose-hipped Negroes lounging in dim doorways, watching the car go by with the whites of their eyes. Dark storefronts gray-shuttered against the fog, their slatternly galleries overhanging the wooden sidewalks, kinky-headed Negresses looking down. Mules lined up at a hitching rail. *Bureau de Poste.* A weed-grown *parc* where the statue of Toussaint L'Ouverture clapped a cockaded hat to breast and sadly regarded the village's neglect and decay. The arched doorway of a *brasserie* where Haitians in straw sombreros looked up from marble-topped tables to gape at a white man hanging to a spare tire. *"Blanc!"* John Ranier caught snatches of outcry. *"Cochon! Tiens la—"* Black shadows and shanties huddled like toadstools.

In the weaving mist everything steamed, dripped. Palm-fronds were islands suspended in watery upper currents and patches of candleshine came through cracked shutters and seemed to float. Some scared pickaninnies huddled around the cinnamon smudge of a bonfire. An enormous Mammy with a kerosene can perched on her turban, a rooster under her arm, hugged against a Mother Goose picket fence and shook her fist and Creole imprecations after the speeding car. Swaying recklessly on a turn, the fender at Ranier's elbow scraped the hub of a two-wheeled cart, and Ranier cursed almost as frantically as the crone who shrieked from the driver's seat. *Bankety-bank-bank-bank* across a second bridge. A fleeting glimpse into the blue-walled courtyard of a building marked *Gendarmerie* where a black soldier in faded brown canvas leaned yawning on his rifle.

A vine-covered railway shed and *wham-slam* across the glistening metals of a grade crossing; then the car was tunneling white night on open road, jungle sweeping by on both sides.

John Ranier set his teeth. Anyone should know better than to give a Haitian the wheel of a car. That fellow Marcelline would kill them all, and Mr. Haarman, who wanted gentle handling, must certainly be already dead from that bumping along the beach.

Improved highway was worse. The tires hummed on new macadam, axles screeching with strain at every curve. Cramped in a hoop of rubber, John Ranier could see nothing of the road save the little patch illuminated by the tail light, shiny and wet, a streak of black silk that whistled rearward under his heels and slipped aft into formless vapor.

The road climbed and wound. Now the village window-lights were a cluster of luminous oranges adrift to the left and below in pooling haze; gone. Where the devil was that black Barney Oldfield driving them? Five miles north to the hospital, Hyacinth Lucien had said. But Haitians were as careless with time and distance as they were with the speedometer of a car; five miles on a road in Haiti could be fifty to a white man, especially when the map was obscured in wool-thick mist and you were going sixty miles an hour on a spare tire. John Ranier suffered a certainty the Winton had left the road and was racing off into the sky. Monsieur Marcelline had missed a curve in the night and was steering for the moon. Lucky no celestial pedestrians were afoot on this cloudy highway; their fate would have been the same as that skunk's back there, no more than a brief acrid whiff in the nostrils. *Creeeeee*—another hairpin turn like that and the hack would lose a wheel. Presently they should sight the north star, for Ranier saw they'd just passed the Pleiades.

He marked the constellation clearly as it whizzed aft in blank space, a little cluster of twinkles above the road on an invisible hill, like candles burning on some cosmic birthday cake. Ranier wondered what the captain of the cruise ship would say when he explained his absence by claiming he'd whizzed by the Pleiades on a worn-out Firestone tire. "Drunk again!" probably. And, "You're fired." That red-jowled navigator would never believe the entrance to the famous constellation was a ghostly roadside arch marked "Cemetery" and the Pleiades were not stars but candles keeping vigil in a lonesome Haitian graveyard.

THE ROAD dipped, climbed, swerved. Blackness swept in behind the car, rushed by on both sides. Night mixed with fog and ceiling zero, all landmarks vanished. Ranier could guess the forest without seeing it; could sense the cliffs of timber massed on either side of the road, walls of vine, underbrush, close-packed trunks looming blacker than the darkness. He's been smart, all right. If this relic didn't leap an unnoticed precipice he'd end up in mountain wilderness, miles from anywhere in Caribbean jungle with a party of panic-stricken tourists, a dead man and a homicidal expert who made butcher knives disappear in thin air. These Haitian limberlosts would be duck soup for anyone with criminal talent, and that glimpse of the village below with its yawning *Gendarmerie* had not been any reassurance. In a republic which beat goatskin drums to ward off wandering dead men, the law might be equally phantasmal. Haarman's assassin had certainly picked his spot.

Or was Haarman's assassin a her? That peroxide blonde didn't look capable of anything worse than kissing a Pekinese or gobbling four pounds of bonbons in a lace bed littered with pink ribbons and tabloids. Still, these faded violets were the tantrum type. There'd been that blood-letting in Philadelphia—back in the old ambulance-interne days. Dame looked soft as a bag of marshmallows, and cut her husband's throat from ear to ear. And Daisy had been seated nearest this case—

Brown next nearest, yet the Ohio real estate man (somewhere on the cruise he'd dropped remarks about Columbus and real estate) looked more overweight than dangerous, too. Golf knickers and dumpling cheeks didn't go with knives; and murderers, of course, seldom looked the part. But Mr. Brown didn't seem the sort to stab his fellow-man in the back.

Nor did Professor Schlitz appear capable of any violence greater than sticking a bug on a hatpin. Too jittery for this cool-blooded job. Spent his life classifying butterflies and lecturing on mosquitoes at some obscure college, reciting limericks for relaxation. Those pince-nez spectacled eyes weren't the eyes of a killer. If they'd reflected the truth—

Carpetsi, on the other hand, fitted the part. Something oily and unsavory about the Broadway boy, and truth wasn't in his Latin eyeballs. But courage wasn't, either, and he'd been sitting too far down the table. While Mr. Coolidge of the cauliflowered ears, Mack Truck jaw and monkey brow—a specimen who looked willing to choke his grandmother to death if the price was right—had been seated even farther away.

That left Marcelline and Kavanaugh. Inside the café, the dusky Haitian had sat at table's head, quite beyond knife-reach; he'd gone outside once to fetch the car, park it near the door and stand gazing into the window at Haarman's chair. Nothing in that. Six feet from the window his tracks had halted, and it was another ten feet inside to that fatal chair. You couldn't stab a man sitting sixteen feet away. But you might see blood on his chair-back, and you might walk into the room afterwards and talk about something else. The *Garde d'Haiti,* when and if they came, would do well to cross examine Monsieur Marcelline.

And they might find an Irishman in the woodpile. If anyone in this tourist batch looked competent to engineer someone's demise, the narrow-lipped Kavanaugh did. He'd admittedly organized the shore party, and Mr. Haarman had joined the ride on Mr. Kavanaugh's invitation. The man had a cold, direct eye and a cool alibi, and by midnight would probably be in touch with a lawyer. There was a ruthless, self-assurance in this sugar company executive which made him appear quite capable of severing another's spinal cord with nicety and aplomb. Mentally, John Ranier shook his head. Characters under suspicion always turned out to be innocent, didn't they? At least it was that way in mystery plays. Only this wasn't any mystery play, and Kavanaugh, two chairs down the table from Haarman, hadn't left his seat throughout the evening.

Hyacinth Lucien had served a last round of drinks, Ranier remembered, then retired to his bottle-washing behind the bar. He couldn't possibly have juggled a knife and a tray of rum-glasses at the same time. There it was. No one could have done it. Someone had. When had that blade whisked in and out of the Dutchman's back? Hard to tell, because he'd begun that paralytic stare in the forepart of the evening, before the others came in. What had been the matter with him then? Why had he thrown Ranier out?

John Ranier decided with an oath as the Winton's tires screeled on a curve, that he didn't give a damn who stabbed that Dutchman—that he'd let his imagination get away with him—and that he'd drop out the minute this joy-ride slowed to forty an hour.

HIS DECISION to drop out, right then, was taken out of his hands. *Screeee—am!* Jammed brakes gave out a stench of burning grease as the car took a side road on two wheels; *thump!* a sudden halt flung John Ranier from his perch and left him sitting upright on a roadway that was certainly not paved with clouds. There could be no doubt about it; the car and John Ranier were on solid ground.

Twelve feet beyond him the sedan smoked to a halt; voices broke loose in the night. Too dazed for action other than spitting a dislodged tooth, John Ranier sat on burning posterior while his vision cleared. Black shrubbery hedged the driveway where he'd come to earth: there was the vegetal sultriness, the close-hemmed feeling of jungle around. The sedan had stoped before a screened verandah that fronted a long, two-story frame building, the wings of which stretched off into misting darkness. Headlights of the car streamed through murk to finger through the verandah screen and circle the front door with a wan luminescence.

John Ranier saw the building was painted white, and unlike

the average country place in Haiti showed evidence of being in repair. A planter's villa from the old days, judging by the gingerbread and gargoyles running around the upper gallery. Great sablier trees extended moss-bearded limbs above the gallery rail, and in the drifting scud, opalescent with ghostly rays diffused from the car lights, the dark roof-line seemed to swim along in the night.

He saw a light in an upper window, as if someone were studying late.

He saw there was a pale lamp burning in the reception hall.

He saw a neat, black-lettered sign on the front door—*Ludwig Eberhardt, Docteur en Médecine.*

He saw the doors burst open on the Winston; Kavanaugh leaped to the ground, raced to the verandah, and started an urgent pounding on the door. Excitement shrilled from the car; the knocks echoed off into the drugged mountain stillness; it seemed a long three minutes before Ranier saw the door come open.

A girl was standing there. A slim girl, cool in a white linen dressing robe, with a gray tabby cat hugged in her arms. The car lights brushed gleams from tumbled, brown-gold hair, caught the blue of wide eyes in a cool tanned face, the carmine red of lips parted a little in surprise.

John Ranier scarcely heard Kavanaugh's rapping, authoritative outburst. "Let us in! Quickly! Been an accident! Man out here's dying—"

John Ranier saw the girl standing there in the door-frame facing Kavanaugh, and *aguardiente* or not, his heart skipped four beats and left him icy sober. Suddenly he knew that whether he wanted to or no, he wasn't going to leave that girl facing Mr. Kavanaugh and Daisy, Professor Schlitz and Monsieur Marcelline, Mr. Brown, Mr. Coolidge and Mr. Carpetsi with the remains of Mr. Haarman on this lonely mountainside in Haiti.

CHAPTER V

SOMETHING TERRIBLE—

CANVAS SHOES MADE no sound on gravel as they moved John Ranier across the driveway, and melted, unobserved, in the shadowy brush. In a bed of rank tropical fern, he crouched, listening, eyes on the sedan, the house. One thing was plausible. If anyone in that party was secreting a knife, he'd get rid of it before police were summoned; the nooks and crannies of that 1919 Winton would be logical for the hiding of cutlery. Ranier told himself he'd feel better when he located that knife, and his first move would be to search the sedan.

Then he heard Kavanaugh's shouting. "Hurry it, can't you? The man's bleeding to death! For God's sake, Daisy, get out of the way, and if you're going to faint again, get into the house where the young lady can look after you! Hold his head, Professor! Brown, you and Carpetsi help carry him. Coolidge, stay out there in the car with Marcelline. The girl says there's no telephone, here, and you may have to drive back to the village for the police—"

Ranier muttered under his breath, parting the ferns before his face for better view. She was holding open the screen to admit the scramble that charged across the driveway carrying Haarman; but Kavanaugh's tall shoulders, in front of her, blocked Ranier's sight.

Emitting a babble of sticky sobs, the Daisy woman was first to reach the verandah where, feminine-fashion, she lost no time in having a nervous breakdown. Ranier could hear the girl's voice low in quick sympathy as she put an arm around the weeping Broadway belle and led her into the dim hall. A stampede of feet on the verandah as Schlitz, Carpetsi and Brown blundered Haarman's body to the door, leaving in their track a spotty, winding trail, as if they'd been carrying between them a cake of drippy ice.

From somewhere in a back hall the girl's voice called: "This room. In here—"

Kavanaugh shouted back at the car: "Do as I told you, you two! We'll be in the emergency room with Haarman. I'll talk to this doctor. Ten minutes at the longest—"

"Take your time," Coolidge called. "We'll be on the job."

The door slammed. In the mountain's stillness only the muffled chugging of the car. Then the engine was cut off, the headlamps switched out; the silence was absolute. Ranier listened. He could hear no sound from the house. He peered in the direction of the car. In swimming blackness, Winton and its two remaining passengers might have been absorbed. A match broke this illusion; a brief blue-red splutter which showed Mr. Coolidge standing on the running board lighting a cigarette, his eyes under jaunty cap brim fixedly regarding the villa's front. He moved his head casually to speak down to Marcelline whose face was thrust from the driver's seat. There was a conversational murmur too subdued for Ranier to catch; the match died; there was only the spark of a cigarette some dozen paces away.

Ranier turned his attention to the hazed silhouette of the house. Except for the hall lamp and that yellow upper window, the villa remained in darkness, which meant Haarman had been hustled to some room at the back. No chance to go knife-hunting with those two watchdogs waiting in the sedan, but he might get a look at what was happening in Dr. Eberhardt's. Carefully he started through the ferns. Fog curled around him; invisible tentacles of moisture fingering his face. His movements whispered in the watery underbrush. A marshy odor, heavy with the scent of jungle plants; the air too torpid for breathing. Like picking your way along the weed-grown bottom of an aquarium. It was dark going with a feeling there might be snakes.

UNREASONABLY, HE felt a lot better when he skirted the trunk of a sablier, lofted like an apparition in the night, and put the wing of the verandah between himself and the spark of Coolidge's cigarette. Looking back from the corner of the villa, he could see nothing. The side of the villa sprawled along a slope where the scrub had been cleared and there seemed to be a lawn.

Feeling his way along the dark side-wall, he moved swiftly under a row of black windows that were probably hospital rooms. When he paused to consider a black obstruction that was only a thick-trunked, lily-padded vine, he thought he could detect an odor of formaldehyde. The thick breath of a sick room. Smell of leprosy? What sort of place would this Dr. Eberhardt be running here?

Voices!

John Ranier flattened himself against the wall.

—"Lay him on his back. The pressure stops, sometimes, the bleeding. A knife, you say? How terrible! In a moment this hot water will be on, and the doctor should be here from his laboratory. If one of you would just start removing those bandages—" The girl's voice. Drifting around… the corner of the building from somewhere at the rear. Hurried, yet controlled, with a faint throat-huskiness shading into the least foreign accent. Somehow John Ranier knew her voice would be like that.

Daisy's voice: "Ohmygod, it's awful. That terrible road up the mountain. This awful country. I thought we'd never get here alive. I thought we'd go off the road. I want to get out of here. I—I—I—"

Brown's voice: "Y'see we was all in this café havin' a few drinks before we started to drive to Port-au-Prince, and poor Haarman just sittin' there with his back to a window, and—"

Kavanaugh's voice: "Save it for the police, Brown. And can't you hurry Dr. Eberhardt, miss? If this man dies—"

The voices came more distinctly as Ranier stole along the

sidewall; at the corner of the building he stopped with a gasp. Light washed through the screen of a window at the back, spread out fan-wise in the fog-drift. The window was broad and open; by standing away a little and craning his neck, Ranier, concealed in a clump of Poinsettias, had an unobstructed view of the brightly lighted room. Two hurricane lamps with nickel reflectors shed a glare from white-washed walls that made faces bent over an operating table look greenish and unnatural. Brown, Carpetsi and Schlitz were fumbling with Haarman, who lay face up on the cushioned table, which was in the middle of the room. Kavanaugh, his coat open, belts dangling, stood with a cigarette in a doorway to a corridor. Daisy, her hat on her knees, hair in haystack disarray over cornflower eyes, sniveled make-up and tears into a handkerchief and work a rocking chair in a corner. The sleeves of her linen robe rolled to the elbow, the slim girl stood at the taps of a washstand at the side, her back to the room, talking over her shoulder above the pour of running water.

To Ranier, familiar with the scrupulous tile of Bellevue and asceptic glass of Johns Hopkins, the room looked hopelessly inadequate and third rate—combination war-time dressing station, country doctor's office and old-fashioned apothecary shop. A shelf laden with a barber-shop assortment of colored bottles. Tin cabinet of surgical instruments. The outmoded operating table a cross between a dentist's chair and an ironing board. Moths blundered around the lamps and some dead insects clung to the window screen. Dr. Eberhardt's hospital was evidently not up with the Mayo Brothers.

But there was nothing wrong with the way that girl handled herself. Ranier liked the practiced way she scoured her hands; shook back her gold-glinted hair. Nurse's training. Lining up the case for the doctor. Not her first emergency; and a girl had stuffing to take up nursing in one of these tropic backwaters. Ranier liked that. He liked the firm brown look of sun-tanned arms, and the slim curves revealed by the tight-drawn robe. He didn't like the way Kavanaugh stood smoking, looking at her.

"Can't you ring for that doctor again?"

She nodded; reached for a push-button like a doorbell set in the wall. "He always comes at once when I ring it. If he is working hard, though, sometimes he does not hear the first time. He will come."

Schlitz turned from the table, unclasping his pince-nez. His eyes looked pink in a pinched face. "The bandages are undone. My God," his voice shook with appeal, "who would have thought this terrible consequence would have resulted from our planned shore excursion. Poor Mr. Haarman! Stabbed! Why," his voice shrilled as if it had just occurred to him, "with no more compunction than one might impale a Lepidoptera—"

"We'll all be murdered!" the sobs burst from Daisy. "I just knew something dreadful would happen when—"

Brown's voice chattered, "Honest to God, Kavanaugh—"

"Miss," Kavanaugh snapped at the girl, "will you ring for that doctor, again? Are you sure he's in?"

Her hand was on the call bell. "I was upstairs in my room asleep when you came," Ranier heard her tell Kavanaugh. "I saw a light under his door as I ran downstairs. I do not think he would go out and leave the laboratory light."

"Nnnnnnyuh!" the groan was a sound that startled the room.

Carpetsi leapt back from the table, white-lipped. "The guy's comin' around—"

"He ain't dead yet!" Brown gasped. Ranier had a glimpse of the pudgy man's face, pop-eyed. "He's still alive!"

Kavanaugh lashed out from the corridor doorway, "Miss, if you could get whoever's running this place down here, this man might have a chance!" and only the girl seemed to retain her presence of mind, darting from the washbowl to slip past the Irishman at the door.

"I will get Dr. Eberhardt," she said breathlessly. "The bell, sometimes it does not work if the battery is down. One moment, please."

Ranier, looking into the room from his station in the shrub, had a queer impression that when the girl's white shadow slipped into the corridor and disappeared from view on a whisper of running feet, another shadow entered the room. Something intangible, not to be seen but felt. Something that crossed Kavanaugh's face as he walked forward to gaze down on the operating table and its patient. Something that made Carpetsi stare at Brown, Brown glare at Schlitz, the professor peer about and wring his hands. Now the girl was gone they didn't like being left together alone. There was only the nervous squeaking of the woman's rocking chair; the pour of water from the basin taps.

Then, from deep within the house, the girl's voice screamed.

"Oh—come, somebody! Come quickly! Something terrible has happened to my uncle the doctor!"

CHAPTER VI

DEATH OF A DEAD MAN

HE COULD HEAR feet pounding through the house as he skirted the dark wing, and he raced with no thought for a broken instep to beat them to the front. He knew her scream had come from that lighted upper room.

Coolidge shouted, "Hey!" from the direction of the car when he broke through the ferns and ran plunging along the line of the verandah. John Ranier didn't stop. Taking the verandah in two strides, he slammed through the front door, stumbled into the pale-lit reception hall. He saw the stairway, the balcony above, the girl's stricken face looking down from the upper-hall gloom; and he was on the fourth step going up when the others came out of the back corridor and ran shouting into the hall.

Kavanaugh saw him and yelled, "What th'—where the hell did *you* come from?" Schlitz, Brown, Carpetsi and Daisy were banging along behind Kavanaugh; at the same time Coolidge and Marcelline charged in from the front.

Coolidge bawled. "It's the doc from th' ship! He just run around from behind th' house!"

The hall filled with uproar. Ranier ignored the crash of boots coming behind him, bending every sinew to mount the staircase and be first to reach the girl. "What's happened here? What's wrong?"

Her frightened eyes reminded him she had never seen him before and his unexpected appearance must be alarming. He must look like a maniac. Muddied, disheveled, sea cap askew.

Face oil-smoked from that spare-tire ride, abrasions on his palms and the seat half out of his pants from that jounce in the road. He caught her arm.

"It's all right! I'm from the ship like the rest of these people! I came with them here—I'm the ship's doctor! Where's Dr. Eberhardt?"

She gasped, "He is not there—something terrible must have happened—" pointing down the balcony to a wide-open door. Lamplight streamed yellow from the door and some papers blew over the doorsill and scurried out on the balcony carpet.

Ranier started for the door, conscious of tumult coming up the stairs, oaths, puffs of winded breath, steps clattering like cavalry. The girl was close behind him. He heard her voice catch on a sob, appealing for quiet. "Oh—please. There are some very sick patients downstairs. We must not wake them—The laboratory—this is Dr. Eberhardt's laboratory."

Ranier halted on the threshold; stared into the lighted room. He was aware of the girl beside him; aware of her fear-darkened eyes and tremulous breathing. Kavanaugh was on the other side, features sharp, eyes cold steel under his downsnapped hat brim; and a coolness under his shoulder blades told him Marcelline and Coolidge were crowding up behind. He had to shake off a feeling he was surrounded; center his attention on this room.

"The doctor is not here," the girl breathed. "Something must have happened to him. Something has happened here—"

SOMETHING HAD happened in the room, all right. There might have been an explosion in this laboratory. The window that looked out on the gallery and driveway below was open, the screen out. The breeze that rippled a gray, dissolving curtain of fog over the sill, stirred a thresh of scattered note-papers, fever charts, record blanks and loose leaves across the floor. On the left-hand wall, shelved with a drugstore array of colored bottles, a score of bottles had been uncorked and overturned, dripping glisteny cascades of acid, powders and chemicals. A case of books—Ranier recognized Lister, Semmelweis, Pinel, Thorwaldsen's *Tropical Diseases* and Ringold's *Anatomy*—dumped its contents to join the mess, and surgical instruments were everywhere.

Near the door at his elbow an old fashioned roll-top desk might have experienced a hurricane, inkwell upended, pigeonholes in disorder.

Along the right-hand wall a lab table was strewn with all manner of topsy-turvy, a scramble of test tubes, mortars, rubber hose, chemical jars, microscope lying on its side, glass cannisters overturned spilling glutinous messes of bacteriological culture. At one end of the table a big glass tank filled with live frogs gave off shimmering greenish light-rays as the amphibians—there must have been two thousand of them—sped, dived and darted in crazed schools against the glass. In that corner a human skeleton dangled like a marionette; turned slowly in the breeze with a faint clinking of hinged bones, and grinned at the green maelstrom in the aquarium.

"Hell!" Ranier said.

"He was up here by himself all evening," the girl whispered. "He was in here when I went to bed at eight o'clock because I am alone on call tonight with the patients. He was so very busy, so much to do with no one to assist—" Her voice choked. "He was experimenting—something so important he works on—a theory he could revive dead cells with adrenalin. Tonight he was to finish, to make the vital discovery. He told me not to call him unless for emergency. He said he would go out only if the case was extreme."

"Revive dead cells?" Ranier echoed. "Experimenting with—"

She whispered, "He has worked for years. I thought he was in here when I went down to answer the door. Look! His laboratory in ruins! What has done this? Where is Dr. Eberhardt? Never does he go out without leaving a written message to tell me where he goes. Always he leaves a note for me. On that—"

She was pointing at a white enamel table in the center of the tumbled room. Pointing at a small metal standard, on one corner of the table, a lead base with a thin five-inch spike such as housewives use for pinning a stack of milk bills and notes to the ice man. There was no little note pinned to this spike. A plump green bullfrog had been impaled on the standard. The frog's mouth was open like a purse, its eyes bulging. It worked its hind legs feebly. It was still alive.

But John Ranier wasn't looking at the frog. He was looking at a glass bowl set in the center of the table. There was a Bunsen burner flaming under the bowl, and the clear liquid in the bowl simmered and bubbled and gave off a pungence of something cooking. The odor filled the room. A faint flavor of boiled beef. John Ranier didn't like that center-piece. There were, in that bubbling bowl, two human hands. In the boiling water they swam and dodged about and rapped red knuckles on the glass as if they were alive.

NOBODY COULD speak. Then the girl, staring at the opened window where the fog surged, whispered: "We must find Dr. Eberhardt! We must!"

John Ranier said huskily, "That bullfrog's still alive. This couldn't've happened very long ago. What time did you say he—"

Kavanaugh snarled, "It must've happened before we came! Otherwise we'd of heard the noise!" His fingers gripped Ranier's arm, shook. "You were outside there just now! Did you see anybody on that gallery out there? Did you see anybody around?"

"I was at the back of the house." Ranier wrenched away. "Why?"

"We didn't hear nothing at the front," Coolidge put in hoarsely. "Out in the car me and Marcelline—"

Marcelline blurted, "Regard! A frog there! *Sacré nom de Dieu!* It is the Voodoo! That frog—"

Everybody was pushing in. "Say," Brown's voice aghast, "ain't them somebody's hands there in that bowl?"

"Hands! A skeleton!" Daisy's scream soared soprano above mounting babble. "Ohmygod! Ohmygod! Ohmy—"

"Kavanaugh," Coolidge implored, "I think me and Marcelline

better get started while my nerves hold out. We'll take Brown with us. It's a long way in the dark. This Eberhardt doctor ain't around, an' if we're goin' for the cops—"

Buzzzzzzzzzzzsz!

Everybody heard it. Stood rooted. Stared.

Buzzzzzzzzzzzzz!

There it was again, drilling the baited silence. Coming from a panel in the wall above the laboratory table. A short, insistent drone that lit a tiny red light-bulb in the panel.

Buzzzzzzzzzzzzz!

The small bulb glowing again, on red, off red, like a firefly.

"Why—" the girl at Ranier's elbow gasped convulsively. "Why—that is the call bell from the emergency room. That is the buzzer from the room where we left the wounded man!"

"Whaaat?" It was Kavanaugh who whirled, eyes glowing. Face shocked for the first time that night. "By God, who—we left Haarman down there alone!"

A sensation of cold seemed to flow under John Ranier's scalp. Swept in the rush for the stairs, he tried to fight back fear; a seventh-sense feeling that unknown quantities had invaded the shadows around him and something diabolic and occult was loose in the fog-hung Haitian night. A man stabbed in the back and his table companions do not see it. Cryptic figures and the name Dr. Eberhardt scrawled on an envelope from the stabbed man's pocket. A Dr. Eberhardt's hospital near the scene of crime, a lonely mountain villa and a beautiful girl. Dr. Eberhardt missing, his laboratory wrecked. A frog jammed on a spike.

Those three drones from the buzzer seemed the final terror. Three calls from a room where a man lay dying on an operating table, and alone. Who had pushed that bell to start them downstairs in stampede? John Ranier seemed to run in a cold wind. He could see the tuck was out of Kavanaugh, now. All the hardness was gone from the Irishman's face and his skin was niveous, cheekbones glistening as if under the icy spray of the morgue.

The girl's fear sickened him. Somehow—he didn't know

how—his arm was about her waist as they followed Kavanaugh down the hall to the back corridor: he could feel her tenseness as they ran. *Thump, thump, thump,* the others were coming.

Then they were panting in the doorway of the emergency room, Kavanaugh holding them back, glaring. John Ranier saw the room was as they had left it. Only Haarman was there, on the operating table. The man's knees were drawn up as if in spasm, his left hand was clenched on his chest, his right arm hung limp, palm open. His face stared at the ceiling, an unseeing glassy stare. His mouth was open and his tongue showed.

"He's dead," Ranier said. "He must've just died."

It was the girl who gave the low-pitched, breathless cry.

"No—No—No—!"

Everybody looked at the girl. All color had fled from her face. Her eyes were wide, white-circled, appalled. She stood rigid, one hand clutched in the gold-brown thicket of her hair, the other pointing at Haarman's corpse on the operating table.

"What's the matter?" Ranier asked.

"That man!" the girl's voice was barely audible, a gray whisper in her convulsed throat. "His face—the scar on his right hand—I did not notice when they first brought him in tonight—I know that man! His name is Adolph Perl! Adolph Perl!" Her voice rose on the wings of terror. *"He couldn't have died just now! He died fourteen years ago in this very room! He died here in Haiti—Dr. Eberhardt buried him in the graveyard down the mountain—fourteen years ago—"*

Fog creamed and curled against the window screen, opaque, wraith-like, silent. Not quite silent. Somewhere far out in the smothered night there was a low, sullen throbbing of wooden drums.

CHAPTER VII

THE GIRL'S STORY

THE ROOM HAD stopped breathing. In the corridor, the halls, the stair-bannisters, upper rooms, dark passageways behind, all the normal night-sounds of a house asleep, all the nocturnal squeakings of floor-crack, of hinges straining in release, of timbers expanding after heat of the day, had stopped. Every clock, dripping faucet, mouse, might have died. The villa held its breath. Something in the air had quit. It seemed to Ranier as if the night itself was held in the grip of shock, like a great crouching beast muscle-locked in an ictus. Only its pulse was going, a low, dulled throb from the abeyant dark, no louder than the tapping of a fainted man's heart.

Nobody moved. In the shadowless glare of the hurricane lamps, the room with its bottles and operating table was stark; the body on the operating table, the people in the doorway like dressed figures in stone. But the girl with her right hand caught in her hair, her left hand extended in that awful attitude of pointing, was shivering. An imperceptible trembling that shook her lips, quivered down the soft curve of her throat, shook the slim lines of her figure, down the brown unstockinged ankles to her white tennis shoes. In the white of her face her eyes, glowing at the body on the table, were almost black. Ranier had never seen such eyes. Wider. Wider. The room dwindled in his own vision, other faces blurring into background. It was as if only the two alone were there—the staring girl, the contorted dead man in midroom. And the girl was shivering and shivering.

He must put a stop to this. He must break that shock before it broke the girl.

He hardly knew he moved. He hardly knew he moved through that immense silence, stepped to the operating table, consulted the taffy-haired man's lifeless pulse, pulled a blood-stained coat over the dead face. He hardly knew he walked, then, to the girl; caught her wrists to her sides, spun her rigid body in an about-face from the table, and commanded angrily, "Stop it! Stop it!"

His voice broke the spell; cut the overtaut nerves of tension; smashed the ice in the air. Figures came to life around him as if released; everybody seemed to yell at once. Kavanaugh was shouting at the girl, "What do you mean? What do you mean by saying Haarman died here in Haiti fourteen years ago?"

It was communicated to Ranier's sensitized skin that the Irishman's assurance had returned, and he had to admire the man's grit. Panic reacted in the others, but the tall, self-sure man had recovered his steely personality and was pointing that domineering finger again. His tone implied, "What the devil do you mean, trying to scare Dave Kavanaugh?"

"She made a mistake," Ranier said grimly across his shoulder. "Of course you did," he spoke directly to the trembling girl. "This Mr. Haarman came down on the cruise ship with us from New York. Someone stabbed him in that café down in the village, and he died a few minutes ago while we were upstairs in that laboratory. He must have revived in one of those spasms of strength that come sometimes just before death; staggered over to push that call button on the wall; then pulled himself back up on the operating table. Effort that finished him. You can see he's not been dead three minutes. You've mistaken him for somebody else."

The girl's eyes moved in dilated fascination to the lifeless shape on the table, and he could feel her wrists grow rigid in his grip.

Lais Engles slumped to the floor

She whispered, "I am not mistaken. It is he. Adolph Perl. He died here fourteen years ago. I saw him die."

SOMEBODY SWORE and somebody made a sound like a whinny, and the look on the girl's face put an ache in the roots of John Ranier's hair.

Kavanaugh, who had walked to the operating table, spun furiously. "Well, he's dead, all right, all right.... What is this, an insane asylum? Girl tryin' to tell us Haarman is a guy she saw die once before!"

"She's mistaken him for someone she once knew," Ranier insisted.

"I am not mistaken. That scar on his palm. Shaped like the English letter Z." Her low voice reminded Ranier of the other-worldish murmuring of a person talking out of sleep. "That scar, it was cut in his hand by an Indian in Para, Brazil. The face I would know anywhere. Thinner, older, but the face of Adolph Perl. It was the last summer of the War, I met him. He was mate on my uncle's schooner, and then we were four years lost up the Amazon—"

Kavanaugh stared at the girl from under stretched eyelids. "The Amazon River in South America? Two seconds ago you said he died here in Haiti!"

"It was on our way back to Europe. Adolph Perl died when the schooner came ashore in Haiti. That was in 1922. And it is Adolph Perl, here now—on the very operating table where he—"

She put her face in her hands and began to cry softly; and an alto from the doorway moaned, "*Zombie!*" and nothing of this was real but the echo of those drums far off in the night. Even Kavanaugh became unreal, his cheekbones sultry, his eyes blue sparks, cocking his thumb like a trigger and aiming his finger at the stunned audience in the doorway, bawling suddenly;

"Well, what are you standing there for? You don't believe this nutty girl, do you? You realize there'll be a murder charge here, and all of us held up under one hell of an investigation? Haarman's dead and we've got to get a move on. Brown!"

The fleshy man designated by Kavanaugh's finger made a timid step forward. His spectacles looked owlish, and his lips made the sound of "Wh" twice.

"Snap out of it," Kavanaugh told him. "When you get to the village down below, call the American consul at Port-au-Prince on the phone. Tell him what's happened here, and to hop in a car and get here fast. Use my name, understand?

"Whuh—when I get to the village?"

"Marcelline will drive the car. Coolidge, you go, too. While Brown's phoning, you get out those police. And bring 'em back on the jump." He whipped back his cuff to inspect strap watch. "It's nine-thirty. Don't forget, all three of you are in this under suspicion. Try any funny stuff and it'll be just too bad. If you aren't back by ten, I'll swear out warrants for your arrest."

Angelo Carpetsi whimpered, "I'll go with them, Mr. Kavanaugh."

"Like hell," the Italian was corrected harshly. "You'll stick here with the rest of us till the cops come. Okay, you three. Go!"

They went. Pug-nosed Mr. Coolidge with his nerves, plump Mr. Brown and bugeyed Monsieur Marcelline. There was something in the sound of their fast departing heels that left no doubt about their being grateful to leave. Distantly the doors of the Winton were heard to bang; followed the hammering of an engine, the squeal of a car bending a driveway on precarious wheels, zooming off down a mountain road in night.

John Ranier was thinking: "Now I've only got to watch the blonde mess, the professor, the Dago and Kavanaugh. Find Eberhardt and do something about this girl—"

Kavanaugh cut into his thoughts with:

"So now, ladies and gentlemen—" slurring the "gentlemen" as his eyes went coldly at Ranier—"the Haitian police will be here soon, and meanwhile we can wait right here where it's cozy and we can keep an eye on each other. And maybe the girl can tell us what's become of the doctor who runs this establishment, and explain this crazy nonsense about Mr. Haarman!"

If the Irishman's tone chewed a brittle suggestion of threat through his teeth, the girl at Ranier's side did not notice it.

"There were five of them who died," she whispered. "Five who died besides Adolph Perl. It was here they were stricken by the mauve death from Brazil, and here on this coast they were buried. And that man on the operating table was buried in the cemetery three miles down the road—"

CEMETERY THREE miles down the road? Sweat beads bunched on John Ranier's forehead as he recalled the little cluster of candle-lit gravemounds constellating the fog-cloaked mountainside. He couldn't help a side-glance at the body on the operating table; a glance that moved hastily to Kavanaugh's scowling face, to the faces hovering in the doorway—Professor Schlitz's fear-cartooned features ridiculous in a sun helmet; the blonde woman a portrait of misery scribbled in rouge and powder; Angelo Carpetsi's terrified black eyes. An hour ago they'd been bored American tourists seeing the Caribbean littoral through the bottom of a grog-bottle; now they were peopling a nightmare in which a member of their party had been slain by an invisible knife, only to be identified by a nurse in this jungle-locked retreat as a man who had died four years after the World War.

He looked sharply at the girl. Whispering through her fingers, her voice had been barely louder than the fog-muffled tumpings that were as counted heart beats from the whitewashed night. She must have sensed the thought behind his scrutiny, for she dropped her hands from her marble-white face, let them fall inertly to her sides.

She whispered, "*Nein,* I am not mad. How it can be, I do not know, but it is the same man. I would have known him anywhere—anywhere—"

"But it *can't* be the same man," Ranier assured her. "People don't die twice, Miss—Miss—"

"My name is Laïs Engles. I came to the Americas from Griefswald, Germany—on a schooner with that man. It was the last year of the War, and I was six years old. My mother was dead and my father had been killed in the Battle of Jutland—it was my uncle, Captain Friederich, who took me on his schooner because the orphan asylums of Germany were crowded—there was no place for me to go. Adolph Perl—*he*—was mate of that schooner!"

Brushing past Ranier to confront the girl, Kavanaugh snarled: "If you've got to spin us a yarn, Miss What's-your-name, you might keep it straight while you're spinning it. While back you called Dr. Eberhardt your uncle; now it's some Kraut skipper during the War!"

"Captain Friederich was my real uncle. Dr. Eberhardt, who raised me here in his hospital after Captain Friederich died—him I call Uncle Doktor." Fingers clenched, she turned to send a dilated stare at the body on the operating table.

"That was in 1918, but I remember as if it were yesterday. My uncle's schooner was the *Kronprinz Albrecht,* very fast and with hidden engines. A blockade runner, like the famous *Emden,* it was to sail through the British fleet, cross the Atlantic, travel up the Amazon on a secret mission for the Kaiser's government. Do you understand? It was camouflaged as a tramp ship flying the flag of Holland; no one to suspect it was the German Navy. Another reason for taking me—a child on board would put the vessel above suspicion. And the crew were hand-picked volunteers." Her eyes shone strangely and she pushed a hand across her forehead. "Do you think I could forget this man—this man who was mate of that schooner?"

Kavanaugh's lip curled. "This happened when you were six years old?"

"So you think I would not remember? The long Atlantic voyage? The day we sailed into the Amazon at Para, where the mate—Adolph Perl—went ashore and got in a fight with an Indian who slashed that scar in his hand? *Nein,*" her eyes, fixed on that frowsty operating table, grew. "I remember well. My uncle, Captain Friederich, confined him for three weeks in irons because of that fight. Brazil had declared war on Germany, and it was dangerous for us to attract attention. That is how I could never mistake that scar—"

Ranier looked at the body that was stark under the hurricane lamps. Flies were walking on the coat that covered the taffy-haired man's face, and his hanging arm looked stiffer than it had a few moments ago. Already the dead hand had discolored a little. He jerked his eyes from the Z-cut scar to surprise a venomous expression on the face of Mr. Kavanaugh. Scorn fought with unbelief across the Irishman's hard-chiseled features; his eyes were twinkling at the girl under fanning lids; and, as was usual in domineering types, the man's doubt crystallized into anger.

He lashed at the girl, "Even if Haarman was the man you think was the mate of that schooner—which he wasn't!—just what would a German ship be doing, exploring up the Amazon in war time?"

She whispered, "Germany was desperate. All the world was leagued against her. The Kaiser wanted a secret pact with Chile, one of the few countries that was neutral. In the mountains of Chile were nitrates for explosives. Our mission was to reach Chile somewhere in the headwaters of the Amazon, to bribe the Chilean diplomats to declare war on our side against Brazil and Peru. From Para we sailed up the Amazon, across the interior of South America, deep in the vast river wilderness through thousand miles of jungle, such a voyage as no schooner had made before. But we did not reach Chile. In those miles and miles of floating wilderness we became lost. How could I mistake anyone who was in that little handful of German sailors?"

Kavanaugh said harshly, "The mythical expedition gets lost in the Amazon and turns up in Haiti. Two times two makes six!"

But the girl's voice went on, low, appalled: "We were four years lost on the Amazon. Unexplored tributaries. Yellow channels everywhere. I think it was on the Rio Madeira tributary my uncle lost the way, deep in the heart of South America. Our schooner went aground and we camped in the jungle for months, waiting for floods to float her. Brazil was enemy country and we dared send no message for help. Our wireless went to pieces, too. From Berlin we had no word of news, and the sailors of the *Kronprinz Albrecht* almost forgot Germany or such a place as Europe. The primitive Indians of the Rio Madeira had never heard of the War; only Captain Friederich and Colonel Otto, the Prussian envoy in charge of the mission, refused to turn back. They had promised the Imperial High Command to reach Chile, a mission that might save their Fatherland. They were German officers of the old school. Adolph Perl—the mate—was a German of the old school. *Nein,* we pushed on until the schooner was rotting to pieces, the crew starving, only a few of us remained. Our gear was rusted, clocks stopped for lack of oil, time was lost track of. There was an old woman who had come with us from Germany to look after me—Old Gramma Sou. She used to tell me stories of Germany, and Adolph Perl, the mate, would stand listening. *'Herr Gott!'* he used to say. 'If only

I could see the girls on the *Unter den Linden* again.' How many, many times have I thought of it!"

LISTENING TO the girl's haunted voice as it spoke just then, John Ranier could almost forget this was a hospital in Haiti and she was talking of a cruise passenger who'd been murdered, stabbed that night in a waterfront café a few miles away. He could almost forget this strange bright room with its sinister fog-curtained window, its company of frightened tourists, its undertone echo of Negroid drums. He was seeing a river in far-off South America, a vast brown flood slipping through endless green, a tattered schooner manned by desperate men, a little German girl with yellow pigtails and round blue eyes. What incredible distances the vibrations of the War had traveled. She'd been six, and he sixteen—a boy in the muds of France, crawling through barbed wire with a smashed foot—a a child with pigtails in the lost jungles of Brazil—

"After four years hunting for a way to Chile, my uncle had to turn back for supplies, for engine oil. We found our way to a place called Porto Velho. There were a few English and Americans there; a little camp in the jungle, building a railroad to Bolivia, they said. How they stared at us—all that was left of us. We thought them soldiers, but they were not soldiers. They said the War was over long ago. Can you imagine the feelings of Captain Friederich and his men? It was 1922—all those terrible miles of journey, those months in the jungle for nothing. I will never forget how Adolph Perl raved and cursed. How, when the schooner returned to Para, my uncle wept on learning Germany lay beaten, the Kaiser's government was no more; and in answer to his cable to Berlin came an order from an admiral he had never heard of. It was thought our ship had gone down long ago. So the *Kronprinz Albrecht* was ordered back to Germany at once, still under secret orders, and we started up the Caribbean. But a terrible storm drove us close to Haiti, drove us into this Gulf of Gonaives; our ship ran up on the beach of the village below. Fourteen years ago, that was. That night I first saw Dr.

Eberhardt. That night—" her voice shook—"that night came the mauve death."

"The mauve death?" Ranier questioned hollowly. "What was that?"

"So Dr. Eberhardt called it," she murmured huskily. "A rare tropical disease with symptoms like beri-beri. Terribly contagious, it is, and kills within two hours of infection. The—the skin turns violet. Our—our schooner had brought it from the jungles of Brazil."

She pulled her linen robe tighter as if the room were suddenly cold; and John Ranier, watching her closely, felt a slow malignant dread begin to creep up his spine. Had sight of that wizardish laboratory upstairs, and the added shock of this emergency case, deranged the girl's mind? Carried her back to some terrible childhood experience which a stunned mind was translating into the present? Shock did queer things to people. Inspired hallucinations. But the girl looked sane—terrified, not deranged—

"Verstehen-zie?" she panted. "That awful germ, that mauve death must have been carried by our schooner, for Dr. Eberhardt said it had never before been in Haiti, and the night of the storm with our schooner on the beach, the disease broke out among us. I was then ten years old, and never could I forget that night. I could not! The darkness. The strange island. Bonfires on the beach. The Haitians crowding to see the ship. We came ashore in a lifeboat—all that was left of our pitiful expedition—with what luggage we could save. Dr. Eberhardt was among the Negroes; ran up to see if he could help. When he discovered we were Germans, he spoke to us delighted—but, *nein!* he stared suddenly at Colonel Otto and cried, '*Lieber Gott!* you must get out of this crowd at once; you must all come at once to my hospital!'"

Ranier said thickly, "But Miss Engles—" and she lifted a hand in protest, whispering, "Please! I must tell you! I must tell you what happened that night to us—to *that* man! Dr. Eberhardt—he brought us here to this hospital, and Colonel Otto was dead before we got here. My uncle, Captain Friederich was next to die—an hour later. Then Old Gramma Sou, my nurse, whom I had grown to love as my mother. Nothing could save them. Dr. Eberhardt could not save them. 'It is the mauve death,' he told me that night. 'It is the mauve death that strikes like the lightning and spreads like the wind. You must be a brave little girl, my child. Some of your friends will never leave Haiti alive.'"

She stopped to draw a shuddery breath, and Kavanaugh's voice quarreled: "So this Eberhardt was in Haiti at that time, was he?"

"He has spent his life here in Haiti," her lips gripped back a sob. "Dr. Eberhardt is a great man, a scientist. He came here before the War, and when the fighting broke across Europe he refused to go back to Germany. His life is devoted to medicine, to his experiments, to his work among the Negroes. That night he was terrified for fear the mauve death would spread, and he fought to stop the contagion, knowing plague and panic would destroy all his work. It was terrible! Terrible! The American Marines were in Haiti at the time, and there was a Marine sergeant at the hospital. Dr. Eberhardt sent him down to the beach with orders to burn the schooner. *Ja,* the American soldier burned our schooner that night, and gave his life to do it. The plague took him, too. He returned to the hospital—died!"

FISTS CLENCHED, eyes wide, she moved so suddenly at Kavanaugh that the Irishman, startled, sidestepped into Ranier. Off-balanced by his lame foot, Ranier swung against Professor Schlitz, and the thin insectologist shrieked as if tagged by a ghost. The white, mourgish room dizzied on John Ranier's vision as he heard the girl's low-pitched words flung at Kavanaugh:

"Do you think I could forget one detail of that horrible night? Mistake anyone who was there? *Nein,* I remember every detail. How Colonel Otto, when he died, asked to be buried in his Potsdam uniform. Old Gramma Sou dying in the taffeta dress she had saved from the schooner—the dress she had brought from Berlin to wear at the embassy in Chile. Captain Friederich dying with 'God save the Fatherland!' on his lips. That Marine sergeant—his name was O'Grady. A huge man over six feet tall, he was, and he fell to his face out there on the verandah, his cheeks all lavender, and he had a red moustache. Dying. Dying and singing a wild American song!

"How could I forget that brave man or any one of those brave Germans who gave their lives for the Fatherland four years too late, killed by the plague they had brought from Brazil. My uncle, Captain Friederich, blamed himself because the mission to Chile had failed; *ja,* he thought that was why Germany had lost the war. He cursed the death that was striking him down in Haiti, the death that would prevent him from carrying out his government's last order. He called Dr. Eberhardt that night. 'You must carry on for us!' he told the doctor. 'If the mate, Adolph Perl, dies also, *you* must carry on!' He told Dr. Eberhardt the story of the secret mission. He gave Dr. Eberhardt a suitcase of papers, something of great value to Germany that should have been delivered to the diplomats in Chile. Now Captain Friederich had been ordered to return that suitcase to Berlin. Dying he begged the doctor to look after me, but first he made him promise to take charge of the suitcase; Dr. Eberhardt must swear as a German to return that valuable case to the German government. And Adolph Perl was weeping. Weeping that night. 'I will not die,' he cried. 'I will carry on for the Fatherland!' It was right out there in the hall. I was listening at a door, and I overheard."

Her fingers, pointing at the door, brought cries of fear from the tourists dummified in the frame. "Out there in the hall," she repeated. "Fourteen years ago. Colonel Otto, Captain Friederich, Old Gramma Sou—dead! And that American Marine on the verandah—fourth to die. And an Anglican missionary from a little village down the coast was fifth. An Angelican missionary who had stopped in to pray for the dying, and in two hours he, with them, was dead. *Ja,* it was a fatal disease, that mauve death. Dr. Eberhardt locked all the doors, let nobody enter after that. If word got loose there was a plague in the hospital, the Haitians would have rioted and murdered all the whites. Those of us from the schooner—all that had survived—we waited to be next. There were only three of us left. A sailor named Hans Blücher—myself—the mate, Adolph Perl. We waited for death to take us. In this very room we waited."

Turning slowly, fearfully, the girl pointed at the fogblurred window across the room. "Dr. Eberhardt and the house-boy, Polypheme, they were in the stable back there behind the hospital. We could hear them sawing and hammering. Building coffins. I wept in fear, because I was little and it was late at night and I did not understand. I only knew the bodies were in a row out there in the front hall, waiting. And Hans Blücher, the sailor, wept too. And Adolph Perl, the mate, walked up and down cursing. I can see it now, as I saw it then.

"Hans Blücher said he was feeling sick, and he crept out into the corridor. We sat in this room together, Adolph Perl and I. We waited. Hans did not come back. In a minute Adolph Perl said, 'I am going after that man!' and went out into the corridor. I waited alone. The pounding of the coffins went on and on, like those drums you hear beating on the mountain tonight. After a while Adolph Perl returned. 'Hans Blücher had fled the hospital,' he told me. 'The scoundrel has run away.' Then Adolph Perl began to stagger and cough. He put his hand to his throat—his scarred hand. *'Heilegegott!'* he screamed. 'I have caught it from going out there. Now I, too, am going to die!' He climbed up on that operating table—that very table where you see him now—and lay there gasping—"

THERE WAS a sensation of frost forming on John Ranier's temples; it was too late at night for this sort of thing. Something in the girl's voice convinced him she was speaking truth, and her breathless words, whispering out of memory, described a scene more real than present actuality. The dread in her eyes, fixed now on Haarman's stiffening body, was no pretense. There was sanity in the white struggle of her lips to go on, as if the words were being dragged from her throat at great effort of will.

"Adolph Perl lay where you see him now, and Dr. Eberhardt

ran in from the corridor, very angry. 'Who left the front door open?' And Adolph Perl lifted his hand, the hand with the scar. 'Blücher ran away!' he swore. 'I saw him running for the jungle. He was afraid he would get the contagion. Now I have caught the mauve death from going out there in the hall.' He was weeping, coughing, and he described the symptoms the others had suffered. He begged Dr. Eberhardt to take him out in the hall. 'Lay me between Captain Friederich and Colonel Otto. I want to die between my officers!'

"Dr. Eberhardt carried Adolph Perl into the hall and put him on the floor between the dead officers. Adolph Perl lay writhing. Then he lay still. Dr. Eberhardt looked down at him and groaned, 'He is dead. We must bury them quickly and secretly.' The doctor had been giving me injections, and he gave me another and told me, 'You are not going to die. You must help me now and not cry out or the Haitians will hear you. We must turn out all the lights so the Negroes will not see us.' The coffins were there in the hall. The lights were turned out. Moonlight came through. Dr. Eberhardt put all the bodies in the big yellow rough-boxes in a row. He said the bodies must be buried at once and he told me to take a last look at my friends; then he ran outside to help Polypheme hitch up the wagon. I was afraid to wait there in the hall alone, and I ran upstairs to the laboratory and hid. When the wagon came, I crept downstairs again. I had to help nail on the wooden lids. It was terrible, nailing on those lids. Dr. Eberhardt had covered all the faces with handkerchiefs in the dark, and—I am telling you this because—because—"

Hand to forehead, she stared at the operating table. "Because there was a streak of moonlight," she whispered, "and it fell across Adolph Perl's hand as we nailed up the coffin, and the last thing I saw was that brown, Z-shaped scar. Then I watched Polypheme and the doctor load the wagon. There were six coffins. 'We must hurry,' Dr. Eberhardt said. 'We must distribute them at different cemeteries along the coast so the natives will not see a lot of new graves together and suspect anything.' I remember how he climbed up on the wagon and wrote the names on the coffins with a pencil. How he held me on his lap. How we started off in the moonlight, Polypheme whipping the horses—"

Once more the girl was shivering. Lips colorless; face marble; eyes shining, narcotic. She cried, "Adolph Perl was buried that night. In the cemetery down the road—near the village. I saw it. I saw Dr. Eberhardt dig the grave. White with exhaustion, he was, but he dug every one of those graves, choosing sandy soil to make it easy for the shovel, digging, digging, while Polypheme held the lantern. *Ja,* then Polypheme would fill them, and the wagon would go on. We put Old Gramma Sou in the graveyard east of here, and the American Marine sergeant in the soldier's cemetery beyond. The missionary in his own churchyard; then Colonel Otto at Bois Legone; and my uncle, Captain Friederich, last, at a place high on the *morne* overlooking the coast. But Adolph Perl was buried in the graveyard three miles below here, *ja*—I saw him buried—you can see the marker. He died of the mauve death that night, and I saw him buried—*and this man you have brought here tonight,*" she finished with a sob, *"is that same Adolph Perl!"*

"Ohmygod!"

Miss Daisy May was on the floor again.

CHAPTER VIII

THE WEBBED FOOT

AND THE GIRL, herself, might have fallen if John Ranier hadn't caught her in time. She swayed, and he steadied her, wondering about his own knees and doubting his sanity. He was imagining this. He'd had one drink too many down there at Hyacinth Lucien's, and *aguardiente* had gone to his brain. But the girl's slim body quivering against him was real enough, as the past, the dark scenes her husky-throated words had conjured to his vision were gone, and he was conscious of the present, tonight, Haiti outside, jungle and mountain close around, a villa smothered under breathless fog. White walls of a make-shift hospital room, and moths flitting under lamps. Kavanaugh's shoulder beside him, that fainted female on the floor, Carpetsi's pistachio-tinged face sweating, and Professor Schlitz's pince-nez, silly with fear.

It was a charade, a spell cast by the muffled *tumpy-bum-bum* that pulsed from the fog-bank beyond the window screen and came into the room like a dead march for the body on the shabby operating table. The fog-bank was a ghost looking in, and there were ghosts in the room that couldn't be seen. Ranier could feel their fingers in his hair. He knew he ought to do something about it, but he could only stand there, muddied, disreputable, sea-cap aslant, supporting a slim girl in white linen with gold lights in her hair and blue terror in her eyes; could only stand there glaring from the girl to the dead man in midroom, the cruise passenger named Haarman who'd been stabbed to death tonight—a man this girl had seen buried fourteen years ago!

It was the insectologist who broke that cataleptic charade. Eyes popping the glasses from his nose. Voice climbing a ladder in his throat to a windy peak of falsetto.

"You hear what she says? You hear what this girl says?" waving his hands. "That man Haarman—she knew him during the war—she saw him die in Haiti in 1922! But he got on our boat from New York—! Was sharing my stateroom on this cruise! He told me he'd never been to sea before. Said he was German—yes!—but born in America—in the artichoke business in New York City. Artichokes!" the professor screeched. "He told me that! And he said he was taking this cruise for his health! His *health!* My God! How pale he always was! So horribly *pale!* His *health!*"

"And always walkin' around by himself!" Carpetsi said, staring frantically at the table and rabidly biting at a hangnail on his finger. "He'd never come into the bar, or—"

"And he'd always walk the deck in carpet slippers," the professor shrilled, as if the fact held some evil significance. "Carpet slippers! You'd be standing at the rail and he'd go by and you'd hardly hear him. As if—as if—"

"Who stabbed him in that café? No knife or nothin'! Marcelline said there was a face, didn't he? Didn't Marcelline say—"

"Those *zombie* things! The guides in Cape Haitian mentioned them, too. Dead men brought to life, and—"

A whimper broke from the Italian boy, jumping him around in the doorway. "Holy Jees, I'm gettin' out of here!" And then Kavanaugh's voice was crashing with the authority of gunfire, hammering, "Stand still, you fool! All of you, shut up! Nobody's going to leave." Striding across the floor, he jerked Carpetsi back from the corridor, shoved the thin man aside, blocked the exit. "Nobody's getting out of here, see? At least, not until those three fools come back with the police!"

FEET PLANTED apart, body bowed a little at the middle, the Irishman let his eyes circle the room with an uncompromising glare that came to rest on John Ranier and the girl at his side.

Kavanaugh aimed his finger at Laïs Engles. "Get this!" he told her in a grating tone. "There's a murder been pulled off tonight, and no crackbrained ghost story is going to run me out of here before I'm cleared. I don't know you, see? And I don't know your reason for dishing out this yarn. Much obliged for an interesting tale to take up the time. Thanks. But I don't believe any of it."

"It's true," she whispered.

"Sure," Kavanaugh grinned. "This guy from New York was a German naval officer up the Amazon. He told us he never went to sea before and his name's Haarman, but he was a mate on a blockade runner, named Perl."

"I know him."

"He died of a stab-wound after we brought him here tonight, but he's the same man who died in this hospital fourteen years ago!"

"I saw him buried."

Kavanaugh sneered, "Oh, sure. Some of these black island witch doctors raised him from the dead and he goes up to New York and runs an artichoke business, and then he takes this Caribbean cruise back to Haiti for his health. But all this time he's a living dead man, eh? He's one of these *zombies*—"

"I don't know," she put her face in her hands. "I don't know—"

"I suppose this Dr. Eberhardt who runs this hospital would remember all about this German expedition who died of th' plague from Brazil? I suppose Dr. Eberhardt would recognize this guy?"

"Dr. Eberhardt only saw him that one night, but I am sure—"

"And where *is* Dr. Eberhardt?" Kavanaugh demanded. "Why isn't he here?"

"I don't know."

"Well, I know," the tall Irishman rasped. "Maybe there's such a thing as corpses coming back to life and going into the vegetable trade after fourteen years in the grave, but not in my bailiwick! I know Mr. Haarman got on this cruise ship in New York City ten days ago. I know he had a few drinks with me on deck and told me about his business in New York. I know he asked me if he could join a motor ride from here to Port-au-Prince, and chipped in his share for the automobile. I know he was alive back there in that damned dirty café where we were going to start out, and I know somebody stabbed him. I don't know why he was stabbed or who did it or how, but I know it's murder and he died in this hospital of yours for the first time in his life, see? If you think you can throw a scare in me with all this *zombie* rubbish, you're wrong."

He turned a thin smile at John Ranier. "And what does our ship's doctor think?"

John Ranier thought: "The man's talking sense, but he doesn't see this girl believes her own words."

He said slowly: "I'm sure Miss Engles has had a shock. Whatever happened tonight upstairs in Dr. Eberhardt's laboratory frightened her, and her imagination is overwrought." He touched the girl's arm. "There are such things as close resemblances. Many people look alike. After all, you haven't seen the man, Adolph Perl, in fourteen years, and you were a child when you last saw him. As for the scar on Mr. Haarman's hand, why that may be coincidence, too."

"The thing isn't worth bothering about," was Kavanaugh's harsh comment. "Telling us Mr. Haarman is a German naval officer she saw buried in 1922. She hasn't the slightest bit of proof—"

The girl's head came up, her wide dark eyes met the man's scoffing stare. "I have proof."

"Just because you saw that scar—"

"There is more than the scar."

Kavanaugh said in a low fury, "Listen, Mr. Haarman was never in Haiti before and you never saw him before and he isn't anybody named Adolph Perl and you know it!"

"Very well," her tone was weak with strain. "If the man is not Adolph Perl there is proof. In South America the sailors on my uncle's ship went barefooted. The left foot of Adolph Perl fascinated me as a child. The crew nicknamed him The Duck. The toes of Adolph Perl were joined by a membrane. Perl had a webbed foot—"

Every eye in the room was drawn by that same icy magnetism. That body on the operating table. The dead man's shoes. High-laced brown shoes, thick-soled, awkward in the outspread, loose-ankle posture of death. John Ranier heard Kavanaugh's half-throttled oath. Professor Schlitz made a gargling sound. Even the Daisy woman roused to her feet at this climax to cling on Carpetsi's sleeve and stare with eyes like doughnuts, whimpering.

The girl's white lips murmured, "If the left foot is webbed—"

John Ranier walked to the table, unlaced and juggled off the shoe, pulled off the sock; expecting, naturally, to find the left foot of Mr. Haarman was not webbed.

It was webbed.

CHAPTER IX

BE HE ALIVE OR BE HE DEAD

THEY RAN. THEY fled that anamorphosis, went into the corridor as if that grotesque bare foot had kicked them wholesale through the door. John Ranier went with them because he could see no reason to remain behind with a Mr. Haarman whose naked pedal extremity showed an eczematous heel, a pallid callus-scabbed sole, a fallen arch, five dead toes pointed at the ceiling and that batwing-like membrane between the toes. Mr. Haarman, dead with a webbed foot, did not invite companionship. The case, Ranier felt, was beyond a ship doctor's chirurgery. It might even have baffled a chiropodist.

Half way down the corridor he discovered Mr. Haarman's left shoe was in his hand, and the *bang!* it gave when he dropped it brought Kavanaugh around as if he'd fired a gun. The girl cried, "Oh!" running with her fingers across her mouth; and at the corridor's turn he could not help looking back, half expecting to see Mr. Haarman in the doorway, coming after his shoe.

Always to Ranier there'd been something of the eerie about a hospital at night, something beyond the calculations of *materia medica.* There could be a "witching hour" in medicine when the most hard-boiled and scientific practitioner sat back with folded hands to wait. For what? For something not in the book. Something outside the realm of test-tube, nostrum and pledget. Something that stirred through the hushed hallways or entered a dim-lit ward, barely moving the window curtains, to choose a patient for the "turn." The Unseen impulse that stemmed the tide of a hopeless hemorrhage to rescue the moribund for another day. The Caprice that stole into an adjoining room to beckon bony-fingered at a simple tonsillectomy case, and whisper, "You—"

It was there. In Dr. Eberhardt's hospital, cloaked in mountain isolation and fog. But it was more than the mystery of death or healing behind quiet doors; more than the nocturnal silence of whitewashed walls, the shadows restless under dimmed vigil lamps, the drugged air heavy with sickroom exhalations, germicides. There was, in this shadowy corridor, something invisible and malign.

The front hall was no improvement. The stairway at the side cast a bonelike pattern of bannister-shadows on the opposite wall. The pneumonia pallor of the night-lamp did not reach the upper balcony. Infected by the panic, the gray tabby sped from somewhere and streaked across the hall like a frightened thought. Miss Daisy May jumped the cat with a wail. Mr. Angelo Carpetsi helterskeltered along the bone-shadowed wall, hooked his suspenders on an unsuspected knob and yanked open a closet door. An umbrella, a sun helmet and a black frock coat that might have been Dr. Eberhardt but wasn't, tumbled out of the wall-cupboard to tangle with Professor Schlitz's feet. Professor Schlitz said nothing, but proceeded to go through the front door at a pace undignified for a Ph.D. from Upsala. Seen from behind, he appeared to evaporate in the dark mists of the verandah, a process that was too much for him, for after a half second's contemplation of the fog outside, the professor wheeled and sprang back into the hall, panting like a Spaniel. Where to go when a man with a webbed foot, fourteen years dead, was after you?

Kavanaugh barked, "Upstairs! Quick!" steering the blonde woman around the newel post and dragging her up the steps.

Ranier found himself supporting the slim girl's elbow, and heard himself telling her, "There's nothing to be afraid of!" But he didn't mean it. There was a white blanch to her lips that could not have been there without reason, and she moved in a resistless way, impelled by his hand, as if too frightened to follow her own responses.

THEN THEY were in the laboratory because the lighted room—despite that unappetizing odor of cookery!—was better than any of a number of dark doors off the upper hall. They stood. Angelo Carpetsi with his back to the door as if holding it against an assault of haunts. Kavanaugh fanning the Daisy woman whose haystack head was buried in his shoulder threatening to swoon at any moment. Professor Schlitz handkerchiefing his temples. Laïs Engles trembling. John Ranier fighting a conflict with the muscles in his stomach. You could not have heard a pin drop, but there was only the gurgly bubbling of water boiling in the glass bowl on the white table.

John Ranier walked to the table and turned off the Bunsen flame under the bowl. Two evil objects settled to the bottom of the bowl, and he saw the bullfrog on the near-by spike was dead, and the only sound then was not born of the room, but a faint undertone echo that might have traveled miles through the fog-hushed outer night to enter by the vapor-curtained window and throb in the stifled air. Had the tempo of those mountain drums quickened, or was that the rapid pounding of his own blood?

A shocking thought occurred to him. He said to Laïs Engles, "Those aren't—Dr. Eberhardt's hands?"

She shook her head violently.

But whose-ever they were (he couldn't look at the bowl) they'd want some explaining. So would that pilloried frog. What cannibalistic machination had been in progress up here, and what bizarre violence had disrupted it? That disordered desk; those spilled bottles of Prussic acid, cyanide, strychnine, ammonia; that scattered lab table. He wondered stupidly at the big glass tank swimming with frogs, at the skeleton looking on. The green whirligig in the tank might have been the visual expression of his own thoughts. What sort of experimenter was this old Dr. Eberhardt who had disappeared in this Chamber of Horrors? And how might this have to do with a Leo Haarman, taffy-haired Teutonic artichoke dealer, dead downstairs with membranes between his toes?

He took a turn about the crazy room, limping noticeably as he always did when excited, his thoughts stumbling in his head. Three problems, now. Who stabbed Haarman? How could Haarman be the mate of that Amazon expedition recounted by the girl—a German sailor who died in 1922? And where was Dr. Eberhardt? He paused at the window to pull fresh air into his lungs. Fog and darkness outside. Darkness and fog in his mind. He swung from the window to put a question to the girl, and saw Mr. Kavanaugh push the blonde woman from his shoulder to confront the room with sudden decisiveness.

Kavanaugh's mouth was going angrily, "Now then, now then, what the devil are we running for?" and if someone's insubordination had caused a stampede. The Irishman's eyes were contemptuous. They circled the room with scorn. Narrowed at a bottle upright on one of the vandalized shelves.

He snapped, "Scotch!" Walked to the shelf, uncapped the bottle, and drank off an inch of Sandy Macdonald without coughing. He handed the bottle to the blonde woman, and snapped, "Drink!" The blonde woman tilted her picture hat and drank off an inch. Angelo Carpetsi snatched the bottle, drank, sputtered; passed it to Professor Schlitz who declined with a shudder. Kavanaugh took the bottle and returned it to the shelf. His hard flat cheeks had congested a little. He cocked his thumb and aimed his imperative finger at the door.

"You don't have to hold up that door, Carpetsi; nothing's coming after you. Haarman's dead down there! Dead, understand? He isn't any hoodoo named Adolph Perl, and he didn't croak any fourteen years ago!"

Professor Schlitz moaned out, "The girl said—"

"Never mind," the Irishman cut him off, "what the girl said!" Hands thrust in pockets, he wheeled, regarded Laïs Engles with a direct stare. "Doesn't it strike you as a coincidence that

Dr. Eberhardt, the only person in Haiti who could verify this Adolph Perl yarn of yours, isn't here?"

She gasped, "Yes! Oh, God—What has happened to him? What has happened to Unkle Doktor? That creature you brought here tonight—"

JOHN RANIER stepped to the girl, took her by the arm roughly. "Look here, Miss Engles. Forget that—that man downstairs. You're mistaken about him somehow. We've got to locate Dr. Eberhardt, whatever we do! It looks as if there'd been a fight in his laboratory here. There's mud on that window sill. Somebody came in." He controlled his tone. "Do you know if Dr. Eberhardt had any enemies?"

"Enemies? I—"

"Anyone," Ranier persisted, "who might break in on him, want to do him any harm?"

She sobbed, "He was kind, good to everyone. Established a free clinic. Gave vaccinations. All he wanted was to be left alone. The natives love him who know him. But they are people most superstitious. *Ja,* there are enemies on the Island—"

"Who?"

"The *hougans*—those witch doctors who say he has robbed them of their business, who warn the ignorant blacks against him. There is that ugly Hyacinth Lucien who runs the café down in the village. He is a *bocor* who practises sorcery and sells charms to the deluded Negroes. Several times in the past he has threatened—"

"Hyacinth? He was there in his café all evening, Miss Engles. Anyone else? Did Dr. Eberhardt ever mention anyone? Someone not a native—who might have a reason—"

"*Nein—nein—*" she was crying in her throat, forcing the words through tears. "Who could want to harm Dr. Eberhardt?"

"Listen," Ranier demanded. All at once his tongue felt queer. An electrical taste, transmitting the thought telegraphed from his mind. As if his spinning brain cells, joining in collision, had caused a spark, a definite flash across his mental vision. A hunch that numbed his tongue. He said loudly, "That night fourteen years ago! When you and Adolph Perl and another sailor were waiting down there in the emergency room! All the others had died of that plague, you said, and you three were the only ones left. You and the mate and—?"

"And a sailor named Hans Blücher—"

"That's the one I mean," Ranier flashed. "What became of *him?*"

"That night he ran away. Adolph Perl went after him and said he saw him run from the hospital. He ran away to escape the contagion."

Angelo Carpetsi had edged around the roll-top desk to peep at the bowl which was still simmering on the center table. Temporary courage which had been inspired in the Italian by Kavanaugh's gritty assurance, a shot of Scotch and the door closed on the halt, now left the pink-shirted boy with a loud yell. He whirled on his heels, his complexion pasty as spaghetti. His black eyes glittered at Kavanaugh, at the girl, at Ranier.

"What the hell!" he yelled. "Are we gonna stand around an' talk? Are we gonna stand around here an' talk—with that *thing* downstairs? Dontcha see what's in that bowl, there? Are we gonna *stand* here?" His voice close to hysteria, he hooked frantic fingers on Kavanaugh's sleeve. "It's your fault!" he shouted. "You sent the car away! You wouldn't let me go with Brown an' Coolidge! You wouldn't let me go! I wanna get outa here! Outa here—"

John Ranier was not sorry to see Kavanaugh's knuckles whip up under Carpetsi's jaw, closing the Italian's mouth with a crack that drove him to the wall and left him speechless. The pink-shirted boy had interrupted a thought, and thinking was getting difficult in this nightmare. What had he been asking the girl—

"That sailor who ran away that night. Blücher. Where did he go?"

"I don't know." The girl pressed her forehead and gave Ranier a dazed look. "Nobody knows. Why do you question me about

Hans Blücher? In Haiti he was never seen again. Fearing he would spread the contagion, the doctor was very angry he ran off. That was not all. Hans Blücher was gone in the night, and with him the suitcase Captain Friederich had asked Dr. Eberhardt to send to Germany. Police were called, but Hans Blücher was never caught."

Ranier leaned at her, staring. "You mean—this Blücher ran off with that case belonging to the German government? The devil! Why didn't you tell us that before?" Turning his back on the girl, he paced down the laboratory to the open window, kicking at loose note-papers in his path. Wisps of moisture floated in from the night to finger his face while he stood looking out, his mind racing. Fragmentary thoughts, scenes, went topsy-turvy through his head. Haarman's plaster-cast face in that café. Down there on an operating table, that webbed foot bared. The girl's story knotted in the tangle. Thoughts like live wires whipping about, contacting at some point, creating that flash. Good God, it would be incredible, but—

BACK TOWARD the room, he slipped a hand into his breast pocket; fished out the letters he'd discovered on Haarman earlier that night. Ignoring the inexplicable notations penciled on the stained envelope of one, he thumbed open and read the missives under pretense of leaning from the window for air. Contents told him nothing. A dry cleaner's bill for one white linen suit (it would want more than dry cleaning now!) A circular and note from a travel bureau advising Mr. Haarman that the Adlon in Berlin was a splendid hotel and the Hamburg-American ships were *nonpareil.* Wait! Another thought sparked as he returned the letters to his pocket. Had Haarman been considering Europe, then (frightened, perhaps?) veered to the Caribbean?

He rounded from the window, lips compressed; then, before he could open them to frame the question in his mind, he was interrupted by an oath from Kavanaugh. The Irishman, who'd been stooped in a rubbish-strewn corner, picked a book out of the litter, swung about, elbowed the girl aside and confronted Ranier, narrow-eyed.

"Look here, Dr. Ranier, don't you think we've chattered long enough with this girl? Seems to me the thing to do would be search the hospital for this Dr. Eberhardt who runs the place. Why gabble about this Blücher guy when her story's nutty anyhow?"

"Suppose," Ranier said, "the dead man downstairs were Hans Blücher instead of Adolph Perl."

"Yes, and suppose," Kavanaugh's brows came together, "he's only a murdered man named Haarman!"

"This girl thinks he isn't. At the same time we know he can't be the German mate she says she saw buried in 1922. But," Ranier faced the Irishman's skepticism, "he *could* be somebody who knew that Perl fellow; someone made up, say, to resemble him. Suppose that Blücher, who skipped out that night, shipped up to the States and wanted to disguise himself. Why? The suitcase, let's say documents belonging to the German government; maybe he took 'em to sell a foreign country. He figures the *Wilhelmstrasse* will be after him to get the stuff back. So he takes the identity of a man who's likely dead and at any event won't be known in the U.S.A. or described by the German secret service. He could assume the name of Haarman and the appearance of Adolph Perl. The scar would be easy enough. The toes a matter of grafted skin. Then, after fourteen years, he comes back to Haiti—"

"On a cruise?"

"How do I know? Maybe to silence Dr. Eberhardt and Miss Engles who're the only ones who would know about the stuff he stole? I'm only guessing. Trying to show this girl how Haarman, who seems to look like an Adolph Perl, might be the other sailor who—"

"That could not be!" Laïs Engles cried. "It is Adolph Perl downstairs. Never Hans Blücher disguised to look like him. The scar, the web foot, the face might be disguised. But never the build or color of the eyes." Her dark gaze swerved at those near the door. "Adolph Perl is the man you brought here tonight. Thick-set, heavy shoulders, blue eyes. Hans Blücher was very bony, very thin, taller, with brown eyes. Like you."

Her pointing finger brought a squeal from Professor Schlitz and a stilled oath of disappointment from Ranier. He groped despairingly, "You said there was something valuable in that suitcase—papers, you thought. Didn't you ever know what it contained?"

"Only that it was to have been delivered that time in Chile. Captain Friederich told Dr. Eberhardt what it was. Worth much to Germany. That is all I overheard. Dr. Eberhardt would know."

"And Dr. Eberhardt," Kavanaugh interposed bitingly, "still isn't here! Neither are those damfool black police! So I think it's time to cut all this comedy and get down to facts!" He pivoted at John Ranier; ordered, "Put up your hands!" so unexpectedly that Ranier recoiled backwards, jarred into the laboratory skeleton. The bones clinkled.

Mr. Kavanaugh seemed to copy the skeleton's grin. Mr. Kavanaugh's shoulders were pulled forward, his neck shortened into his trench coat collar, chin jutting, hat-brim down almost to the bridge of his long hard nose. Mr. Kavanaugh's Irish eyes weren't smiling, but were points of hard blue coral sharpening themselves on Ranier's face. Mr. Kavanaugh had transferred the volume he'd salvaged from the floor to his left hand; but he was not pointing that bossy right-hand forefinger this time.

There was a Colt automatic in Mr. Kavanaugh's right hand.

CHAPTER X

ZOMBIES!

JOHN RANIER LOOKED in surprise at the gun and was almost glad to see it there. It was blue-steel, snub-nosed, business like. It looked quick, hard and compact, like the man who aimed it. But its menace was real, a definite focal point for fear, something that brought actuality into this creep-walled, fog-windowed place atmosphered with a whisper of Haitian drums and a wizardish hint of resurrection. It put the cards on the table. An Irishman was something you could get your teeth in.

Ranier lifted his arms. Somehow Kavanaugh's explosive gesture had flicked to his mind that scene in the waterfront café, when he'd picked up Haarman's hand and said, "This man was a con—" meaning to say "consumptive"; and Kavanaugh had interrupted with the same unexpected violence in his voice.

That hard voice had flatted again, commanding, "Come here. Walk towards me and keep your hands up."

"Dave Kavanaugh," the stout blonde screamed, "What are you doing?"

Mr. Kavanaugh banished query and woman with an impatient sideglance; stepped close to John Ranier, ran a quick hand over his coat, ribs, side pockets, hip. "All right, step back and relax," he directed. "You haven't got a gun. Just don't forget, from now on, that I have. That goes for everyone else in this nut factory!"

"I thought we were using knives tonight," Ranier said dryly, meeting those feral Irish eyes. "Where did your artillery come in?"

"Unpacked it from my traveling bag when we motored out here in the Winton. Had an idea I might be able to use it, and it won't be any mysterious mauve death if I do." He waved the gun threateningly. "Stand over there by the girl, will you, Dr. Ranier? You're both under arrest!"

It was an ultimatum as unexpected as the gun; brought an oath from Ranier, an exclamation from the waxworks figure of Professor Schlitz, a gargle from the blonde, a gasp from Angelo Carpetsi. "Say!" jaw hanging limp. "You're gonna arrest them two?"

"Under arrest!" Laïs Engles murmured in a lethargic way, her eyes uncomprehending on the gun.

"Yeah," Kavanaugh informed. "As an American citizen waitin' the protection of this foreign government, I'm taking some law in my hands."

She put her hands to her breast, her eyes bewildered. "I—I do not understand—"

"Then you will," Kavanaugh advised acidly. "Here's a man stabbed in the back and we bring him to your hospital for First Aid, and you let him die. You say you're a nurse for the Dr. Eberhardt who runs this place, but when we call for the doctor you don't know where he is. You tell us you've always lived here with this Dr. Eberhardt; he always leaves word where he goes; then you show us this laboratory smashed to hell. The doc is gone; you don't know how or when it happened—although you sleep on the same floor—and you don't know what's become of him. Is that enough?"

"But I—"

"It's enough," Kavanaugh promised through his teeth, "but it isn't all. We run back downstairs and find Haarman's bled to death. Do you start looking for Dr. Eberhardt, send out a call for help, yell for the servants as one might naturally expect—"

"But there are no servants," the girl shook her head in protest.

"There are only the sleeping patients here; they would know nothing. The old house-boy, Polypheme, went to the village early this evening with the car and will not be back until—"

Kavanaugh lifted his left palm peremptorily. "Save it. Eberhardt's not here, anyway, and you then stall us with a wild bedtime story about Mr. Haarman being a guy you saw die fourteen years ago. A good trick, but it doesn't go down. Any mere than Haarman's web foot proves he was once a German sailor called Adolph Perl, nicknamed The Duck."

JOHN RANIER limped half a step at the man with the gun. "One minute, Kavanaugh! How would this girl know Haarman had a webbed foot unless—"

"Unless you told her?" The man's mouth quirked up the side of his face insinuatingly. "Unless you raced out here ahead of us and tipped her off. You're our ship's medico. Maybe on shipboard you spotted Haarman's phony toes. Tonight, after the stabbing, you scoot out here and wise up this girl. You were on hand when we pulled in with Haarman, weren't you?"

The implication was clear. Ranier said, staggered, "I rode out here on the back of the Winton. Got here the same time you did. As for Miss Engles, why would I tip her off about anything? I never saw her before in my—"

"Didn't you?" Kavanaugh's question came from a contemptuous smile. "You've been doctor on this cruise ship five years, I understand. Sailing around Haiti and making this port every two months or so. You wouldn't, conceivably, have called on your colleague in this God-forsaken spot; struck up a friendship with the beautiful, lonely nurse?"

The girl answered for Ranier, her accent deep-throated, "I do not know this man!" pointing at John Ranier; and he felt a slow flush mount in his cheekbones. No, he'd never called on his colleague in this God-forsaken spot, as one physician on another. Never, in fact, heard of him until tonight. He hadn't struck up a friendship with the beautiful (Kavanaugh's sarcasm was uncalled for on that point) and lonely nurse. The only place he'd visited in this wretched port was the nearest bar. Swigging that damned *aguardiente.* Going to seed. Not that it mattered. Only if he'd been more clearheaded at the start of tonight's madness—

He heard Kavanaugh rasping, "Well, I'm holding the girl for your accomplice, Ranier, and I'm going to turn you over for the murder of Mr. Haarman and maybe Dr. Eberhardt."

Then he could feel the blood running down out of his face, and he was aware that the girl, stricken by the Irishman's malignant accusation, had pressed back to the wall, her hands behind her, shrinking from his nearness, her eyes repelling him with horror. Facing Kavanaugh, his lips went stiff with controlled fury.

"I don't know a damned thing about Eberhardt, or Haarman, either. How could *I* have stabbed Haarman back there in that café?"

Kavanaugh shrugged, bowing a little over his aimed gun. "I'm not saying you did. I'm saving I think you did."

"Why?"

"Why do I think you did?"

"Let's have it."

"I think you did," the Irishman's tone was mockingly judicious, "because you're the only one who was there in that café who could have done it. Logical?"

"I'm listening."

"Have some more." Kavanaugh might have been passing the jelly. "No one of our party at the table could've stabbed Haarman because the others at the table would've seen it. No one at the table went around behind his chair. Only other occupants of the dump were that black bar tender and you. You don't accuse that coon of doing it, do you?"

"He couldn't—"

"That," Kavanaugh smiled, "leaves you."

JOHN RANIER didn't smile. "Does it? I was sitting in an

alcove off the bar, wasn't I? Mr. Haarman was in the middle of the room. How could *I* have stabbed the man?"

"Mr. Haarman was to meet the rest of us in the motoring party at the café, which was to have been our starting point. He went there a half hour ahead of us. You were there when he turned up. Admitted?"

"What do you mean admitted?" Ranier said, angered. He felt he would go cross-eyed staring at the gun which kept his fist from flying at the tall man's mocking teeth. There was a cat-with-mouse attitude about the Irishman that needed a stiff punching. Ranier could only open and shut his hands, glaring, "What do you mean admitted? I said so from the first, didn't I?"

Kavanaugh lifted an admonitory eyebrow, "You also admitted you and Haarman had had a little quarrel?"

"I told you about that, too. He'd been drinking. Ugly when he came into the café. Chucked me out of my chair. He took a pass at me, understand? I never put a hand on him. And what's that got to do with my stabbing the man when the rest of you were there."

"*Before* we got there," was the answer. Kavanaugh's eyes went slantwise at the book he was holding in his left hand. His forehead wrinkled inquiringly. "You might've stabbed Haarman *before* the rest of us arrived. Eh?"

Ranier snapped, "That's a good one, since the man was chatting about the trip with you when you pulled up chairs at his table," but his forehead was wet in a sudden apprehension of the fox-look on the tall man's face; the smirk as he held out the book left-handed, indicating a page under his thumb.

"Haarman might've been stabbed before the rest of us got there," Kavanaugh was repeating softly. "He might've sat there in his chair talkin' to us and havin' a drink. Sure, just as if nothin' had happened. I'd never of thought it possible, till I seen this doctor's book lyin' open on the floor. Just the right paragraph, too. Haarman might have sat there dyin'—just like th' case on this page—*and not even know he'd been stabbed!*"

It was there in the pages of that medical book as it had been printed from the start of that evening in the back of Ranier's mind. Haarman *could* have been stabbed before the others came to the café; could have slumped there in his chair and gone on drinking and talking, never conscious of his fatal wound. There was that Austrian empress who was said to have continued a long walk after being stabbed by a shoemaker's awl, dropping dead without knowing of her wound—the many instances of soldiers going for hours without realizing they'd been hit.

Kavanaugh's voice was purring on: "That explains him talkin' to us when we met him. But he looked bad, sittin' there, all right. Ginned up, too. Never seen you creep up behind him. After he chucked you out, you come in behind him through the window, I suppose. Then went back out over the sill, threw away the shiv-eree, and walked in by the front door."

Ranier said huskily, "It doesn't hold water—"

Kavanaugh nodded agreeably, "Who's talking about water? I'm talking about blood."

"That's what I'm talking about," Ranier appealed to the room. "Cases of people being stabbed without knowing it apply to internal hemorrhage. Haarman's wound bled externally. That much blood, he'd certainly know it. Soaked his jacket across the shoulders. And if he was stabbed before you joined him there at that table, you'd have seen the stains when you took chairs beside him."

"The blood run down the back of his chair," Kavanaugh supplied smoothly. "Since none of us went around behind his chair we didn't see it. The coon who owns the joint didn't see you do it because he was out in back somewhere. All right, Haarman was still ticking when our party arrived. So what? So you see a chance to pin the job on one of us, or maybe blame it on these Voodoo ghosts. That jigaboo Marcelline plays into your hand by having visions and what-not. Also you realize we'll rush Haarman to the nearest hospital, which is Eberhardt's here. You stall around. Still Haarman keeps ticking. Then you tell us you're going to beat it out to the ship and fetch back the captain, but instead of that you take a short-cut, and you're already on hand at the hospital when we arrive. Didn't Coolidge see you tear from behind th' building when this nurse jerked that scream?"

"I tell you," Ranier's tongue felt thick, "I rode out here on the back of your car!"

"Unless, say, you cut up the mountain, an' got here first to forestall this Doc Eberhardt from giving Haarman a transfusion after you'd given him a blood-letting. Then let's say Eberhardt refused to lay off. There's a fight up here in this little museum of his. Was that how you ripped your Sunday pants? Your elbow, too? Look at th' cuts on your hands."

"I fell. I fell off the spare tire of that Winton!"

"Or," Kavanaugh said in his sweetened voice, "did this Doc Eberhardt knock you for a loop up here just before we came. Let's say he did. Then let's say you knocked him for a loop. Say the beautiful lonely nurse runs in. She sees Eberhardt out cold—dead, for the sake of argument. She sees you. I don't say it's love at first sight, y'understand; I say you've known her for some time. I say," Kavanaugh delivered the indictment in the bored tone of a District Attorney summing an obvious case for a stupid jury, "I say you and this girl are hand in glove together. At least, in part of this. Pretending you don't know each other. Huh! But you put Eberhardt out of the way, then cooked up this Adolph Perl gag to scare us off. The girl spins a fairy story about an expedition in Brazil when she was a kid, and Haarman comin' back to haunt her; and you play you're hay-wired by the whole set-up. Well, you can tell it to the bulls, if they ever get here."

KAVANAUGH FLIRTED the gun impatiently; switched his address to the three tourists statue-struck behind him. "It's a pip, isn't it?" showing the book, before throwing it aside. "Poor Haarman was dyin' when we met up with him. Never knew it, either. I wonder what the cops will say when they see those footprints of Ranier's—the ones we saw when Marcelline turned the car around to start for the hospital—those tracks under that café window. Maybe I'm prejudiced," he whipped his aim back at Ranier, "but it seems to me my theory is a damn sight more reasonable than all this living-dead-man stuff!"

Consternation stalled Ranier's tongue. It was reasonable, all right. Reasonable enough to wring a cry from Carpetsi: "Why, th' dirty rat, you oughta let him have one from th' gun!" Reasonable enough to bring a whinny from Professor Schlitz: "Our ship's doctor! Great Scott! He might have murdered us all! I do believe he did stab poor Mr. Haarman!"

"He did," Kavanaugh sneered, "if you happen to be a Christian white man who doesn't believe in Voodoo and all this *zombie* hocus pocus. If—"

The Irishman did not conclude the remark. *Thump!* Sound of a door slammed somewhere in the lower part of the house took the words out of Kavanaugh's mouth; left him tense, beady-eyed, listening. Everybody turned to listen. No denying that below-floors report; unmistakably someone was in the house downstairs, had slammed a door.

A channel of cold air coursed down the back of John Ranier's neck, as if an unseen breeze had entered the room. Laïs Engles might have felt it, too, the way she shivered, staring wide-pupiled toward the hall; and Kavanaugh's face was frosty as he flung around at the girl, white but not so Christian. "Who's that? It's not Coolidge and Brown—we'd of heard the car. Who slammed that door downstairs just now?"

Without replying, the girl made a swift move past the man, snatched open the laboratory door, sent a tremulous call out across the upper balcony glooms. "*Wer da?* Dr. Eberhardt—? Unkle Doktor—? Dr. Eberhardt, is that you—?"

The only answer was the gray cat arriving silently on the threshold, smiling up at the girl, then trotting into the room. Ranier looked at the cat, half-expecting to learn that this was Dr. Eberhardt.

Mouth ugly, eyes glittering, Kavanaugh caught the girl's wrist and twisted her back from the threshold. "Who's downstairs in this place?"

She gasped, "Only the patients. Four. A child with an amputated leg. A man confined in contagion with smallpox. A man dying of *dhangi* fever. A woman bed-ridden, dying of elephantiasis. They could not leave their beds." Her whisper lowered to hardly more than a movement of her lips. "That door—"

Kavanaugh's knuckles showed white from the grip on the gun. Stepping out on the balcony, he sped a quick glance down on the hall below, turned, confronted the laboratory with a grim eye.

"Wait up here! I'll be back in a minute, and I wouldn't worry about shooting the first one of you I caught trying to leave!"

He pulled the door after him; then his shoes made a hurried tattoo on the stairs. Then silence. Silence filled with the blonde woman's alarmed breathing. In which Angelo Carpetsi's skin staled from olive to ptomaine-green while his tie sweat blue through his pink-striped collar. In which Laïs Engles stood rigid against the wall, her hands pressed to the plaster, eyes averted; and Professor Schlitz watched Ranier with the hypnotic stare of a bird confined with a cobra. Anger struggled with apprehension in Ranier's mind. These fools didn't have to be afraid of him; he was as lost in this jabberwok nightmare as they were. A bead of sweat guttered down the side of his nose, and he grimly considered an Anopheles mosquito that had buzzed out of the tainted air to sit on his hand. He pinched the head from the malarial insect, and stood in tension, waiting for sounds below. The gray cat polished itself against his shins.

TWO MINUTES. Three minutes. What the devil was keeping that Irishman? What was going on in this mountain villa?

Had the ambulance party, rushing Haarman to this gloomy asylum, surprised some nefarious enterprise here in the hospital? At the thought, Ranier gave the girl at his side a glance of sudden mistrust. Maybe Kavanaugh had been right and that story of hers was a stall. Her manner was convincing enough, but he'd been fooled by one woman in his life—certainly a trained nurse couldn't believe in ghosts coming back from the grave. Her fear was masking something—something she was holding back? Well, the *Garde d'Haiti* ought to be here any minute now, and this guy Kavanaugh—

The door burst open, and Mr. Kavanaugh was back in the laboratory. Not the same Mr. Kavanaugh who had gone to explore downstairs. Somewhere during that prowl the Irishman had lost his self-possession. Mr. Kavanaugh's cheekbones showed the loss. His lips were pieces of chalk. Eyes glassy. Finger in collar, he seemed to sway in the doorway as if a deck were rocking under him.

"It's Haarman," his lips writhed in chalk-talk. "It's Haarman, and his shoe isn't there in the corridor where Ranier dropped it. He isn't in that room down there. The body—Haarman—he's gone!"

Then, before anyone had time to recoil from that shock, a motor-roar broke in the night outside. The sound grew. Tires skidding on loose gravel. A screech of brakes and wrenched springs as the car came into the driveway under the window. Kavanaugh blurted hoarsely, "The police!" and Ranier listened to boots pound across the verandah with something like Thanksgiving in his heart. Thanksgiving that changed to perspiration on his forehead. It was not the police!

He knew it was not the *Garde d'Haiti,* for that efficient and colorful *gendarme* patrol generally sauntered in pairs, and this new arrival came alone and at high speed.

The police would not have banged through the front door howling, *"M'sieu Docteur! Ma'mselle Laïs! Malheur! Malheur! Mortoo tomboo vient! Au secours!"*

Wild feet came stumbling up the stairs, bringing that frenzy in creole; and Laïs Engles cried in answering dialect:

"Polypheme! Ici! Ici! 'Vitement!" She turned to those in the room. "It's Polypheme—the house-boy—back from the village! He—"

Then there came through the doorway the most terrified darkey John Ranier had ever seen. A little old black man made of rags and licorice with eyes like saucers under the tatter-fringe brim of an enormous straw sombrero. Overwhelmed by the fifty-gallon brim, his face looked not much bigger than a raisin; one guessed he was lost under the hat and frightened by its omnipotence. He wore patchwork trousers and a sleeveless cotton jumper, the right half red, the left half blue, as if he'd sewed the garment from a moth-eaten Haitian flag; and there was a snowy goat-tuft on his chin. He resembled for all the world a black performing goat that had escaped a circus in full costume; and he performed in the laboratory doorway, rocking on hind legs, waving his forefeet at Laïs Engles, eyeballs like burnt matches rolling around in china saucers, mouth bleating, "Nnnnnyaaaaah!" Then, hat and all, he jumped the threshold; flung himself prostrate at the girl's feet.

She cried, *"Lever ou, tout suit!* Stand up, Polyphem! Speak English! Where is Dr. Eberhardt! What have you seen?"

He could stand before her doing a sort of jig, but the English was too much for him' after a gibbered, "No see'm Dr. Eberhardt—Ah been village, come quick!" His linguistic ability, blowing a fuse when it came to what he had seen.

Then Haitian and goat-bleats poured from his mouth, and even his native tongue seemed inadequate. He had to windmill his arms and roll his eyes. His goatee flickered, and the effort brought globes of ink on his forehead. He pointed at the ceiling, at the floor, at the fog-hung window; saw the laboratory tank of bullfrogs and ended with a caterwaul beyond translation.

But it needed no interpreter to make John Ranier understand terror when he heard it. He saw the fear in the little Haitian's eyes reflect in the eyes of the girl. Saw her put hand to throat as if in want of air, and gaze in white transfixion at the window.

"What is it?" Ranier growled. "What does he say?"

"He says," Laïs Engles whispered, "he has just come from the village. A mob is gathering, and the *Rada* drums are signals.

Rumor has started a *zombie* is loose—a dead man walking in the fog. The blacks are angry, and Hyacinth Lucien is spreading word Dr. Eberhardt is a sorcerer, a white magician who has raised this *zombie* from the dead. It was to warn the hospital of danger that Polypheme left the village early. On the way home he passed the graveyard. *Oh, God!*"

She spread one hand against the wall for support, pressing the other to her forehead as if it hurt. "He says—he says he saw near the road an opened grave. An old lady sitting on a coffin. An old lady who is dead. She wears a black bonnet and a taffeta dress, and there is a live frog tied to her wrist. She is the old lady, he says, who came with me from Brazil. Who died in this hospital fourteen years ago. *It is Old Gramma Sou—*"

CHAPTER XI

THE LADY AT THE GRAVE

IF HE SURVIVED to be ten thousand, Ranier knew, the picture of that graveyard would be indelible in his memory, although he never could quite remember how he got there. Afterwards, it had seemed like Kavanaugh's doing. Kavanaugh had yelled like a Choctaw, "Come on!"

There was a tumble down the stairs, led by the Irishman with the gun and followed by all who did not wish to be left behind. A battle to reach the night air. Ranier took time out to sprint to the dark rear corridor and down the corridor to the emergency room in the hopes of finding Mr. Haarman, because Kavanaugh must have been wrong and the dead man had to be there—then wasn't. He could remember racing to join the others at the front; seeing what looked like a small sedan.

From there to the cemetery everything blurred. He stood on the running board, for all the seats were taken—Professor Schlitz squealing with the blonde swamping his lap; Kavanaugh and Carpetsi jammed together; Polypheme at the wheel with Laïs Engles—then no one had wanted to go. The small sedan hadn't wanted to go, either. Made in Detroit, it had suffered hard usage in this tropical environment, and tonight it was worn out. The fog had given it asthma, and its right eye was blind. It bucked spleenishly on leaving the driveway, shied at the turn, shimmied its front wheels when it hit the macadam, then shot on the downhill grade in spiteful abandon. Perhaps it would not have moved at all, if Kavanaugh hadn't muttered something virulent at the driver and flourished his automatic. All right, it would show them.

Ranier had traveled up the mountain on a spare tire; now he was racketing down it on a door. This Model T must have come from the same museum as the Winton, and there was the same sensation of zooming off into space. Night loomed in cliffs that scraped the running boards, and the fog streamed through the cracked windshield and under the wheels so there wasn't any visible road. The car's single eye, its battery dim, was useful solely in showing the curves when the wheels were on them and it was too late to do much about it. But it was no good worrying about accidents. The accidents had happened. If you were a ship's doctor accustomed to only normal miracles and suddenly confronted by vanishing knives and life after death, there wasn't much you could do but hang on.

Ranier hung on.

The woman in the back seat was shrieking like a dame in a roller-coaster as Kavanaugh fired oaths at break-neck turns and Carpetsi loudly remembered saints. Fog funneled by in rushing, fumid whorls; pearl-tinted in the path of the headlight; barrage-thick beyond, as if the night had been everywhere afire and doused, and now the charred blackness was smoking. At the steering wheel Polypheme was a pair of eyeballs, disembodied, with a faint blue shine of a cheekbone, and Ranier could see Laïs Engles' hands, tight-nerved, deathly white, gripping the dashboard just above a dimmed grape-sized light bulb.

IT WAS no time to think about a dead man climbing down off an operating table, leaving the room to retrieve a shoe for his webbed left foot, and slamming the door in departure. Cardiac spasm did peculiar things; *rigor mortis* might cause a cadaver to salute a terrified morgue attendant, or quirk lifeless lips in a grin. But it never walked a dead man out of a hospital, or animated him throughout a Caribbean cruise after fourteen years in the ground.

It was no time, either, to recall the story a French consul in

Port-au-Prince had once told him about the dead men they'd found working at the Hasco plant. Ranier recalled it. Hasco stands for Haitian American Sugar Company, and you can buy Hasco Rum today in any good liquor store in the States. You wouldn't expect the un-dead in a modern industrial plant tinder Yankee capital, but the rumor persisted that *zombies* had been seen there—John Ranier had laughed at the story.

It had been easy to laugh at the story told that time in the suburban country club at Kenscoff where polite waiters served Planter's Punches under Japanese lanterns, and bored tourists capered to a Haitian orchestra butchering the "Black Bottom."

Zooming downhill through fog on this Model T stuffed with terrified tourists in a night alive with the threat of jungle drums, John Ranier didn't laugh. He heard the girl cry faintly, "Hurry, Polypheme—*Vite! Vite!* Oh, God—I've got to see—" and the fog seemed to be blowing in cold blank streams under his scalp. Blowing with the words, "Unreal! Unreal!"

No dead man could walk out of a door. If Haarman could saunter from that downstairs room after epidermal discoloration had set in, all the rules were off, and he might in truth have been buried four years after the War. It gave one's foundations no more substance than this mist in night. Better go back to elixirs, witch-burnings, wands. Accept the "touch-power" of Valentine Greatrakes, the miraculous beds of Cagliostro, and Perkins's tweezer-cure. Hippocrates and Galen were fools in tonight's fog; Pasteur, Jenner and Carrel had built on myths, and this old lady the house-boy claimed to have seen, might be there.

She was there!

A HAITIAN cemetery is, at best, a stage-set for ghosts, with broken masonry and jerrybuilt vaults and the helterskelter parceling of the plots. The little mounds are heaped high with cockle shells; the moss grows green, and there are lizards; there might even be a granite angel with a broken nose. The tombstones have a way of leaning, like bones poked up out of the ground.

Ranier stared. The little old lady—dead for fourteen years—looked very much alive.

The Haitians know who tipped over those stones. They know who tilted that mound at an angle overnight; who blurred the letters once chiseled so deep in the marble. So their cemeteries hug the roads for comfort and burn their penny candles late. But neither candles nor the headlamp of a car were comforting in this particular mountain graveyard.

The headlamp's ray made a swerve across the road, streamed under the cemetery arch and diffused in a cone of misty luminescence that spread uphill in the murk, touching a gleam to wet marbles, creeping across the sleeping mounds. In the vaporous background, the vigil candles were outer moons in a void, each a sentinel to its own patch of earth, and beyond these yellow blurs, the jungle joined with the night in an impenetrable wall.

In the mist that unraveled above them, the dark mounds were smoking. Gray wooden crosses dripped. Vine-clad headstones showed patches of white through glistening creeper, and near the entrance arch one mound was distinguished by a little glass-windowed doghouse where mourners might peep at a wreath made of the departed's hair, a collection of the deceased's belongings, a chromo of Saint Sulpice and a miniature of the departed looking holier than he was. The car-light streamed past this doleful reliquary and touched on something that would have cooled the thick-skinned hearts of Burke and Hare. That Scotch-Irish team of grave robbers would have run for their lives. Even the Model T jumped back.

She was sitting on an overturned coffin, her hack propped against a tombstone at the head of an opened grave, regarding the pile of shoveled red sand heaped alongside, with the solemn interest. She was frail, and old-fashioned, and the fog-shawl wrapped about her shoulders blew in tatters and wisps that floated away. Her black taffeta dress was the same stuff as the fog, delicate as cobweb, and the black kid gloves in her lap wanted mending. Some bright beads glinted from a crumbled reticule at her feet; and her shoes, styled of another period, high-buttoned like those of Mrs. Katzenjammer, were mossy from too long in the damp. But her granny's bonnet, fastened beneath her chin by an enormous bow, was almost jaunty. Her spectacles were bright. She looked spry. An old lady—the words occurred to Ranier with a taste of zinc in his mouth—well preserved.

Very well preserved. Approaching her on legs that moved through no volition of his own, John Ranier was sure she was alive. She was sitting there composing an elegy. She had come there with flowers and sat down to rest; come there out of the long ago, and was tired from the long walk. Ought to have chosen a better seat, though. That coffin-bottom was pretty well gone. In the darkness she'd mistaken it for a bench. She'd better go. That shawl of fog was draughty for frail shoulders, and the taffeta so thin it wore into holes and tatters as one watched.

There! She nodded at Ranier. Quaintly the bonnet nodded twice. Good evening, young man. Plain as could be. Then he saw the movement came from a fat green bullfrog tethered to her wrist by a length of string. When the frog jumped, her head moved. Tied by a hind leg, the frog made another restricted hop, and the old lady reproved her pet with a perky nod. Some flakes crumbled from the satin bow under her chin, and her glasses went awry. You wouldn't have expected Mother Goose in Haiti—

"Old Gramma Sou—!"

"Don't!" Ranier pulled the girl back, and she stood against him, hiding her face in his shoulder. Mindless, he stood in the headlamp's gray-yellow path, arm about the girl, while shadows charged by him, struggled together at the grave-edge. Professor Schlitz, after one appalled look, tottered backwards over two mounds, fell against the little doghouse near the entrance arch, ramming an elbow through one of the windows. Automatic hanging at his side, Kavanaugh went in a prowl around the opened grave, circling it twice, cursing in a harsh guttural monotone, coming at last to a stand beside the old lady in black. In the wet rays of the car light his face was marble. His eyes were cat-green. Inadvertently he touched the coffin with his boot toe, and the wood crumbled like punk. Oaths snarled from his teeth. Typically, the Irishman's fear appeared to translate itself into rage.

ANGELO CARPETSI was on hands and knees, staring down into the raw excavation. The blonde woman stumbled up to Kavanaugh, holding her skirts up to one knee, slipping and sliding in the soft loam. Too late Ranier thought of footprints. That old lady, no matter how spry, could not have shoveled her way out without assistance. Someone else had been there. That length of string on her wrist looked new. The bullfrog could not break from the leash, although his desperate leaps reduced the glove holding him to leather fragments. It was better to think that someone had been there earlier tonight, someone who had arranged this necromantic old lady in that pose. Whoever it had been, the footprints would be blotted by this rush. Tightening his arm about Laïs Engles, Ranier could feel her shivers running up and down his own skin. His teeth jiggled. He heard glass jangle as the Professor rebounded from the housed grave; heard sounds something like words blurt from the Italian boy— "Empty— How'd that old woman—! Holy Mother—!" Heard Kavanaugh's tooth-ground oaths. Only the old lady sitting there in frayed taffeta remained composed.

The blonde woman began to scream. She clutched Kavanaugh's sleeve, pulling him toward the car, screeching into his agate face. "Get me awaaaay!" her voice ascending as if in rage. "I've had enough of this! Enough of this, understand? That man murdered—! *This*—! I won't have it—! You've got to get me out of this—! You said there wouldn't be any danger—! Just a ride, you said, and you'd take care of ev—!"

She slipped to her plush knees, dragging him almost down on top of her, as his free hand smote across her mouth, stopping her outcry with an infuriated smack. "Get into the car!" he yanked her to her feet; shoved. "Get back into that car, by Judas, before I—" He sucked in his breath, green-lit eyeballs following her hysterical gallop through the archway; then wiped his lips on his wrist and wheeled to face the grave.

Carpetsi turned and rose from his knees with a corkscrew motion that brought him around to face Kavanaugh. Greasy hair slid in a raven's wing across his left eye. His right eye, black, glitterous, moved from side to side under a sickly lid. He whispered, "What the hell, Kavanaugh?" in a voice that seemed to come from a cramped stomach. Three times at Kavanaugh, as if the Irishman should have some answer.

Kavanaugh shook his head, panting, "I don't know how—I don't know how that body—"

Staring across the gold lights in Laïs Engles' hair, John Ranier growled, "Somebody did this! Somebody exhumed this—old lady! Yes, and propped her up against that tombstone—tied that live frog there!"

His own reaction now was anger. He'd let his imagination make him a fool. Heat dried pallidness on his forehead in an upsurge of rage against the vandals who had roused an old lady from her last sleep.

"Damn! Maybe I'm wrong, Kavanaugh, but I'll bet the one who stole Haarman's body out of the hospital tonight is the same filthy rat responsible for *this!*"

"Stole Haarman's—" Kavanaugh's teeth came together with

a click. "By Judas! Sure! Well, Ranier, how much do you know about that?"

"I don't know anything about it. I'm going to find out."

Carpetsi pushed hair from his left eye; stepped toward the Irishman. "This ain't no time to talk, Kavanaugh. I'm gettin'—"

"Shut up!" Flinging the command at the Italian from the side of his mouth, Kavanaugh kept his gaze focused on Ranier. "Just who do you think snatched Haarman's body?" His voice was harsh, threatening. "If you've got *any* ideas, let's have 'em. And about this!" He jerked his chin at the grave.

Ranier shook his head. "All I know is, that frog looks like one of the batch from the tank in Eberhardt's laboratory."

Carpetsi interrupted in a raw voice, "Kavanaugh! I'm goin'!"

"We'd all better go," Ranier snarled. "For the police."

"Like hell! After what that black goat in the car told us about the riot in the village?" Kavanaugh's mouth went up at one corner, baring teeth. "Those boogs would tear your beautiful nurse to pieces. Besides," he twisted at Carpetsi, "Coolidge and Brown went for those *gendarmes,* and they're due any minute. Pull yourself together, boy! I'll handle this! We're going back to the hospital, that's where. But first we're going to settle something."

SLIPPING THE automatic into a pocket of his khaki waterproof, Kavanaugh stepped close to Ranier, stopped in front of him, glared down at Laïs Engles, his hard eyes fixed on the back of the girl's neck. "First," he repeated, aiming his finger at the girl, "we're going to settle something. She claims Haarman is a guy named Adolph Perl, a man she saw buried in Haiti fourteen years ago. I don't know the game, see? I don't know the Hallowe'en racket! But as long as she's stickin' to her Haarman-Perl story, maybe she can show us *that* grave?"

Ranier gripped the girl's shoulder. "Miss Engles—"

Slowly she wheeled in his grasp. Gems of moisture glimmered in her hair, and her face was gardenia-white in the wreathing fog.

Confronting that rectangular black pit and the frail watcher at the grave-side, she shut her eyes, swayed. Ranier held her firm.

"That Perl fellow, Miss Engles. We'd like to see *his* grave."

She whispered, "The tombstone—look at the tombstone—!" pointing.

Carpetsi uttered a strangled yelp, turning swiftly to see; and Kavanaugh's eyes swerved between wolfish slits, the pupils glinting yellow-green through quivering lashes. Aghast, John Ranier saw the girl's finger indicated the tombstone employed as a back-rest by that appalling old lady. The slab at the head of the opened grave. The old lady leaning against the edge of the slab gave a nod as if in confirmation, and settled against the stone a little more comfortably, her bonnet sliding down rakishly over her forehead.

The hazed headlamp of the car did not afford enough light for reading the weathered stone. Ranier snatched for his flashlight; sent a wan ray leaping across the excavation. The misty circle brought the slab into spectral relief, its legend clearly legible.

HIER RUHET IN GOTT
ADOLPH PERL
Gest. 3 Januar 1922
ICH HATTE EINST
EIN SCHONES VATERLAND

Professor Schlitz translated in a wizardish tremulo, "Here rests in God—Adolph Perl—Died third January, 1922—I once had a buh-beautiful Fatherland."

Laïs Engles cried, "I had that inscription put on for him, myself. *That* is Adolph Perl's grave! The old lady—that is Old Gramma Sou, who was buried in the cemetery three miles from here!"

Her chin touched her breast sleepily, and she slowly went to the ground through Ranier's nerveless hands.

CHAPTER XII

DRUMS SPELL DISASTER

"BY HEAVEN! IF that *is* Perl's grave!"—"I told you, Kavanaugh!"—"What's this old woman doin' here when—?" "You can see it's just been dug up!"—"Where's Perl, then? He ain't here, is he? That means Haarman *was*—!" "If anybody thinks they can do this to me, Dave Kavanaugh—" "How *she* get here? If this dame was buried in some bone-orchard three miles away—?"

Voices. Voices banging, snarling, caterwauling in Ranier's ears, a pyrotechnic of words, sentences exploded unfinished, hanging fire in the air. Impossible to follow that play of expressions. Impossible to think. Fog seemed to swirl through Ranier's head as if doors had blown open in his frontal lobe, and his thoughts went scattering about his brain like the papers on the floor of that scrambled hospital laboratory. Voices were bats whisking through his brain-doors in erratic flight, and somewhere in his subconscious, drums were muttering.

He discovered his mouth was open, inhaling mould. He closed it, and dropped to one knee beside the girl. Chafed her wrists. Heard himself wheedling, "Take it easy! Take it easy!" in an insincere way. Like asking someone to have some ice cream in a catacomb. But it was hard to effect a bedside manner at the edge of a freshly-opened grave in a foggy cemetery; particularly when the rightful owner of the plot wasn't there, and the visitor sitting on the absentee's coffin was an old lady from a neighboring necropolis.

Bad enough to believe her above ground in her own graveyard without learning she was three miles from home. He'd thought Adolph Perl (if any) securely anchored in some burying ground nearer the village. What unearthly power had transported the old lady to this foreign field, dead with a live pet bullfrog? What was she doing at Perl's grave, and where was its original inheritor?

Kavanaugh was bawling in the direction of the car, "You get this, Daisy? Keep screamin' like that and you'll have everybody in Haiti down on top of us! The body that oughta be here ain't here, that's all. If you'll close that trap of yours and give me a chance to think—"

From the car Professor Schlitz's voice went piccolo, *"Perl's* grave! *Perl's!* Then Haarman *is* Perl—Of course he w-wouldn't be in his grave! It's precisely as the girl told us, don't you see? Don't you see?" The piccolo in his throat struck High G. "He was a *zombie!* In my stateroom! Dead tonight and walked off again. *Again!* Oh, my! He'll be roaming—!"

The insectologist's screech conjured visions of Mr. Haarman strolling down the night, vacant eyes staring, dead face expressionless, blood creeping from that hole in his back—perhaps carrying his shoe in a lifeless hand and walking on that exposed duck foot.

You could see things that way in the fog. Adolph Perl's grave empty. Haarman being Adolph Perl. As sensible as any of tonight's wizardries, with that café stabbing in broad lamplight; that crytogram on Haarman's mail; Dr. Eberhardt's disappearance from a laboratory where hands cooked; Haarman's walk-out after death. The girl had said Haarman was Perl and Perl was missing from his grave and an old lady from another cemetery was here to pay her respects to the departed. It fitted with the girl's war story and the legends of Monsieur Marcelline. No denying that old lady, well preserved though she was, had been buried a long time—

Helping Laïs Engles to her feet, John Ranier shied a glance at the visitor across the excavation; would not have been surprised to see her stand up briskly, adjust bonnet and specs, bid them a hoarse goodbye, and lead her bullfrog off into shreds of mist.

Drawing the girl aside, he asked huskily, "Feel all right now?" At sound of his voice, Kavanaugh and the Italian stopped shouting blurred words and looked toward him.

Laïs Engles shuddered, "Please—I will be—all right."

Ranier said dryly, "Don't look again, but—are you certain that's the—the old lady who was on the German expedition with—"

"Oh, it is—it is—!"

He said under his breath, "This is terrible!" Aloud: "Where's the cemetery the old lady came from?"

The girl whispered, "Beyond the hospital. Back up the road the way we came. About a mile the—the other side of the hospital."

"The other side of the hospital?" Kavanaugh shouted the word "other", shouldering forward. "Direction *away* from the town? Impossible!"

Ranier's tone was grim. "We're going there to look. Right now! We're going to the cemetery where the old lady, here, was buried."

"We ain't!" the snarl was surprising, coming from Angelo Carpetsi. The Italian boy's face was surprising. Pushing oily hair from his black eyes, he made a sudden lunge between Ranier and Kavanaugh, stood glaring from one to the other, his fog-drenched features glistening, wrenched. His pink silk shirt, pasted to his breast, pumped up and down. He cat-spat at Ranier, "You keep outa this!"

Ranier said through his teeth, "We're going to the cemetery where that old lady was buried!"

"We're goin' to find Brown an' Coolidge!" the Italian boy corrected. His eyes glittered. His face puckered like Mussolini's in the gnashing bombast of a speech. He pinched his fingertips together and sawed the gesture up and down under Ranier's nose, spitting, "If you know what's good for you, quack, you'll keep your puss outa this! I say we're goin' to catch up with Coolidge and Brown!"

He wrenched around at Kavanaugh. "You've stalled long enough. Yeah. I know the racket. I'm on to you, see? If it wasn't a stall, you'd be huntin' damn quick for Brown an' Coolidge an' that shine they went off with, instead of—"

Kavanaugh's eyes were barbarous as he plunged his hand into trench-coat pocket, shoved the bulge at Carpetsi and broke in with, "You greasy little wop, you've lost your head! I don't know any more about this than you do!"

"Yah?" the Italian boy was screaming now. "You're smart, ain't you, Kavanaugh? Too damn smart! Well, you ain't goin' to get away with it. I know you're in this with the ship's doc. You fixed it for this quack to be in that café when we started tonight. You're workin' this with him. Sure, you are!"

KAVANAUGH SQUINTED through the yellow-lit mist as if it were acrid and stung his eyes. Squinted from Carpetsi to Ranier while his sharp features registered wrathful amazement. "Can you beat that? He thinks," he scoffed at Ranier, "I'm hand in glove with *you!*"

"You betcha you are!" Carpetsi howled. "You're workin' together with this murderous sawbones, or you'd have knocked him off after Haarman was bumped. You dirty double-crosser, I suppose you think you're gonna smudge *me* out? Yah, it'll be me next. Me! All the while you're pretending you don't know a thing about this set-up in the graveyard, here—"

Kavanaugh put his face close to the Italian's; squalled, "It'll be you next, all right, if you don't close that yap! You'll have every boog in Haiti on our necks!"

"Let 'em come! Let 'em come!" Carpetsi's expression was close to rabies. His fingers scratched the air before Kavanaugh's face. "You can't put this over on me, you big mick! By God, I see the trick you're pullin'! I'm gonna spill your beans, Kavanaugh—"

Kavanaugh told him in a deadly voice, "You're going to shut

up! You're going to shut up, Angelo, and go over and sit in the car. You'll shut up, or I'll shut you up!"

"Yaaah!" the Italian's face was the shade of liverwurst. "You'd knock me off now, if you dared, but you don't dare! Too many witnesses you'd have to dust off. I won't shut up! I'll spill your beans! If you think that stunt of sendin' off Brown and Coolidge—"

There was an interruption, then, that suspended the Italian's screeching in mid air.

John Ranier, standing back with the girl, too dazed by Carpetsi's outburst at Kavanaugh to move, heard a shout from somewhere beyond the car. A full-lunged bellow that came from the darkness on the road, its source invisible in the mist.

"Hey, there! Who wants Coolidge?"

It spun Kavanaugh in a crouch. Sent Carpetsi reeling on his heels as if struck by a fist, combing wild fingers through his Dance Palace hair. Thrusting the girl sideways, Ranier glared in bewilderment toward the car under the cemetery arch where the blonde woman had trilled a coloratura shriek and the Professor was blatting, "Did you bring the police?"

Then boots came pounding under the fog-drizzled arch, crackled over the cockle shells of a grave mound, and Coolidge formed in the lighted area before the headlamp. It was not the same Coolidge who had gone for the police two hours ago in this nightmare. The man's appearance was that of a rhino flushed by big game hunters from a swamp. The tourist attire that had been incongruous on his Mack truck frame was plastered, shapeless with mud. His shoes were swollen with clay, pants mired to the knees, sleeves brown to the elbows.

Blinking in the misty light-bath, he faced the group at the grave-side and scowled from one to the next, stupidly. Gold gleams ricocheted from his teeth as his mouth pulled lungfuls of breath and his chest puffed like a blacksmith's bellows.

"I was leggin' it back to the hospital," he panted at Kavanaugh. "Seen you go by in th' flivver. Damn near run me down in th' fog, and you was by before I could yell. Got here fast as I could." Plucking off the cap he had hung on one doorknob ear, he mopped his face and forehead with the cap, rotary motion, panting, rolling his eyes. "There's been an accident, see? I'm a mass of nerves! Justa mass of nerves!"

KAVANAUGH SAID, "I'll say there's been an accident!" pacing up to the big man in a way that made Ranier think of a terrier accosting a Great Dane. He shoved his pocketed gun into Coolidge's muddy midriff, and Coolidge looked down at the Irishman's nudging pocket, and scowled, and began to walk backwards. Kavanaugh followed him, walking forwards.

Coolidge blurted, "What the hell—!" as Kavanaugh walked him out of the headlamp's path, drove him stumbling away from the car, pushed him at a tangent toward the foot of the graveyard. In the fogged darkness, still walking, the two men were gray, half-melted shapes.

Clinging to John Ranier's arm, Laïs Engles peered into the vapour-screen where the men had dissolved to a merged shadow, and whispered, "What is happening? What is happening?"

Ranier said, "Wait and see."

He heard the Irishman's voice bang, "Tell your story, big boy, and tell it quick!" the bang lowering to a menacing rapidfire undertone, muffled words punctuated with oaths, too inaudible for listeners to catch. Coolidge replied in gushing whispers, evidently pleading. Their voices bleared to a smothered mumbling from which Ranier's ears caught fragments. Kavanaugh haggling, accusing. Coolidge groaning, panting, denying. Coolidge shouted, "Holy Jumping Judas!" and Ranier could see the white oval of his face as he stretched his neck to look past his inquisitor at the opened grave. Twice Kavanaugh caught the big man's lapel, seemed to be shaking him; several times the Irishman looked back, glinty-eyed. Ranier heard his own name spoken, Professor Schlitz's, the girl's.

It seemed to him the whispered inquisition was lasting a long time, but he stood at the foot of the grave with the girl, nerves tight, waiting because there was nothing else to do. Everything was ravelling off into mists, facts dissolving, swimming through his fingers before he could clench them on anything certain. Bad dreams were like this—figures formed; faded; changed features; cut illogical capers that in the dream seemed logical. Like one of those nightmares where you walked in jeopardy through a forest of unseen perils, only it wasn't a forest and you were falling through limitless space. But he wasn't falling through space. He was standing in a Haitian graveyard with a frightened girl. A frightened Italian was rooted near-by, making throat-sounds like whimpering. A frightened Negro, a frightened blonde and a frightened college professor were parked in a frightened Model T under the cemetery arch. Two frightened men were arguing in violent whispers off in the fog; and the only one present who wasn't frightened was the little old lady jaunty against the tombstone—uncaring because she was dead.

What had become of the Winton? Of Brown and the Haitian, Marcelline? But those would be easy answers compared to: What became of Haarman? Was he dead when he was killed? Was he Adolph Perl buried fourteen years ago, and if he wasn't why had Perl vanished from his grave? Simple answers compared to: How did this old lady travel three miles on those mossy shoes? Who brought her here and why? How the hell can I get this frightened girl out of this? Has that mob started from the village? Where's Eberhardt?

EBERHARDT! QUEER! The name kept prowling through his subconsciousness with the insistence of those drum-beats tunneling the fog. He wondered if he'd spoken it aloud. No; that was Kavanaugh's voice. They were coming back into the light; the Irishman moving with swift, purposeful strides; the muddied Coolidge wiping his battered face on his cap.

"We're getting out of here," Kavanaugh came shouting, "right now! Everybody into the car!"

Angelo Carpetsi raised a whimper. "I ain't going."

"Don't be a fool," was Kavanaugh's tongue-lashing command.

"Stay behind here in this bone-yard and the black mob that's coming from the village will tear you to mince. We're moving out! Quick!"

He strode at Ranier, pointing toward the road, talking with the up-pitched momentum of a radio announcer. "Smash up! The Winton! That damned coon Marcelline crashed the sedan in a swamp a mile this side of the village. Marcelline and Brown went on. Beat it on foot the rest of the way to get the police. Coolidge says the car's smashed to junk, and there's hell to pay down there. Gunshots in the village and drums going like express trains. There's a riot, all right. Marcelline told him to run back and warn the hospital. Coolidge says he passed this graveyard on the way up, but he didn't see anything because it was all he could do to keep his feet on the macadam."

"If I'd known what was here, I'd of never come back," the big man promised. "I'd of never come back after you passed me up the road in the flivver. I'm justa mass of nerves!"

Kavanaugh panted, "We'll be more than a mass of nerves if we don't get out of here!" And suddenly his hand was on Ranier's shoulder, his hard voice cracked, shaken, his manner conciliatory. "This is getting me, Ranier—sorry my nerves blew up a while ago. That goes for the girl, too. Lost my head the way the Italian kid lost his at me. Can't blame the boy, with things popping like they are. Now on, we got to stick together. Stand by me, will you?"

They were running for the car. Ranier, hand clasped over Laïs Engles' hand, nodded blankly at the Irishman beside him, and tried to remember something he had wanted to do. Kavanaugh reminded him.

"And you're right, Doc. We'll go to the graveyard where the girl says that old lady was buried. Try to find some clue—!"

Looking back from the Model T's running board, Ranier saw the old lady had assumed a more comfortable pose against Adolph Perl's headstone. Her glasses had dropped to her lap, bonnet tipped over her eyes, chin fallen to her breast. Wrapped in a cocoon of fog, she might have resumed her interrupted immortal doze. A cadence of low-boomed drums drifted through the cemetery vapours, and the old lady's chin sank further, as if lulled.

But she was not quite asleep. As the car charged off with pounding cylinders, Ranier saw her head nod perkily, twice—goodbye.

CHAPTER XIII

THE SECOND GRAVE

ON THE ROAD the fog had thickened. Surging across the highway's surface as if the macadam were afire. Bushing up from the roadside. Rolling in white woolly bales before the headlight; boiling blackly astern. Where the road dodged between high embankments, the stagnated mist was the consistency of evaporating milk. Landscape, sky and night were blotted out. Jungles had dissolved to steam; solids turned into white, watery gas and set adrift. That a car from Detroit could stay on this nebulous milky way in Haiti was not the least of tonight's miracles.

But the car climbed and plowed through the vapour-blizzard with a disregard for safety that had its passengers howling. If it once slowed to forty it was not the driver's fault. The little black man at the wheel yanked the gas lever down to the last notch on its quadrant. Whatever those native drums had told him, he didn't like it. No need to wipe the steamed windshield. Under the brim of his giant sombrero, Polypheme's eyes were occult headlights that discovered a road the half-blind car couldn't see.

And once more Ranier was assailed by a sense of dream-like unreality. This race to escape an undertone muttering of drums. This desperate dash from cemetery to cemetery to inquire why an old lady, fourteen years underground, had tonight deserted her tomb. Skidding, rocking, slewing on unseen curves, threatening to fly into fragments at every turn, the car boiled on through invisibility, and only the girl's fingers locked with Ranier's seemed real. He could not see the running board supporting him. He could only guess Mr. Coolidge was clinging on the opposite side, from occasional shouted references to nerves. Polypheme was a shadow with a pair of eyes, and the jam in the back seat a formless blur of shapes and outcries—groans from the Professor, caterwauls from the blonde, howls by Carpetsi and oaths from Kavanaugh.

He could not see or hear the girl. Clutching the windshield post with his right hand, he locked his left hand with the girl's in reassuring pressure. She was there. In the front seat, and trembling, her invisible fingers icy cold. But he wasn't dreaming their frightened grip, and they were something human to hang to when the car screeched on an unseen curve. It was strange as hell. Why hold the girl's hand? He hadn't held a woman's hand like that in all of five years. His grip wasn't fatherly, either. Why in the name of God should he try to reassure this girl? Who was she, after all? What was he doing in this nightmare, working up a protective instinct over a girl he'd never heard of three hours before, when he ought to concentrate on saving his own skin?

Ranier withdrew his fingers and fastened them on the doorframe. Was he going insane? A ship's passenger had been murdered; stabbed before his eyes! Body-snatchers were loose in the night, and a black mob was coming, and for all he knew—

Well, it was no time for romancing. For all he knew, the girl's lovely hand might have a part in this dirty business. Certainly when Kavanaugh had questioned her she'd held something back. Something concerning Dr. Eberhardt—that hospital?

As if summoned by his thought, the hospital loomed ghostly at the left of the road, and as the car raced past the entrance, Ranier had a glimpse of that lighted laboratory window shining Hallowe'en yellow through the black upper branches of the sablier tree. In the fog the place looked dismal as an owl-hoot. The car did not slow down, and the outsprawled villa was a misshapen shadow surrounded by the ghosts of trees, there and gone in the mist.

John Ranier looked back, wondering if Haarman's body were

roaming that spectral place. Hell with that! Native voodoo might dig up the dead, but it couldn't animate them, even on a night like this. Someone had stolen the Haarman cadaver for good reasons that weren't so good. To do away with the evidence? Hide the fact of homicide? You couldn't bring a murder charge when you couldn't produce the corpse.

Or had the taffy-haired tourist's body been appropriated for some darker purpose than concealment, some necrologic experiment conceived in this Haitian limberlost?

REMEMBERED WORDS phrased themselves through Ranier's mind. "He was experimenting—something so important he works on—a theory he could revive dead cells with adrenalin—tonight he was to finish, to make the vital discovery—" The girl's words, spoken when they'd found the wrecked hospital lab, the doctor absent. Dr. Eberhardt, again! Could this mysterious and as yet unseen physician be back of tonight's witcheries? Some half loony scientist, demented by years of isolation in this Caribbean backwater, bent on resurrectionism?

There was Eberhardt's name on that envelope from the murdered tourist's pocket. There was the girl's assertion the stabbed tourist was someone Eberhardt had buried fourteen years ago. There was that little old lady, another of that long-ago funeral party, transplanted to a robbed grave. There was the possibility that Eberhardt, missing in the night, had returned to the hospital, pilfered Haarman's body from the emergency room, slammed that downstairs door. What sort of doctor would walk off and leave dissected hands boiling over a Bunsen flame?

Ranier's imagination began to picture a dark figure chasing down the night with shovel and wheel barrow, hunting likely cemetery-subjects for experiments. The sort of creature who, in cone-shaped astrologer's hat and alchemist's robes, would conjure at midnight in a laboratory, a dabbler in mummy-dust and usnea, (moss scraped from the head of a criminal who had been hanging for weeks on a gallows.)

Whew! Ranier shook off a shiver. No moment to go wool-gathering with that sort of material; better quit thinking until the next shock came along. Ten to one, he'd fall off this running board flying through nothingness, come to earth with a bang, and wake up back in the Blue Kitty Café, banging his chin on Hyacinth Lucien's floor.

But the ride went on. Climbing. Banking. Tunneling through jungles of vapour. Dipping through smothered undercuts. Taking unseen curves on two wheels. Uphill and down-dale through the dissolving, white-blanketed night; across an aerial trestle that had no more foundation than a rainbow, its girders merely shadows suspended in mist; between black rustling walls of timber that slashed invisible overhangs of foliage at Ranier's face; past the half-formed shapes of boulders, the half-seen trunks of great trees. Once the gray ghost of a donkey went by in the cloudy backwash like some waterlogged carcass seen from a ship's rail at night; and once there was a horse's skull on a post, like a rural mailbox at the roadside, a frowsty death's-head signalling Haitian voodoo. In the momentary light of the headlamp, the eye holes steamed, and, as the car slewed past, the horse-teeth bit at the seat of Ranier's pants.

The ride went on; and the next shock came after the girl cried out of darkness, "Polypheme! *Ici!*" and the car skidded to a standstill with screeching brake-bands. Wiping mist from his vision, Ranier made out a rift in the jungle's wall, a little bay in the creaming forest, an open glade beyond the edge of the road. The fog was thinner in this clearing, as if held back on three sides by the close-packed trees, and the car light spread across the vale a moony illumination. Grassy and sequestered, it might have been a picnic spot, save the knolls were mounds and the mossy rocks were tombstones and there were tilted wooden crosses and a scattering of late-burning candles.

No, it was not quite the place for jelly sandwiches. There was a path led in from the roadside, a sandy lane that picked its way among the mounds, and about twenty feet in from the road the path was blocked by a sand pile. There was an excavation. There was an uncovered coffin grounded alongside the excavation. There was a round-shouldered tombstone at the head of the excavation. From the roadside John Ranier could read the epitaph.

HIER RUHET IN GOTT
GROSSMUTTER SOU
Gest. 3 Januar 1922
ICH HATTE EINST
EIN SCHONES VATERLAND

But the figure sprawled beside the unlidded coffin was not resting in God. Neither was it Grandmother Sou.

Before he was half way up the path, Ranier knew who it was.

CHAPTER XIV

THE DEAD MARINE

SHATTERPATED, JOHN RANIER stared down at the thing while the fibres of his skin twitched with repulsion and a cold passed through him and made his lamed foot ache. It was lying beside the empty coffin, an elbow negligently hooked over the coffin's cowling, its long legs outstretched in the weeds, one foot in the grave.

The mummified face under the faded campaign hat was distinguished from Tutankhamen's only by the wispy remains of a red moustache. One surmised it had not always been gaunt, for the uniform fitted loosely and the leather-faced leggings had sprung from the dwindled calves. The tunic was no more than a mustard colored gauze, a delicate garment spun by a khaki spider, and the bronze sharpshooter's medal was sewed to the breast pocket by cobwebs, and the webbed bullet belt, unhooked from rusty buckle, had lost its cartridges.

John Ranier had seen that O.D. uniform before, that globe-and-anchor insignia above the hatband. He had seen it before, and in similar disrepair. Once he had stepped on it in the leaf-mould of Belleau Wood, and there'd been another in the wire at Cantigny. They seeded the earth from the home of Montezuma to the shores of Tripoli, these soldiers of the sea, but Ranier would have wagered this leatherneck was the first to rise from a grave after fourteen years, mascotted by a bullfrog. The frog was tied to the bullet belt by a length of grocery string, and it did not want to play mascot for a tough marine, a three striper of the breed that wouldn't stay down—

Ranier retreated, backing slowly down the path, step by step. Shadows retreated with him, gesturing maniacal motions with their arms, colliding and bumping in precipitate retreat, bombarding the rancid dusk with senseless cries.

Ranier was glad to get back to the road, let the fog pull the wool over his eyes. People stumbled and shouted around him, hugging the car for safety, darting wild glances off at the wallowing white night. Kavanaugh had his automatic clutched in his hand, and his long-jawed face seemed infuriated. Moving his head from side to side, he stood against the running board of the car like a captain defending a quarter deck against an expected rush of mutineers. When the insectologist made a leap to gain the back seat, the Irishman struck him aside with an elbow and a look of annoyance, snarling:

"Nobody's going yet! Nobody's going yet!"

The blonde Daisy woman pushed back her picture hat, put her face in her hands, began to bawl. Angelo Carpetsi's teeth were audible in a flour-and-water face; and the big Mr. Coolidge walked up and down the road's edge, panting, "Holy Jumpin' Judas! Holy Jumpin' Judas!" towelling his face on his cap, revolving ox-like eyes.

Unconsciously, Ranier had halted beside Laïs Engles who was standing in suspended animation, canvas shoes rooted in the myrtle at the bottom of the path, one hand to her throat, white face averted from that object in the weeds. He couldn't look at her. Not yet. He could only stand with fingers clenched in dry palms, his mind quivering, his ears only half aware of the uproar breaking around him like the clamor of a hundred skunk-panicked hens, his eyes held by that scene in the fog-hemmed glade.

Then Kavanaugh snapped, "Everybody wait!" in sudden decision, and, ramming pistol into pocket, sprinted up the path for another look. They could see him scouting around the rectangular crater, stooping to scrutinize the vacant longbox, peering gingerly at the mummy beside the box. He snatched back his cuff to examine his strap watch, then glared off toward the highway in the direction they had come. He struck a match on his shank, held a palm-cupped glimmer above the marble headstone, as if convinced the moony light from the car had played tricks with the epitaph; read the name on the stone aloud. Then he skirted the sand pile, kicking at the fresh-turned loam.

He called, "Footprints, but too smudged to make out. Might be one man or ten. You, Coolidge," aiming his forefinger, "come up here."

Grudgingly the big man ascended the path. Kavanaugh handed him a penny box of matches, and they knelt over the excavation; conferred in quarrelsome whispers while the Brooklyn truck driver scratched and held wax matches over the trench.

WATCHING THAT shadowplay, not looking at the girl, Ranier fumbled for her wrist, fastened his fingers around it, pulled her craftily to him so that their shoulders touched.

"Talk low. That's the marine?"

"Yes," she breathed.

"Who fired the plague ship from Brazil? Who died of the mauve death that night your German expedition landed in Haiti?"

"Yes."

"The mate, Adolph Perl, was buried first in that cemetery down by the village; the old lady we saw there tonight was buried here?"

"Yes—I—"

"This marine, those others who died that night together, they were all buried in different cemeteries by Dr. Eberhardt and Polypheme because the doctor didn't want a lot of new graves together, didn't want the Haitians to know there'd been the plague—?"

"Dr. Eberhardt feared a panic among the natives who were hostile to his work and—"

"Eberhardt and Polypheme," Ranier nodded toward the Negro huddled in the car, "buried those people? Polypheme would remember?"

"He drove the wagon with the rough-boxes. Filled the graves that night—fourteen years ago. He would remember that."

"Would he remember the people who were buried?"

"No—he—he did not know them. He did not see them that night before they died."

Ranier suggested in a low, grinding mutter, "But Dr. Eberhardt might have remembered them. Dr. Eberhardt tended them before they died, laid them out, managed that midnight funeral. Do you see what I'm driving at?"

He could feel her arm harden in his grasp. She whispered, "No."

"Listen," his eyes were directed straight ahead, but his murmur deflected at the girl, "you've got to tell me everything you know about Eberhardt and tell it quick. That tourist Haarman who was stabbed in the Blue Kitty Café and died in your hospital—that murdered man had an envelope in his pocket with Eberhardt's name scrawled on it and the figures, 'one million m, four million dollar sign.' Make anything of that?"

She shook her head.

"Haarman was stabbed this evening some time around seven-thirty. Was Dr. Eberhardt in his hospital at that hour?"

"I don't know. I go to bed at seven because I am on night duty with the patients. He was in his laboratory then."

"So he might've ducked out without you knowing it," Ranier deduced, rubbing the words off his lips with the back of his hand. "And some time in there his lab was scuttled. Where'd he usually spend his evenings?"

"Laboratory. Tonight he planned to stay in; let Polypheme take the car. He was very engrossed—experimenting—" her voice trembled.

"Experimenting," Ranier nodded soddenly. "Adrenalin, you said, reviving—trying to revive—dead cells. And a man who looks like a dead man comes to Haiti and is murdered. Then his body disappears. The body of the man he looks like is exhumed, missing. An old lady, disinterred, is transferred to *that* grave and we find this marine at hers. All the while Eberhardt's missing. It doesn't rhyme. It's crazy as hell. But there's this much. Eberhardt's the only one in Haiti who might mistake Haarman for Perl; the only one, besides you, who knows the location of all these victims who were buried that night in 1922."

HER PAINFUL breathing came to a stop, and there was a momentary silence between them when she might not have been there. Her stricken inertia, impelled by his last statement, filled him with new uneasiness; and at the same time he became aware of Angelo Carpetsi's regard, noticed the Italian youth had sidled nearer in the fog to eye him covertly from where he stood beside the stalled car. But Carpetsi could not have heard much, what with the incoherent wailing of the blonde collapsed against a fender, and the falsetto obligato of Professor Schlitz demanding someone to tell him over and over again why he had ever quit the cruise steamer to go motor-touring at night down this baneful Haitian coast.

Detecting the Italian's baleful espionage, John Ranier kept his eyes fixed on the fog-blurred pair conferring in mid-graveyard, and tugged the girl's sleeve to back her along the road's edge into deeper shadow. The fog drank them in. Beyond the car light they were in that outer void, known by the sailors of Columbus to have been in these latitudes, where the night begins. The moony graveyard with its moony inhabitants, the parked car and the people there like a frenzied accident-crowd, were in another world. In the fog-bank Ranier stopped just in time. Another step backwards and he might have gone over the Edge.

Standing with him, there, the girl was weeping. Tears of quicksilver moving in silence down the shine of her cheek. She was looking up at him, lips moving, and her husked words struggling against sobs, barely reached his ear.

"I know what you are thinking. I cannot help it—I did not want to tell you. Dr. Eberhardt—from that terrible night when all my friends died and left me homeless on this coast—has been a father to me. He saved me from the mauve death that night. Brought me up, taught me nursing—I was going to study medicine—some day take over his work. Oh, I cannot tell this of him—I cannot—!"

Ranier whispered, "You must! What are you trying to tell?"

"Last summer," she breathed. "Fever. He has been ill. Worked so hard, no rest, miles to see his patients, night after night with the sick, operations—Fighting disease, ignorance, poverty among the mountain people—all by himself and no money to do it with and never stopping—locking himself in that laboratory. I've begged him to let up, and he would laugh. No time to let up in medicine, he would say. A doctor never lets up."

Ranier's lips twitched at the corners, husking, "Then you think—?" and she put an arm across her forehead as if to fend off the idea, shaking her head unhappily. "I cannot think. Tonight before supper he was—all right. But so worn, so white—ate nothing. Rushed up to his experiments on the verge of exhaustion. Lately—sometimes—he has done strange things—"

"What things?"

"Forgotten where he left his instruments. Misplaced prescriptions. Violent headaches, too."

Ranier thought, "Migraine," and averted his eyes from the pain reflected in the girl's. She was whispering miserably, "And he talks strangely about—about death. Serums to revive the dead—believes science will some day do it. Oh," her whisper broke, "it is horrible of me to imply—I was not going to tell you. But when I saw his laboratory tonight—his papers scattered, cultures spilled, those hands, that frog on the spike where he was always so careful to leave me a note where he has gone—*Lieber Gott!* but one night last summer when he was in a delirium of fever he wandered off without—we found him walking in that cemetery where—"

He breathed, "Wait!" and put a restraining hand on her arm with a false, "Don't be afraid, Miss Engles, the *Gardes* will be coming and everything'll be all right!" amplified for the benefit of Kavanaugh who was loping down the sandy path, followed by Mr. Coolidge.

SOME OF the sand might have lodged in the Irishman's teeth. Addressing Ranier, he stood sucking in his cheeks with haggard breaths, his mica eyes shifting between Ranier and the girl. "We aren't waiting for any police," he gritted out. "Brown mayn't get to 'em until morning." His eyes burned, then, steadily at the girl. "Listen. That U.S. Marine up there is the mauve death victim you told us about?"

Ranier answered for her, "I was just checking on it. She says it's the same one—Sergeant O'Grady."

"It's a pip!" Kavanaugh exploded. "A pip! That grave was opened about three hours ago by the looks. Footprints all over the bottom, but try to make 'em out! Smeared. No go. Not a clue but that damned Greenback tied to his belt same as the one tied to the old lady. It's her grave according to that tombstone." Triggering his finger at the girl, "You're sure you saw the old woman buried in this spot?"

"I remember. Old Gramma Sou—"

"Who put up that slab for her?"

"I," Laïs Engles whispered. "For all of them—those Germans from my uncle's ship who died for their Fatherland. Each has the same—the little quotation. But the marine and the—the missionary who died with them, they were cared for by their own people. Dr. Eberhardt bought the stones for—mine."

Kavanaugh deflated his cheeks, and green cords bulged along his jawlines to match green highlights in his cheekbones. "Someone," he lifted his sand and gravel voice for all to hear, "dug up that Perl guy and the old dame and the Leatherneck early this evening. They put the Leatherneck here at the old lady's grave and dropped her off at Perl's. That's how it looks to me. And we got to find the body of that guy Perl."

He paused to let his words drift through the fog, sink in. "We got to find Perl," he went on in a flatted snarl, "because we can't get the answer on Haarman till we do. And we got to get the answer on Haarman or we'll all be up for his murder. My hunch is that Doc Ranier, here, was right. Find the bird who snatched the Perl stiff and we find the guy who killed Haarman—God knows how!—because, maybe, he looked like Perl. So we're going!"

"Going?" The fife-shrill screech was recognized as Professor Schlitz, trilling from the doubtful haven of the car. "Going? Going? Where are we going now?"

"To this marine's graveyard, you fool. And we're sticking together, don't forget that!" Making a pistol of his dexterous hand, the tall man cocked the thumb-trigger and levelled the finger-barrel at Laïs Engles' breast. "Let's have it, girl! Where was this non-com laid away?"

Clasping anguished hands, she shrank against Ranier as if afraid of the Irishman's pantomime. "It is not far—to the soldier's grave. A little way, on up the road. You will see the barracks of the marines."

"Holy Jumpin' Judas!" Coolidge unexpectedly roared. "Y'mean to say there's leathernecks somewhere up the pike? Marines? U.S. Marines?"

Kavanaugh lashed out, "Why the devil didn't you tell us there were some United States soldiers—"

"There are no soldiers there," Laïs Engles cried. "There are no soldiers who can help us. The marines were removed from Haiti when Herr Roosevelt became president in America. The Haitians did not want them, and the occupation was ended three years ago. The barracks you will see standing empty, deserted. There is a little graveyard back of the parade ground. No one has been there for three years."

Kavanaugh's greenish cheekbones glimmered, blistered with

perspiration. He snarled, "Someone was there this evening! Someone who fetched this dead-head from that graveyard to this. We're going to have a look at this marine's grave. Maybe Perl's body is there!"

But the body of Adolph Perl was not in the little marine cemetery up the road where the little marine who was in the old lady's cemetery should have been.

CHAPTER XV

GOING TO JERUSALEM

GHOSTS WERE THERE. Ghosts that trailed the rattletrap Model T driven by Polypheme of the incandescent eyes. Ghosts that rode in, and clung to, the car—an Irish sugar merchant, a Brooklyn mug, an authority on insects, a peroxide blonde, a swart Italian—the ghosts of tourists on a Caribbean cruise. The ghost of a girl with fear's dark light in her eyes; and the ghost of a surgeon who had died young of bitterness and become a frayed ship's doctor soaked in *aguardiente.* Live ghosts.

There were the ghosts of the World War, summoned by Laïs Engles' story to that foreign field—the sailors of the *Kronprinz Albrecht,* blockade runner that had ended its secret mission up the Amazon four years too late, and brought its ghostly survivors—shadelings of the Imperial Navy and the *Wilhelmstrasse*—here to die. Ghosts that refused to be laid.

There was the ghost who had slain Haarman; and the ghost of Haarman, web-footed, vanished in the night; and the ghost of unseen Dr. Eberhardt who might be foaming mad.

The night, itself, was a ghost, fuming and blowing, trailing its gauzy veils across field and road, stalking in moist white cerements through the jungle, blindfolded with eerie bandages, muffled in cotton, embracing with clammy half-liquid arms the earthy ghosts of black Haiti. You could hear its bloodless pulse when the car engine stopped, and in that moment when everyone waited for someone else to move. Pulsations faint as the first heart-beats starting life in a chicken's egg.

Ranier stared at that abandoned marine barracks and knew they had found the headquarters of all loose banshees. Here was the spot. The house was haunted, and most of the spectres were home.

Set back from the road the low frame building, seen in fog, was like a carcass half consumed in a spider web, its framework showing in skeletal patches where the tar paper covering had been eaten away. The building—like American intervention—had not been favored by the tropics. Damp rot had spoiled its lumber. Its flesh-and-blood defenders had been withdrawn, and the spirits of Haiti had attacked the outpost, pried off the door to force an entry, and staved in the roof. The corral was overrun with weeds, outbuildings undermined and ambushed, the jungle closing in. You could see the spectral inmates passing and repassing behind the broken shutters, floating about the empty rooms; and when the car turned into the dooryard a horde of shadows fled around the corner, escaping into a boarded-up mess hall.

The ghosts here were American. Ghosts from the days of Benoit Batraville and Guillaume Sam and the Caco insurrections. Shades of Smedley Butler! Fog foaming across the weed-grown parade ground was the smoke of Springfields in a soundless battle of wraiths; and Ranier almost listened for a faint bugle echo to summon phantom stalwarts of the Corps, red-skinned and roaring, the words of "*Mademoiselle*" on their curse-baked lips, charging the fog with reckless bayonets.

Rounding the corner of that abandoned outpost in Haiti, he would have welcomed a few marines. Light from the one-eyed flivver didn't go very far in the surrounding fog. The girl indicated a footpath leading across the parade ground, and there was no telling what might greet them on that steamed-over field. You couldn't see five inches through the churning cream, and somebody's voice jittered, "Whoosh! Bats!"

BUT BATS hadn't left those boot-tracks in the mud. Visitors had been on that path before them; heel-marked the way. But the spongy loam had bleared the prints so that it was impossible to guess whose or how many shoes had been up that path ahead of them.

Kavanaugh swore at the smudged tracks: "They been here and gone!" yanking out his .45 to snap off the safety catch. "Everybody together, now. Where's the grave?"

"At the end of the path," the girl pointed, "across the field. You will see the crosses under a big silk-cotton tree."

Ranier hoped those early birds had gone. Or had one man left those splotched prints? Or was it a man? He cleared his throat, training the flashlight on the obscure footpath. "I'll go first. Come on." Swinging the girl into position behind him, he led off at a jog, and the others followed single file, invisible in the obliterating mist in a way that lifted the dog-hairs on Ranier's neck. He reached back to grasp Laïs Engles' hand; marked Kavanaugh's muttery oaths behind the girl, the others bringing up the rear, Indian fashion. Nobody stayed behind at that haunted barracks.

Somewhere in mid field the Irishman drew abreast of him, scouting the fog-banks ahead with wary gun. And a few paces farther in the clouds, he heard someone take a header in the weeds, Daisy May uncorking a scream and the Professor bawling like a calf, "Wait for me! Wait for me! I can't see!" The trotting line jarred down its length like a string of jolted freight cars, there was a scramble somewhere in the rear, then Coolidge's bellow, "S'all right, go ahead. I'm justa mass of nerves!"

The path bent a little uphill, shook itself out, stopped in a plot of trampled grass; and John Ranier reared up before an enormous phantom, the spirit of a gigantic gray tree formed suddenly before his eyes. A vast-trunked, elephant-hided pillar, swooping skyward, its bearded upper limbs like the hanging gardens of Babylon drifting overhead, its gnarled outspread roots like tentacles feeding in the grass. Fog rolled in white surf through that forest of aerial limbs; swathed the trunk in groping pythons of steam. Man was small in the presence of that ancient jungle monarch. A search-light couldn't have discovered its top. But

Ranier's flashlamp explored the bottom. Microscopic at the feet of this forest Druid were the crosses.

Even in that hour of extremity Ranier found a bur in his throat for that expatriated little squad who hadn't gone home. They held the fort, even when the diplomats in Washington who'd sent them here had forgotten. Unremembered, they carried the flag, a weather-dimmed American flag someone had set in a flower pot under the tree. Their formation was military and their crosses erect, in line.

But the sergeant who should have been at the head of his company wasn't there. The white circle of the flashlight fell suddenly into a black hole; leaped out of the fresh-cut trench to a mound of smoking earth; discovered a corroded longbox; its lid ripped off, thrown sideways across the dirt-pile. The flashlight shook as Ranier sent the scared ray torching to the head of the excavation, revealing the cross that stood there.

SERGEANT EDGAR O'GRADY
U.S.M.C.
Wheeling, W. Va.
DIED OF FEVER

No, the sergeant who should have been there was at the grave of the little old lady who was at the grave of Adolph Perl who looked like (he couldn't be!) Haarman. And it wasn't Adolph Perl at the grave of Sergeant O'Grady. Or anything that might be mistaken for an Adolph Perl.

At first Ranier thought there was nothing at that rifled grave. Then a sound from the unlidded coffin vitalized his hair. *Grumph!* Something slick and green looked over the coffin rim with terrified eyes; gave a leap to escape the white light-ray; flopped back on tethered legs. It was hobbled by a string to a rusty coffin nail, and John Ranier made a mental note never to eat frog's legs again. There was nothing more than that bullfrog in Sergeant O'Grady's coffin. There was, in that coffin, a handful of bones and a celluloid collar.

"The missionary!"

In the confused horror of the ensuing moment too many things happened at once. Afterwards, thinking back through the nightmare, Ranier could never quite sort the incidents in sequence. He could remember grabbing up a clod from the dirt-pile, breaking the earth in his fingers, shouting: "This sod wasn't turned an hour ago!" He could remember turning his horrified flashlight at the great, ghostly tree as if expecting it to embrace him with its arms. He could remember Coolidge lumbering forward with matches; Kavanaugh striding around the grave, glaring, gesturing his automatic. Daisy May was somewhere in the fog with Professor Schlitz, both wailing like babes in the wood, and Laïs Engles cried out through babbling pandemonium.

"—but the missionary was buried at Morne Cuyamel! At the crossroads a kilometer from here! In the churchyard of the Anglican mission at Morne Cuyamel—!"

"Zombies!" Polypheme howled. *"Cultedesmmorts! Zombies là!"*

Kavanaugh skirted the grave, ran past Ranier with a roar. "To the churchyard, then! Get back to the car, all of you! We'll go back to the grave of this missionary!"

Shadows raced about in the dark vapour, and Ranier wheeled on the girl with a low-voiced, "Wait! Don't leave my sight for a second! I've found out something here—something that's—" His voice stopped behind clenched teeth. The shadow before him was not the girl. His left hand swept out, gripped an arm. Silk tore in his steeled fingers.

"Doc!" Carpetsi's guttural words were oil-coated, seeping out of mist. "For God's sake, don't spot me with that flashlight." He was there like a secret, gripping Ranier's lapel with his free hand. "Gotta talk to you—alone—make a chance—"

"Now," Ranier gritted. He could feel the Italian's body quivering. The answer was scarcely audible to his ear; choked syllables and a scent of garlic.

"No, no—careful—I know, see? I know who killed Haarman,

and I know who's playin' Goin' to Jerusalem with these corpses. I'd be killed in a second if—"

The Italian's whisper was bitten off short. Interrupted by a sound of hammer-blows somewhere in distance. *Tonk-tonk-tonk!* Metallic concussions somewhere far in the fog's sceneless void.

Kavanaugh's voice squalled, "Shots!" Laïs Engles cried, "Up the mountain somewhere! Up on Morne Cuyamel where the Anglican mission—!"

Everybody was running.

CHAPTER XVI

EAR TO EAR

EVERYBODY WAS RUNNING, phantoms across that fog-smothered parade ground, but there was nothing phantom about those reports which had echoed down through the smothered stillness. Three shots Ranier had counted. Gunfire on Morne Cuyamel where the Anglican missionary who occupied the sergeant's coffin had been buried. The sergeant was A.W.O.L. and that celluloid collar was occupying his place. But the bones of the missionary under that giant silk cotton tree had told Ranier something that jelled the sweat on his forehead. When he learned Angelo Carpetsi's version he might know the answer to this jabberwok graveyard relay, and meantime he mustn't let Laïs Engles out of his sight.

In the dash for the car he caught up with the girl, but he had no chance to speak with the Italian. Tourists piled into the back like maniac firemen, aided by boots from the raging Kavanaugh and the howls of nerve-wracked Mr. Coolidge who knew everybody would be shot to hell before they got there. The firing on the *morne* had stopped with sinister abruptness, and there was no noise in the fogged dark now save the car's clattertybang, the yowling of the passengers and the drums you couldn't hear but knew were there.

Balancing on the swaying running board, Ranier interlaced his fingers with the girl's; put his lips close to her damp blowing hair. "Stick close when we get there—! Dangerous, now—!

If shooting starts, they'll fire at the flashlight—! Drop to the ground—!"

"Oh, please." Her fingers squeezed his in appeal. He stooped his head to hear. Above the rushing opaque wind and the gasoline-smelling roar of the car he could catch but a fragment of her entreaty. "If it is Unkle Doktor—Dr. Eberhardt—please do not kill—"

Two-wheeling at sixty around a fog-banked curve, the car rocked like a ship; and Ranier, almost thrown from his narrow footing, lost the girl's voice. He muttered a word of assurance, something he did not feel, and concentrated on clinging to the invisible door. Foliage, sharp-thorned, lashed at his legs. Wet wind tore at his cap. There was a narrow underpass with a glimpse of railroad girders overhead where the fenders struck sparks from the concrete sidewall and Ranier only saved himself from being sandpapered off his perch by flinging his head and shoulders into the car.

That black gnome under the Pancho Villa sombrero was driving as if the Legions of Eblis were hugging his exhaust pipe. "Faster! Faster!" That was Kavanaugh's shouting. If Polypheme failed to comprehend the Irishman's English, he understood the pistol-muzzle nudging his neck. Ranier weighed the advantages of being crash-piled on a hairpin turn or dying at the dank hands of some homicidal ghoul, and found neither to his exact taste. But it was no time to indulge twinged nerves. He could only hope the gunmen behind that fusillade had run out of ammunition, and he might discover from Carpetsi who it was. He hitched along the running board, cursing a corrugated stretch of macadam that loosened his teeth. Hands clutched his coat, pulling him inboard.

"Save me!" Professor Schlitz screeched. "Save me, Dr. Ranier! You're an officer from the ship! Don't let them go to this place! We'll all be murdered in our tracks! Murdered in our tracks!"

Ranier fought the insectologist off, cuffing, slapping. "Pull yourself together! Nobody's going to be hurt—!"

"Somebody's going to be hurt," Kavanaugh roared, "if they don't stop kicking me in the face! By God, Daisy, if you don't sit quiet I'll throw you out of the car!"

No chance to sneak a word with the Italian in that jammed uproar of hysteria and back-seat driving. He could glimpse Angelo Carpetsi's gray profile and glowing black eyes in the center of the crush, and those eyes radiated fear. Meeting his, they flashed a message of silence, an unmistakable warning to keep mum until an opportune time.

Ranier felt his way back to the windshield post, the Italian boy's whispered confession echoing in his mind. "I know who killed Haarman, and I know who's playin' Goin' to Jerusalem with these corpses—" Did the pink-shirted Dago really know? If so, why hadn't he told Kavanaugh, Brown, Coolidge; revealed the murderer back there in the café? Why that strange verbal flare-up with Kavanaugh back there in the graveyard near the village? And why the clandestine confession to him, Ranier, in the burying ground deserted by the U.S. Marines? Did Angelo actually know anything, or was that another play in this underground game of vanishing corpses and scrambled graves?

SUDDEN APPLICATION of the brakes put an end to these speculations. An end John Ranier could hardly have foreseen. Caromed off the front fender, he found himself in the road at the side of a low stone wall as unexpected on that jungled mountain as cocoanut palms would have been in Devonshire. Fog washed along the wall, obliterating lengths of its precise masonry, but when the white tide reached the iron gate it stopped, as if it realized its malarial breath did not belong there. The car's headlamp traveled through the gate which was standing ajar, and advanced across a grassy churchyard to the steps of a white mission house that was certainly, with its gothic door and pointed steeple, a copy of something north of England.

An infiltration of moonlight soaked the scene in a pale blue gloaming, and John Ranier stared at that church in the wildwood with his mouth open a little. It opened a little farther

The German colonel was sitting beside the grave

when he saw a mud-caked car, twin of Polypheme's job, parked in the rolling roadside smother beyond the gateway. The car was parked without lights, the driver's door hanging open, no owner in sight. Someone visiting the mission? No light in any window of the church, and its yard of tombstones still as death. Mosquitoes buzzed, augmenting the silence; foliage steamed and dripped. Everybody peered; listened. Even the drums were inaudible in that hundred-ton hush.

But gunfire had echoed in that moon-soaked stillness and its memory remained like soundless thunder in the air. Any moment now, and the rector in nightcap and gaiters should come fussing out of the church door to know the trouble. Had he come he would have learned it soon enough.

Ranier learned it when, instinctively keeping his head below the line of the wall, he limped to the gate; looked in. There was a faint flavor of gunpowder in the mist that floated around the gatepost. Ranier shocked back from the entry with a yell.

The grave was two mounds distant inside the gateway; and

he was sitting, that German officer, with his back against a shoulder of the tombstone, in a pose John Ranier had seen before. There was a familiar arrangement, a patterned design to the layout—pile of fresh-spaded sand, raw-lipped excavation, uprooted coffin turned turtle among the peaceful neighboring graves—that displayed a consistent technique in the artist's veiled hand. The officer, himself, seemed familiar, almost expected in his shreds of a Potsdam uniform threadbare as gray moonshine, his tarnished buckles and moth-eaten tabs, mouldy boots outstretched in languor, green leather helmet like an inverted goblet lopped over one skullish ear. He was grinning like a Jolly Roger, and one might have believed him to be humming until one spied the cloud of midges that made black spots before his eyes. A German *Kommandant* on duty would not hum. The Iron Cross dangled from his skeleton throat, and stars on the bleached tunic collar proclaimed him a *Stabsoffizier* of high rank.

"Colonel Otto!"

But Laïs Engles' hand-smothered cry was not a necessary introduction. He had suspected the name of that Death's Head Hussar, even before his eyes discovered the tombstone legend which had nothing to do with the occupant of the lot. The headstone marking that violated grave was legible in misty moonlight; its epitaph singularly ominous.

REV. ARCHIBALD DAVIS
R.I.P.
DIED OF FEVER

3 January 1922

A Moment, Stranger, As You Pass By,
As You Are Now, So Once Was I.
As I Am Now, So You Will Be.
Prepare For Death, And Follow Me.

It was Coolidge who read the epitaph aloud, and it seemed nobody in the hugged crowd on that churchyard's threshold was willing to take that sombre advice. They weren't prepared for death, and the prospect of following the missionary left them cold. The blonde woman uttered the sounds of a strangling parrot. Kavanaugh's oaths were sulphurous. Professor Schlitz came, saw and was conquered—that was one limerick he didn't like! He backed out of the gateway with nervous prostration on his scholarly visage; wheeling like a mare, and bolting for invisibility down the road.

Ranier said, "Hell! Hell!" and put out a sweaty arm to hold back the girl. He wasn't prepared for death, either. At least, not in the form it had taken in this magic-lantern churchyard scene. The artist had not signed this picture with a bullfrog, but the object affixed to the skeleton's hand was just as good.

RANIER STARED at the automatic pistol in that knuckly fist of bones, and his blood ran thinner than the hint of powder-smoke in the air. The colonel was in no condition to have fired the weapon. But that pungance in the damp persisted; and the .45, balanced on his knee, was aimed into the trench beside him as if he'd lounged there idly pot-shooting at rats.

Ranier shuffled unwilling feet to the grave-edge, anxious to know what the bony marksman might have been sniping. Finding out, he damned his curiosity.

The Haitian *gendarme* had been shot through the head three times. On the sandy grave bottom he lay face up, mouth wide as a slice of watermelon, staring sightlessly at the obscured sky. A little landslide of sand had partly covered his legs, and there was a footprint clearly recorded on the breast of his khaki blouse. A glance at that shoe-shined black face told Ranier its wearer was dead. Horror bulging from those white-circled African eyes could only have been matched by the electric-light shock in his own.

"Murdered!" It was Kavanaugh at his elbow, and the Irishman's eyes were hailstones. "A cop, by heaven! There'll be holy hell breakin' for this! That," he pointed at the skeletal sharpshooter at ease against the tombstone, "—that couldn'ta done it! Can you match this, Ranier? Can you match it?"

Ranier said thickly, "Those shots we heard—killed this *gendarme.* Not ten minutes ago. Grave robber who did this—that *gendarme* must've driven up and come on him at work. He fired at the *Garde* before the fellow had a chance—!"

"Brown," Kavanaugh suggested hoarsely. "Brown and Marcelline got to the police in that village. That's how it was. They reached the headquarters down there, and the fool police captain telephoned some post up in this neck of the woods. God! They sent one man! *One* man!"

"His car's headed toward the hospital. Maybe you're right. He was passing the churchyard. Saw this infernal—" Bringing his teeth together on an oath, Ranier clipped off the speculation; pointed a shaky finger at the reasty human residue across the grave. "The gun!"

"I seen it."

"It's not the German's. He'd have carried a Lüger. It's," Ranier husked, "like yours. Colt .45."

The Irishman nodded, white-faced. "These body snatchers or who's doin' this, they knocked over this cop, dumped him into the ground and left the cannon in that skeleton's fist. Someone stepped on the cop, too."

Ranier circled the grave, dog-legged. It wanted some resolution to relieve that officer of his pistol. Dropping it into his side pocket, he told Kavanaugh, "I'll take it along; might be fingerprints. It's a U.S. Army gun. That marine sergeant's name on the butt. Get it?"

"What the hell—"

"Yes," John Ranier whispered fiercely, "what the hell." He scrubbed clamminess from his forehead with a shaky palm, his eyes dry and hot on the Irishman's haggard face. "I'll tell you what the hell. Somebody robbed the dead topkick of his gun; fetched it here. The bloody thing jammed on the third shot or it wouldn't have been discarded, you can bet on that. These ghouls are going to stop at nothing. Nothing. They—it—whatever it is, murdered Haarman. This *gendarme.* Any of us may be next. Adolph Perl, that old lady, the Marine, the missionary, this German officer—do you see what's happening? Those people who died of that mauve death fourteen years ago, one after another they're being dug up. Know where we'll find the next—?"

KAVANAUGH INTERRUPTED, "What I wanta know is why they're bein' spaded up like this and shifted around. What's anybody want with these corpses?"

"This thing isn't as mad as it looks, Kavanaugh. It's following some sort of plan, some devilish routine, but I've got a hunch there's something screwy with the routine. Listen. The next episode's going on right now, my life on it! In the cemetery where this Potsdam colonel ought to be." He called toward shadows hovering at the gate, "Miss Engles? We want to know where you saw this colonel buried."

"Bois Legone," her answer came faintly. "The little village half way up the mountain beyond here. There is a fork in the road and one takes the dirt road to the right. It is near the market place, a big cathedral—"

He brushed hairs of mist from his eyes; ordering, "Tell Polypheme to crank the car. And send Mr. Carpetsi in here, will you? Before we leave—Mr. Kavanaugh and I want a word with him."

Kavanaugh said from the side of his mouth, "The Wop? What for?"

"He's got something to say. You might be interested."

A hippogrif's shadow formed at the gate, moved forward on squee-geeing wet shoes and came into focus as Mr. Coolidge, cap mopping a worried forehead, serious sobriety in his eyes. He puffed, "I heard you pagin' Carpetsi. He ain't in the car. He ain't there."

John Ranier didn't like the way he said it. Kavanaugh demanded, aiming a finger, "What do you mean, he ain't there?"

"Angy ain't waitin' in the car," the big man informed glumly.

"Couple minutes ago he told me he was a mass of nerves, and when I looked around to answer he wasn't nowhere in sight." His eyes slid sidewise from the tableau behind Ranier. "Don't say as I can blame him for takin' a run-out powder, or that louse-collector, either. See, they ducked in the fog. Angy's gone."

Kavanaugh bawled, "Get him!" thunderously; jabbing his gunbarrel finger into the big man's solar plexus to send him in an arm-swinging backwards stagger, dissolving into shadow as he went, out through the gate. "Bring back that ginzo! He can't have gone far in that soup out there. Get him!" He spat at Ranier, "So the slicker had something to spill, did he? Give you an idea what it was?"

Ranier's eyes strained at the curdled darkness of the road where Coolidge's boots could be heard galloping along invisible macadam. The big man was hallooing, "Hey, Angelo! Angy! They wantcha back here!" in a hide-and-go-seek quaver, striking futile safety matches that drowned in the surfed murk like sparks in a quiet ocean.

"He said he'd be killed if he told," Ranier muttered.

"He'll be killed if he doesn't," the Irishman proposed flatly. "I knew that spaghetti-swallower was keepin' something back. Yeah. This isn't the time, by all that's holy! for any of—hey, Coolidge!"

Boots on the road had stopped. Stopped as if the clattering truck driver had been snuffed out by a wand-touch in the mist, brogans and all.

"Coolidge?" Kavanaugh stretched his neck with a shout. "Are you there?"

About forty paces from the parked police car a match spluttered feebly, exhibiting the Coolidge face as a spoiled cabbage, disembodied and afloat in the toadstool-colored eddy. The match signalled frantically, and the big man's face, blue in distress, was screwed up like an infant's gathering breath for a colic howl.

"Where's Carpetsi?" Kavanaugh could have been heard in India. "Did you get him?"

The match expired to a spark that floated groundward. The face disappeared, and the howl came from Nothingness where it had been.

"He's been got!"

GOT! IT was a mild word for what had happened to Angelo Carpetsi. A sickly euphemism flattering the thing that had overtaken the Italian youth out there in the glucose-thick woolpack of the road; the red butchery that had struck in silence, stealthily, without mercy, feeling its victim and tip-toeing off, unseen in invisible mantles of mist.

There had been no struggle. Nothing. Fifty feet down the roadway waited the shadow-shape of Polypheme's car, its myopic eye pouring light at the churchyard gate. Nearer, parked in the opposite direction, the blacked-in shade of the driverless police car. Not a pebble-throw distant, no more than a curtain-fog between, was the churchyard, moon-drugged with its own noisome mystery. And while Ranier and Kavanaugh had been stalking that moon-lit stage-set of death and tombstones, here in the dank darkness of the wings, obscured by ambient night, it had happened.

"He's been got!"

On the dewy black macadam Angelo Carpetsi, face up, stomach arched, fingers curling on the unyielding road-surface. Looking up into the flashlight's ray, the eyes already losing their Latin lustre. The agonized lips were lemon-color; the forehead, under a shock of polished hair, painted battleship gray. The shirt-front was dyed a deeper hue of pink; the highwaisted trousers mud-stained; and the patent leather shoes that had attempted escape were splayed as if the ankles had broken—had tangoed their last dance. Feebly they kicked for traction as the curled fingers strove to push up, but the road there was slippery. More slippery than any dance floor.

Ranier whispered, "Good God! It's an artery!" and it seemed an hour, the minutes dragging by in chains, he stood there staring, fettered by horror of the scene. The fog. The silence. The prostrate figure bleeding to its death. Coolidge squatting at the dying man's head, babbling like a child over a broken doll, lamely attempting to stem that arterial gusher with a handkerchief. The big man's hands were red mittens, his coat polkadotted maroon. As well have tried to cork a Holland dyke with a Dutch boy's thumb.

Ranier had to wait thirty seconds. Thirty seconds for his marrow to thaw. Was that murderer lurking off-side in the fog, watching, gloating at his handiwork, selecting his next subject? Better turn his back on that thought. That terrible spurting must have clocked a dozen minutes already on the bill, and it was slowing as if the power was being turned off. He saw there was nothing he could do; then he did it.

Thrust his flashlight into Kavanaugh's hand. Shouted at the girl, "The car! We're rushing him to the hospital!" Shed his jacket, peeled his shirt, ripped bandage out of the cotton sleeves. Drove the blubbering truck driver aside with a blow; attacked death with a shirt sleeve, blindly, mechanically going through the motions. Amazing Carpetsi had survived this long—amazing, in this red-fogged ollapodrida of necrology and murder, any of them remained alive.

"Who did it! Who the hell?" That was Kavanaugh, pacing, juggling the flashlight, teeth bared, eyes feral, a panther caged by the fog.

"Ohmygod!" That was the fainting blonde.

"Holy Jumpin' Judas!" Coolidge, making faces at his hands.

"Creeeech!" The Model T streaking to a standstill beside the victim. The voice of Laïs Engles, *"Hätte ich es doch gewusst!* I saw him run off—!" The pulse thumping in the night. Whispering mist. Weaving light. Ranier's own voice speaking, unfamiliar, rusty, care-worn. "Lift him now. We're taking the flivver. Kavanaugh—you and the others in that *gendarme's* car. Better follow us to the hospital with—"

"Hospital, hell!" With a ferocious expletive the tall man swooped at something glinting in the road. Something that had been lying beneath Carpetsi's body. Something the Irishman snatched up, held in grassy fingers under the mist-drenched ray of the pocket torch. "Hospital, hell! Do you know whose glasses these are?"

There was blood on the black silk ribbon. The little gold nippers between the eyes had been crushed as if at some time underheel, and from the right lens a piece had been broken to leave a crescent of optical glass, a pixie scimitar of crystal, sharp-edged as a razor. Ruby gleams shimmered on the razor-edge.

"Aw," Coolidge mourned. "I never did trust that goof."

"Where—" Kavanaugh wrenched his head from left to right, lips flattened over his teeth, "Where *is* that college professor?"

The thin insectologist wasn't there. He gave no answer from the fog. In those mephitic vapours Professor Schlitz had gone, leaving behind his glasses. Had those glasses cut the throat of Angelo Carpetsi from ear to ear? He'd been going to tell who had played Going to Jerusalem with those corpses. He wouldn't talk, now. He was Going to Jerusalem, himself.

CHAPTER XVII

THE BENEVOLENT SPY

NERVOUS SYSTEMS IN human bodies are made to withstand a certain voltage. Push shock beyond that point, and the nerve-ends are burned out, the system electrocuted, reflexes may go in reverse. So coroners chuckle at their work, sophomores from divinity school shriek laughter shooting at other sophomores from divinity school in bombing planes, ladies giggle at funerals, and hangmen smile at the sight of hemp.

On that ambulance run to the hospital, starting from a churchyard where a ghost from the *Wilhelmstrasse* sat guard over a dead Haitian *gendarme* in an Anglican missionary's grave—racing through fog past a burial ground for U.S. Marines where the missionary usurped the coffin of a topkick—on past the woodsy cemetery in which the sergeant napped at the old lady's tomb—sixty an hour through a black steam-bath with Carpetsi's head, glaucous and dying, in his lap—on that midnight race alive with ghosts and the implacable threat of drums, John Ranier felt he'd reached the voltage limit.

Carpetsi's carotid severed by the professor's spectacles! Another gag like that and a man might begin to laugh. There is a point where Horror the Tragedian becomes Horror the Clown. Someone in this charivari of terrors must have a sense of humor.

Ranier discovered his lips curled up in a gibbous grin. Part of this joke was on him. Wanting escape from himself, from doctoring, from tourists and women, he'd come ashore tonight for a quiet bout at the bottle and landed splash in the middle of a devil's broth confected of medicine and tourists and himself with a frightened girl. A witch's brew of embalming fluid and blood (the line occurred to him), made in the shade, stirred with a spade.

Opening with the taffy-haired Mr. Haarman, German-American artichoke dealer, stabbed by an unseen knife in a lighted roomful of people. Reference to a Dr. Eberhardt in the victim's pocket and a cryptogram composed of boxcar figures. Mr. Haarman going (by chance?) to that same Dr. Eberhardt's hospital, locally at hand in Haiti.

Then Eberhardt's mysterious laboratory and more mysterious absence, and the bogey resemblance of the Haarman corpse to a web-footed German navy man buried with a company of plague-victims in Haiti fourteen years before. The girl's war story of a lost Amazon expedition, a stolen suitcase, a homeless child on a burial party. Kavanaugh's accusations and his own self-suspicion dispelled by darker mystery—the dead Mr. Haarman's vanishment.

Then the menace of a Voodoo uprising; a cemetery chase, hare-and-hounds across fog-swathed graveyards; a series of resurrectionisms trademarked by little green frogs; a parade of the long-buried dead and an acrostic of mixed epitaphs, mounting to the murder of a Haitian *gendarme* within sight of a disinterred envoy from Unter den Linden, and this throat-cutting with a pair of pince-nez glasses.

Leading up to what? Ranier didn't know. The answer slumped beside him with its throat cut. Proof enough that Carpetsi had known the answer. Someone had known of the Italian boy's knowledge and thought it best to silence his gutturals for good. Ranier cursed himself for doubting the Italian's intentions, muffing a lead that might have ended this creeping hecatomb. Part of the answer he'd learned for himself in the Marine cemetery under that monstrous-rooted tree. Learned from a handful of that richly-seeded earth, from the gnarled forest giant, from the missionary's misplaced remains. That had told him how.

But, why? and who? Angelo Carpetsi, who might have told him, was dying.

BUT IT was no good crying over spilt blood. Nothing he could do. The wrist between his fingers had almost stopped ticking; when they reached the hospital he'd better give the girl the hypo, instead.

"Too late," he shouted above the wind-cry. "He's going fast. Tell that black boy to slow down before he jumps a cliff. And tell me again who was standing around the car when Carpetsi wandered off."

He could see the gray oval of her face turning to look back at him. Dark refractions of fear from her eyes. "I was there with the woman in the party—she was fainting. The college professor had run down the road. The big man, all mud, said he had better go after the thin one, it was dangerous to be alone on the road. He ran a little way after the professor. It was then—I think—the Italian fled. In the fog I could not see. *Nein,* I did not expect—!"

Ranier put his face near the girl's. "You saw nothing else, heard nothing in the fog out there?"

"Nothing! The Herr Professor with the big man after him, *they* went south on the road. The poor Italian ran north—off by himself. In the mist they—they disappeared. I was looking at the churchyard, then."

The car skated on a curve, zigzagged wildly, decided to remain upright and let the girl go on.

"In a few moments the big man returned. He said the Herr Professor was gone and he did not dare remain alone in the fog. With the woman we waited at the gateway, watching you. *Aber,* I thought the professor and the Italian boy would come back—"

Ranier assured her grimly, "The professor will come back. If anyone can land that insectologist, the Irishman can. How far from that Morne Cuyamel mission is Bois Legone—the place where you say the colonel was buried?"

Her answer drifted back, "Perhaps a kilometer." But five-eighths of a mile could be a thousand on this blindfolded coastal highway where murder was marching to the boom of Afro-Caribbean drums. Would Kavanaugh and Coolidge, the blonde propped howling between them, ever reach the next village? Driving off, back there, in the dead *gendarme's* car, the Irishman's promise had been virulent.

"Don't worry, Ranier, we'll get him. That spindle-legged school teacher can't murder a guy in hot blood under *my* nose! We're goin' to Bois Legone and take a slant at what's happened there, and I'll call out every cop in the place. I'll get that killer for this if I have to burn down Haiti to do it! Wait at the hospital! Be with you in half an hour!"

Half an hour. Ranier calculated the distance in what was left of his mind. Measured it as three miles between the hospital and the English mission, an added kilometer to Bois Legone. Four miles. An empyreumatic four miles littered with the bones exhumed by someone, bloody-handed, bent on digging up the past. Someone celebrating a Satanic holiday with the femurs, clavicles and drum-sticks of those plague-victims buried by Dr. Eberhardt and a small German orphan on the night of January 3, 1922. Somebody looking for someone? Who? And for whom?

Yaaaaaahaaaaaa! The blatt of the automobile horn and a hair-brained swerve to avoid some visitation in the road, flung Ranier off the rear cushions, tangling with Carpetsi on the floor. But it was only a cow meandering in the mist; and another race-track curve, wrenching of metal and screeching brakes brought them alongside the verandah of the hospital, docked in the fog at Dr. Eberhardt's front steps.

If the doctor was in, the yellow upper window, the water-logged lower extensions of the villa gave no sign. In the pale entrance hall, spook-shadowed, silent, with its prowling staircase and dim second floor balcony, Ranier deposited his soggy burden on the settee near the hatrack and told the girl to wait with Polypheme. Damp-fingered, he took the gun that had belonged to Sergeant O'Grady from his pocket, and scouted the back hall, the emergency room. He found the bandage and cotton he wanted; scurried back to give them to the girl;

mounted the stairway to the second floor, expecting anything to happen. But the laboratory was as he had last seen it save for the minor detail of the cat which was, when he entered the room, scrooched on the center table industriously eating the frog left impaled on the spike.

When he returned to the lower hall with a dressing and antiseptics, he found Carpetsi dead.

And Polypheme, looking like a worn-out umbrella, with a Winchester 30-30 in his hands.

Laïs Engles was gone.

A WITNESS to that scene—the little Haitian Negro ambushed under that colossal straw hat with a rifle almost as long as he was tall; the haggard ship's doctor, heavy-handed with bottles and gauze and jammed automatic, stymied at the feet of a dead man, eyes fixed on the place where the girl had been—a witness might have had difficulty telling which man was most scared. The black man, the white man, the dead man—fear identical in the eye of each.

Rrrrrrr-bong! *Rrrrrrr*-bong! The wall clock, itself, striking two in that appalled charade of silence, had to clear a nervous throat before speaking.

Then Ranier broke from lethargy with a roar, dropping things from his hands to make a lightning snatch at the black man's unexpected gun. "Where is she?" twisting the Winchester loose with a savagery that almost brought the house-boy's fingers away with the barrel. "I'll kill you if you've harmed a hair of her! Where's that girl? Where'd she go!"

The Negro's lower lip hung and jiggled while his butterplated eyes brayed silently at the fury on Ranier's face. Ranier shouted, "Miss Engles! Miss Engles!" and his voice choked out in the hospitalized silence, leaving a medicinal hush in the echoes' train. He swung back the rifle, golf-club posture, keeping his eye on Polypheme's palsied face.

"What've you done with her? By God, I'll bat your head off, you—!"

"Dr. Ranier—!"

He saw her, then, in a door that had opened down the hall. Towel on wrist, basin in hand, she ran quickly forward; seized his arm.

"Was ist's? What is wrong?"

He lowered the rifle shakily, expelling a breath of relief. She was all right, except for those woeful circles under her eyes, and now that he could see her there it occurred to him he'd been bellowing like a movie hero over the girl, too concerned about her presence or absence. This midnight Hallowe'en was getting him. Somebody walked around a corner and his nerves popped like roman candles. A flat feeling in his stomach angered him. Liquor dying in his digestion and the shock of the girl's disappearance had left him a little sick. Ranier found a second to marvel at his concern for her safety. He wondered, sardonically, what had happened to the hard-boiled ship's doctor who'd been impervious to everything.

He told Laïs Engles almost sullenly, "Don't do that. Walk off like that. Not in a place where anything can happen. Where'd the black boy get this rifle?"

"Unkle Doktor," she indicated an anteroom across the dim hall, "kept it in there. I told Polypheme to wait with the gun while I—" her glance went to the settee, and her explanation concluded on a stifled, "Oh!"

"He's dead," Ranier bluntly agreed, giving Angelo Carpetsi a farewell scowl. Propping the Winchester against the banisters, he stooped to collect the grave-robbed army automatic, bandage and a bottle of merthiolate from the floor. He stowed gun and medicaments into his pocket, then turned to take the basin and towel from the girl.

"The ginny can't use any first aid where *he's* gone." Ranier covered the staring face with the towel; confronted Laïs Engles in swift decision. "And we're leaving, too. I've got some things to do. Come on, we're checking out of here."

"Nein." She moved backwards from his outreached hand.

Ranier protested harshly, "But you can't stay here. Nothing we can do for Angelo," he grated a short humorless laugh, "since people don't seem to stay buried in this country. And I'm not going to hang around here twiddling my thumbs waiting for Kavanaugh to come back. He may not come back. That village mob may come instead. I'm going up there to Bois Legone and taking you with me. I'll leave you at the *Gendarmerie* or the nearest white planter for protection."

"There is no *Gendarmerie,*" the girl said, "at Bois Legone. Even if there was—I cannot go."

"You've got to. I want a look at the cemetery where that Prussian colonel was buried."

"Go, then. I will remain here."

"You can't," he snapped hotly. "I tell you, I've got to see that Bois Legone graveyard and see it quick. You think you could stay all by yourself in this howling madhouse?"

"Polypheme will be with me. We will have the rifle. It is not a madhouse." She drew herself up, and in the algid hall-light her face was marble carved in determination. "It is a hospital. Dr. Eberhardt is—is out; and there are the patients."

"Patients!" Rainer's eyebrows came together, eyes glaring.

"In the excitement—I forgot. Too long already I have left them unattended. There is smallpox here, a Negress dying, a child very sick."

Smallpox! A moribund Negress! A dying pickaninny! As if there wasn't enough hell in this murderous mumbojumbo! He flipped an impatient hand.

"All right, I'll look at them. Right now. Then we'll leave Polypheme to tend them, and you'll go with me. Where are the beds?"

She said wearily, "*Nein.* Go. At two-thirty I must give an intravenous injection. *Ja,* I have done it before," she answered the unbelief on his face. "Other cases. When Dr. Eberhardt was overworked. So I will be on duty here."

"After all you've been through? Good God!"

"I am a nurse."

HE WANTED to shake her. Make her listen to reason. Anger at heroics that seemed unreasonable saw-edged his speech. "Listen to me. I've got to go to that next cemetery because it's our only chance to catch up with the killer who's behind tonight's job. We've got to stop that murderer or it may mean our lives. This isn't any Voodoo racket. It's deeper. Something to do with that German wartime expedition to Brazil that you were with, that's plain. Those people who died fourteen years ago—Perl, the old lady, the rest of them—had something this ghoul is after. Whoever the devil is, he'd decapitate his own mother to get it. God knows where the next strike will hit."

Apprehension switched his eyes to the front door where a moist draught had opened the door a little. Tendrils of mist were clammy fingers curling around the inside knob, the gauzy and secret fingers of a wraith trying to force an entrance. Drumbeats walked in measured tread through the opening, padded softly down the hall in a monkish processional, unseen, and whispered off into dark recesses at the villa's back. The tremor beat under his hair.

He went on furiously, "Believe me, our lives aren't worth a nickel while this killer's on the rampage. And you're involved with that expedition. If it's Eberhardt—maybe mad, trying some crazy experiment—we've got to stop him. Brown and that fellow Marcelline—they never got to the police!—where are *they?* Kavanaugh, Coolidge, the blonde—I wouldn't trust any of them with the lights out—and this loco bug-expert on the loose! Add that outfit to a gang of body-snatchers—"

He stopped pacing, arrested by an idea. Turned at the girl in an excitement that lowered his voice to a slurred monotone. "Judas! I'm dumb. Why didn't I think of it before. Listen, Laïs!"

"*Ja,* I am listening."

"You know where those body-snatchers are, right now? Well, they weren't far ahead of us when we got to Morne Cuyamel. They were on their way to the colonel's cemetery at Bois Legone.

Right now they're leaving Bois Legone, and I'd stake my life on it they're headed for *Captain Friederich's grave.* Sure! Wasn't that captain of your German expedition last to be buried? Well, they've gone right down the line so far. Get it? We can cut them off by going to that *last* grave before they get there. Where was that captain buried?"

She said tonelessly, "My uncle, Captain Friederich was buried on the mountain-top above Bois Legone. A tiny cemetery there, overlooking the coast, on the main road to Port-au-Prince. You will know the entrance by stone urns which stand beside the road. My uncle's body lies in a mausoleum."

"A mausoleum!"

"It belonged to Dr. Eberhardt who bought it from a French planter. That night of 1922—the Herr Doktor gave it to me for my uncle's—"

Ranier blazed, "*That's* where we'll go! We'll head off the rats, by God! Give 'em a dose of that Winchester! Come on—!"

"Take the gun. I will stay. I am not afraid."

"Risk your life for a batch of niggers when—?"

"I cannot leave my patients."

Ranier's veined eyes squinted. "All right. I can't take the time to argue. You know this is a dangerous spot. I told you the only chance to stop this pogrom was to head off these jackals at your uncle's tomb," he warned roughly, "and that's where I'm going. It doesn't seem the moment to pull any of this Christian-duty stuff. You'd better save your own life and stick with me. It's madness to stay here!"

Direct, unwavering, the girl's eyes met his. "You are a doctor, *mein herr.* You know I must."

HE WAS a fool. He didn't need any little bird to tell him that. He knew it when he steered from the hospital driveway and headed the Model T for Bois Legone when any sane man would have skipped for the nearest timber patch and waited in hiding for the protection of daylight.

He was doubly certain of it when he stopped the flivver five hundred feet down the road, backed off the macadam shoulder into a screen of plantain, switched off the ignition and climbed to earth in the floating darkness. Save for that steady tremor in the night, silence. Smell of soggy loam, mold, closed flowers, vegetal decay. All of Haiti, at night, smelled like rotted floral pieces after a funeral. Around him the darkness foamed and coagulated and clung, the mist blacker than a steam of liquid stove-polish. He might have been a million leagues from Dr. Eberhardt's hospital. And he should have been, if he weren't nine kinds of a fool.

He groped his way along the road-edge. He wasn't seeking a nice, secure hiding place, either. He was limping back to that hospital, going to scout around the villa for a secret look at that German girl, a little sortie to check her actions once she thought him out of sight. That, at least, was his excuse to himself for returning. Trouble was, he knew it was an excuse.

John Ranier had probed too many subconscious motives from secretive neurotics to be able to hide his own inner motivations. Debunking himself had been one of his favorite amusements for the past five years, but in this emergency it was disconcerting to discover himself an idiot. John Ranier, his nerve-ends tuned to a million pricky needle-points of perception, knew he wasn't going back to spy on this girl at all, but to make sure she'd locked all the windows. He wasn't going back there to watch that girl, but to watch over that girl from some place of vantage for espionage on the villa, fearing for her safety.

At the last moment, before leaving her there, he'd gone the rounds to bolt-and-shutter all the windows, and found to his dismay there were neither shutters nor bolts on the emergency room. He'd lugged Angelo's mortal remains to a storeroom and out of her sight, and weakened to the point of visiting the sick beds and giving the Negress with elephantiasis a hypo, stalling, worrying. Worrying about those windows that couldn't be locked.

Then he'd kidded himself. Told himself he was staging a clever act, tricking the girl into believing he wanted her with him, kidding himself into thinking he actually wished to be rid of her.

Matter of fact, it was lucky for him she'd determined to stay behind. Damned lucky. Yet the minute he'd shut the door on her there in that stale hall a sick muscle had closed over his heart, and the sweet-beads of anxiety were still on his face.

Ranier perceived with sardonic grimness the War hadn't taught him what happened to gallants who went out of their way to stick their noses in danger zones. Even that charming experience with a coal baron's daughter had taught him nothing. And here was John Ranier playing Boy Scout over a woman he'd known less than seven hours, going to stand guard all night over a girl who might, herself, have a finger in this grisly Haitian pie, when he ought to be saving his own skin. He ought to have a rose in his teeth. What in God's name was that girl to him?

He hesitated to hunt for the road-edge, warily shading the picayune ray of his flashlight as it sought the wet macadam. Scuffing his heels to keep them on the paving, he went on. He grinned to himself, "Sucker!" Suppose that girl did have a part in this wholesale body-snatching racket? And for that matter, suppose she didn't? Either way he was a fool. If she was part of the racket, he'd make a swell target for that Winchester he'd gallantly left with her. If she wasn't, what difference would it make? Tomorrow the police would come to the rescue, friends would take her away, and John Ranier would be a bum ship's doctor swinging over the horizon on his way to Nowhere. If she were attacked tonight what in God's name could he do about it. Rush cheering to the rescue with a jammed and rusty army automatic?

Even Don Quixote hadn't been such a fool. The romantic Spig had owned sense enough to pick windmills for adversaries. A clogged gun, in this hoodooed night, would be of less avail than Quixote's wooden lance, and he'd be jousting with adversaries something more than windmills, if past indications meant anything.

CHAPTER XVIII

THE SKULL

RANIER PAUSED IN the turbid darkness, peering, listening. Groped forward like a blind man, feeling out the invisible road with uneasy shoes. Deserting that car amounted to cutting off his means of retreat, but if unknown eyes had been watching the hospital, ears listening at the walls, they'd think him on his way to Bois Legone. At least he had that much advantage. If he didn't know where his enemies were, they didn't know where he was.

Sweating, he halted again to listen. Limped a few paces forward. Stopped. Moved on. Those drums didn't seem any nearer, but every second the girl was alone in that fog-cloaked manse her life was in jeopardy. Provided, of course, she was on the level. He quickened his blind-man's walk. Wait a second—

Ranier stopped with sucked breath. In the pitchy murk five inches before his eyes a black shape was waiting. He could almost see its face. His hair stood up. He heard a movement, a faint and sinewy creak, no louder than the sound of a stretched ligament in a flexed forearm.

He struck, left handed, before his galvanized right hand could thumb the switch of his pocket torch. Struck, and grabbed a hairy beard. The thing hit back, a hard little blow tapping him on the point of the chin. Hanging on, he swallowed a yell, and the flashlight came on, spearing its electric ray through the black.

"Hell!"

It wasn't Polypheme, although the caricature resemblance

was remarkable. Ranier was hanging for dear life to the chin whiskers of a black billygoat. There was nothing funny about it.

The goat was dead, stiff-legged, front hoofs brittly out-thrust, hind legs swinging at the height of a man's knees, clear of the ground. Ranier was clutching the animal's chin-tuft, and the animal was hanged by the neck from the fruited lower limb of a sapodilla tree that reached out over the road's edge.

Ranier let go hurriedly and backed away, keeping his light on the hanged goat. In the mist the dead animal revolved slowly and the rope creaked. Flesh contracted along Ranier's spine. He knew the meaning of this bugaboo; had seen such symbols in Haiti, before. A Voodoo warning! The goat had not been dead long. Earlier tonight it hadn't been there. That meant Negroes were in the neighborhood. Some skulking black *papaloi* had crept up in the night and marked the vicinity of Dr. Eberhardt's hospital with a high-sign.

He flicked off the torch with an oath; started down the roadside on a run, left hand outstretched, feeling his way along the sidewall of jungle foliage. A dozen strides beyond the sapodilla, he became aware of opalescence in the fog in front of him. Reflections lighting the mist. He halted, half turned as the mist brightened. A car was coming up behind him. Coming from the direction of Bois Legone and at race-track speed.

Blades of light swept around a black bend in the night, went by him and dissolved in moving vapor clouds ahead. The road's smoking surface became visible. Sound of the engine broke through muffled silence with an abrupt roar. Before he could leap for cover the headlights were on him, picking him out of darkness with a pour of blinding light, yellow eyes racing at him out of night. The car was on top of him with the suddenness of an express train rushing out of a blizzard. At him sixty miles an hour.

A tenth of a second he stood dazed in the onrushing light. Instinct jumped him away from the car's path. He saw the body of the car take form in the smother, the glistening plane of the windshield, the smudged shadow that was the driver's face behind the glass. At the same time the driver must have seen him. He heard the squeal of brakes, the uproar of a quickly throttled engine, the screech of tires skating on macadam.

He thought, "Kavanaugh!" as the car slewed, tilted, came at him sideways, made an oblique swerve to catch him full in the headlamps' glare. The car was still moving toward him, slowing down on the skid, ten feet from him, and he'd lifted a defensive elbow as if to ward it off, when the shooting started. *Spat-spat! Spat-spat-spat!*

He heard the shots in something like astonishment. Surprised at the ruthlessness of it; appalled at himself being the target. Flashes of blue-white flame spitting at him from the car. Glimpse of a wrist, a shadow-hand, an automatic reaching out of the driver's window. *Spat! Spat!* Quick daggers of fire poked at him. An invisible *zzzzzip!* tearing the lobe of his right ear. Instant pain.

Ranier fell. Plunged to the road with his head between his elbows, rolling across the macadam to escape those deadly headlights. *Spat! Spat-spat-spat!* Flame whip-lashed from the car window, the reports deadened by the revving of the engine as gears went into neutral, bullets striking the road around Ranier's writhing body, glancing off the macadam, skittering off into the underbrush. He turned over twice and lay still in roadside weeds, auto lights blazing on his closed eyelids. All over now. The next bullet—

BUT THE car was turning, backing and turning. Clash of meshing gears. Smell of oil-smoke from the exhaust. That gunman was leaving him for dead, wheeling in a reverse turn for a get-away. Light passed across John Ranier's squeezed eyelids; then darkness swept over him; sound of the car driving off. Ranier rolled over and sprang to his feet. Fading up the highway toward Bois Legone in the direction from which it had come was a misty, diminishing, red eyeball—the tail-light of the fleeing sedan.

Oaths boiled to his lips as he watched the dwindling tail-light scooting off into night. He began to swear blasphemously, viciously, hurling silent and scorching names after his departing assailant. Rage swelled in his throat, choking him. His temples burned. Fury mounted as he thought of himself standing unarmed and helpless in front of that murderously unexpected gun-blast; as he remembered the greedy sound of those bullets smacking the road around him, trying to hit him when he was down. Stand here and let that dirty hireling of the devil drive away?

John Ranier was running. Blindly. Crazily. Dashing for the flivver he'd parked up the road, and lighting his way with the pocket torch, aware of folly and uncaring. Cranking, flinging himself behind the agued wheel, slamming out of the undergrowth to the backfire explosions of a moon rocket, Ranier drove the Model T in white hot pursuit of the escaping gunman. He had forgotten his intended vigil over Dr. Eberhardt's ward. Forgotten the girl, the hospital, the storm gathering under the fog, the game of Going to Jerusalem. Rage melted the problem down to a simple basic. There was no involved mystery about the driver of that fleeing sedan. A human hand had triggered those gun shots. The question was only one of identity, and there was the answer racing off into night, wagging his tail-light behind him. *Get him!*

ALONE, STEERING the half-blind rattletrap through blowing cotton, apprehensive of mountain curves and chasms unmarked by guard rails, he would have been slowed to fifteen miles an hour after the first road-bend. Following a car made it easier. The car in the lead had good headlamps, and was making time. Ranier set his jaw, pulled down the gas lever, sloped his shoulders over the wheel and never took his eye from that red point of light marking the route before him.

The red point of light was a star climbing obliquely. A steep grade. It disappeared at the summit; reappeared as a meteor flying downhill. It dipped and vanished. A culvert. Described an arc and went out. A curve. Reappeared on the straightaway, dimming as it lengthened the lead. Cursing, Ranier drove the battered flivver to the limit of its endurance, following the convolutions of that red spark in nothingness ahead.

Somewhere they passed the cemetery where the U.S. Marine occupied the plot of Grossmutter Sou. A handful of candles there and gone in the murk. Farther on, the deserted Marine barracks, the place where a missionary's celluloid collar turned up instead of a topkick's tunic. Moments later Ranier marked the Morne Cuyamel churchyard, fragmentary in fog, the Prussian colonel still lounging by the mission's headstone at the scene of a Haitian *gendarme's* assassination.

Landmarks in the night. Like the unreal surprises in those old-fashioned scenic railways where the gondola rolled suddenly out of blackness into a briefly glimpsed horror-chamber labeled "Orpheus in Hades" or "Blue Beard Boiling his Wife," and women passengers screamed.

Ranier gave the churchyard scene a side-glance, and almost piled the flivver against the stone wall. When he steadied the shimmying front wheels back to mid road, the tail-light in the lead had disappeared. Rounding a quick road-bend, he picked it up again, this time so far in advance it was barely visible through the wrack.

Grimly he yanked the gas lever, goaded to frenzy by the thought of his assailant's escape. It was touch and go, racing a car through the packed fog on a dangerous mountain highway. Beyond Morne Cuyamel the Haitian coast might have been obliterated. The road climbed into a night that had no sky, no earth, no boundaries. Patches of jungle sailed by. Boulders adrift at the roadside. Around the next bend there could be anything or nothing. But Ranier held his eye to that scarlet bull's-eye in front of him and drove in pursuit like a madman, chasing the fugitive spark that stayed ahead of him, climbing, dipping, dodging like some malevolent star racing off through the Milky Way. Nothing phantom about that tail light, though. That car ahead was driven by someone real enough.

But drive as he would, Ranier couldn't close the gap between himself and the gunman's car. In the night's black swirl the tail-light was growing smaller and smaller. Now, far ahead and above him, it was seen as a tiny pinprick soaring through invisibility. He shouted oaths, starting the Model T up a dizzy ascent. The car labored and slowed. *Tap-tap-tap!* Cylinders knocking, exhaust pipe glowing crimson under the floor boards. Single headlamp dimming as the engine struggled. Fog pressing in, churning over the hood in frothing rush, quick to take advantage of the failing headlight.

RANIER CURSED the engineers who had made that grade. The road went up and up. Too steep for antiquated carburetors and spark-coils. Too black. Snorting, pounding, rattling every bolt, fluttering its rust-eaten fenders as if they were striving wings, the senile flivver would never achieve the top. Ranier thrust his head from the window and could no longer make out a red spark in the lead. Ahead steamed Nothingness. Directly in front of the car's mist-hemmed, fainting light was a patch of macadam surrounded by Void. Where daylight might have showed mountain scenery sweeping to distant *massifs* or the far blue of the Gulf of Gonaives there was oblivion. Ahead of him, around him, behind him walls of fog. The car crawled.

He cursed the stalling motor, leaning far out of the window with his flashlight, trying to find the edge of the road. Finding it, he yanked in his head with a yell. That road's edge was closer than he had expected. His wheels were on it. The flashlight's ray, torching ahead of the front tires, had dropped out into space in a way that put a film of frost on John Ranier's forehead. That wasn't the nothingness of fog out there. It was the nothingness of nothing. The light had fallen over the road's rim and dropped to Infinity.

He stopped the car; peered. Wind passed across his face and brushed a rift through the vapor. Moonlight shafted through a hole in the cloudbanks and brought to momentary view the face of a cliff, a silvery Alpine precipice that dropped a sheer two thousand feet in two seconds to a glimpse of beach below. Palm trees down there were no bigger than geraniums, a strand of sand no wider than a string of rice, the surf miniature as cream on a glass of beer. Staring down at that apparitional view, as if at a morsel of land seen from a balloon high in the stratosphere, Ranier felt the strength go out of his marrow. The pull of that abyss made him cry out. Another ten inches forward on this fogged curve above that drop and the front wheel would have gone over.

Clouds boiled over the hole and he was gasping down at thunderheads with moon-bows on their upper surfaces. A rush of rain slapped the windshield. Mist swarmed over the car. Night. The abyss vanished, but he could feel its awful magnetism there. His hands felt like leaves of lettuce, twisting the steering wheel away from the edge, driving the car at snail pace along the inside of the curve.

Putting his teeth together, he went on. If that gunman could make the grade, a look over a cliff-edge in Haiti wouldn't stop the chase. After what had happened earlier tonight, Ranier was certain his nerves would have calloused at a Chinese water-torture. Swearing helped. Slowly the numbness drained from his fingers. Anger, returning, warmed him like wine. Wine? He ran his tongue across gritty teeth. He would have traded his soul to Satan for a glass of *aguardiente.* And for a gun—

Two minutes later, engine picking up speed, the car gained the summit and hit a stretch of gravel. Here the fog had thinned to a consistency of cigarette smoke and streaks of moonlight showed roadway ahead, black-green escarpments of jungly timber on either side. Ranier yanked the gas, two-wheeled the flivver around a bend, jammed on the brakes with a snarl.

The road forked.

There was no sign of the car he had been hounding.

But there were other signs. A decaying sign post stood sentinel at the road-split, pointing its rickety arms in laconic direction. To the left the gravel went smoothly uphill into night.

Port-au-Prince. 105 Km. To the right the road was a discarded washboard bending off through black trees. *Bois Legone. 1 Km.*

There were recent tiremarks on the road to Port-au-Prince, and wheel-tracks as fresh on the muddy side road to Bois Legone. But something was hanging to the Bois Legone pointer on the sign post. Something that looked, in the lunar dimness, like a yellowed hornet's nest dangling on a string. Ranier saw it swaying under the sign post's wooden arm, revolving slowly on a breath of damp wind. He speared it with the ray of his flashlight the better to see.

It was an old ivory. A human skull. Hanging on a length of string that went through the eye-sockets. The wind wound it up slowly, and then it unwound. When it had stopped spinning it was grinning in the direction of the pointer above its polished head. Bois Legone.

Ranier drove his car up the washboard road through the black trees.

CHAPTER XIX

DAGGER IN THE DARK

NIGHT, IN THAT forest of mahogany, sablier, mapou and cedar, was an oppression of blackness only emphasized by the feeble cone of the car light and shafts of moon-ray that seeped through occasional rifts in the foliage overhead. The road was a tunnel, its walls shored up by the boles of giant trees, their upper limbs forming a roof that supported a sky of coal. Gourd vines dangled in loops and spirals, slapping the top of the car. A wormy mahogany that might have crashed of its own weight, lying prone at the roadside, its rotting bulk a feast for parasite fungi and huge toadstools, narrowed the path to the bare width of the car wheels. Ranier squeezed the old sedan between fallen trunks and wedges of timber that loomed like a canyon's side. Perfect spot for an ambush.

The road not even paved with good intentions. Washboard that became a brown paste. Muddy as a quagmire. The tires spun and slewed as the wheels fought for traction. The fog became a drizzle, turned to sooty rain, turned to fog, swarmed out from under the trees in clouds of stagnated steam. Then the car began to chug through breaks in the vapour, openings known to sailors as "fog dogs," where the moon could be seen as a blue-white globe caught in the inky forest-tops, and the trees, tiger-striped, glistening, assumed threatening shapes.

Ranier supposed this nightmare tour of Haiti in blackness, shadow and fog could go on for years. How long since he'd left that beach café to start this hare-and-hounds, this murder-chase across graveyards, through hospitals, uphill and downdale across a Caribbean limberlost that had no compass, along the ledges of terrible chasms, into forest roads pointed out by skulls? Now the excitement of chasing a visible quarry was over, he suffered a letdown. His stomach and his mind began to turn. He was conscious of an ache in his bad foot and pain in his ear, but the bullet wound was nothing, the lobe had stopped bleeding. Only it reminded him of that close call and that his unknown enemy was playing for keeps.

He fought off a reaction of cold fright, forcing his attention to fix itself on the road ahead, his mind grappling with the problem. One thing was certain. That gunman hadn't fired on him by mistake. He'd stood clearly exposed before the assassin's headlamps, and that gun had fired a direct fusillade that had only missed killing him by the grace of God. Which meant the would-be killer had been on an errand. Premeditated homicide, and out to get him.

Why? Because he'd rushed the dying Carpetsi to the hospital? Had the secret hand which cut the Italian's throat back there on the Morne Cuyamel road tried to slaughter him, Ranier, thinking the Dago on a last gasp might have talked? Then who, other than tonight's tourist party, knew him to want to kill him. If that gunman were one of the tourists—

There were Marcelline and Brown, reported as being at that village back down the coast. But the murder car had come from, and fled in, the direction of Bois Legone. Kavanaugh, the blonde woman and Coolidge had left, or said they were leaving, for Bois Legone. Had one of them finished the others and doubled back to silence the ship's doctor?

Professor Schlitz, too; could the vanished thin man be behind this hecatomb? Or had it been Dr. Eberhardt, criminally insane, introducing himself with gunfire?

For the hundredth time since Haarman's impossible stabbing, identification as a man fourteen years dead and subsequent disappearance, John Ranier's brain whirled over the incidents of the past six hours, sorting, deciding, rejecting. Hard to think in a straight line and keep an eye peeled for sudden ambush at the same time. Concentration was difficult when every hair on your skin was crying, "Danger! Danger!" on a road like a spider's dream, and the puzzle turned on impossibilities to begin with.

PRYING INTO blackness ahead, his eyes glittered in febrile suspense, while his mind raced in a frantic hunt for answers. Four things he did know. He knew who Haarman was. He knew how those hopscotched bodies came to be at graves where they didn't belong. He knew there was more of method than madness in this morass of abominations; that a deep cunning rooted under the surface. And he knew Laïs Engles couldn't have fired the broadside which almost killed him twenty minutes ago.

But he didn't know how Haarman could have been stabbed in the back, unobserved; or whose fist had directed the blade. He didn't know how Haarman, scar-marked, web-footed, could be who he was; what had become of his body. Dr. Eberhardt's whereabouts and why remained unsolved. A motive for this welter of resurrectionism remained buried if its subjects didn't. He didn't know the whereabouts of the gunman who had almost murdered him. He didn't know at what moment this Haitian limbo would explode from the concussion of those angered devil-drums.

Was the girl safe?

He cursed himself now for having deserted her, and drove the old car bouncing, jolting, a wild race through the forest; his mind a whirl of confused intentions. To reach Bois Legone and summon some kind of help. To rouse the first house he saw, ask the way to a telephone, and call Port-au-Prince, the American consul, the *Garde d'Haiti.* To locate the Bois Legone cemetery and find out what had become of Mr. Kavanaugh, his girl friend and Mr. Coolidge.

The flivver bounced down a gully steep as a staircase, and he would have been through the mountain village without knowing it, if a brown cow hadn't appeared before his headlamp, forcing him to a jarring stop. Ranier flicked his flashlight; discovered he was in town. Not a street lamp in the place, much less a telephone pole. Jackdaw fences and tin can shanties littered along a mud-rutted alley. Shabby brown walls, shuttered windows, silent doors locked against night. Two-thirty A.M. was not a likely hour in that Haitian community. The huts did not look asleep. There was an air of desertion about those soundless doorsteps that made Ranier wonder if the entire population had gone away. Some bony hounds, surprised by his flashlight, struggled up out of the gutter and crept off in hangdog silence, their starved tails between their legs.

Ranier cut the engine; listened. Not a leaf was stirring. Not a snore. Nothing but the persistent, far-wandering *tumpy-tump-tump* from the night, fog-swathed, tree-muffled in this forest fastness, something that might have been in a vein under his temple. His flashlight made a ghostly white circle, desperately running down the alley from door to door. Nobody home?

He wondered as he waded across the alley toward a hut if he might not be greeted by a blast of gunfire. Had the gunman, who'd tried to eliminate him back there near the hospital, chosen the road to Port-au-Prince or come to this world's end? A number of cars had ploughed the alley mire, and not so long ago, by the looks. Well, he'd have to chance it.

He pounded cautiously on a shuttered window. A scurry on the inside might have been a mouse; then silence. He slogged to the next hut and recklessly belabored the door with a gun-butt. As well have tried to rouse the Sphinx. A wan moon crept out of some black treetops, dragging tresses of greenish cloud, and floated slowly like the face of a drowned woman that had drifted out of weeds. Its rays were like the shafts of light at a pond-bottom, and the scene was done in shades of black, green-black, purple and silver; the buttressed masonry of a church at alley's end coming to view, its outlines watery and blurred as one of those little castles in a fish globe. Keeping in shadow, Ranier sloshed down the alley, shaping his course for the church. Somebody ought to be there.

Somebody was!

NOT IN the church, but in a park to the left where the fog wreathed in orchid tints across untended grass and billowed around the base of a ghostly monument. A thick green hedge, shoulder high, rambled in ragged silhouette around two sides of the park; steep mountain swooped up behind; the church was a gray eminence standing by, and both church and park were fronted by an open square cluttered with deserted market stalls.

Ranier had emerged from the alley mouth and started across the square when he caught that shadowy movement in the park. He flattened against a stall, instantly alert. Around the base of that park monument, as noiseless in the mist as a swimming fish, came the shadow of a man. The shadow hesitated. Advanced into moonlight. Stood with hunched shoulders, intently watching the glooms where Ranier crouched. Ranier could not see the man's face, but the figure was familiar, the sun helmet a give-away.

Professor Schlitz!

And then John Ranier was staring in tripled astonishment, for the professor, evidently convinced he was unobserved, made a quick about-face, turned his back on the village square and went tip-toeing off across the park toward that silhouetted hedge, his torso bent, knees bowed, moving in the gingerly caution of someone stepping on eggs. Thefting toward the hedge as if, net in hand, he had sighted on that wall of foliage some rare and extraordinarily nervous butterfly.

Then, as if he himself were a collector and the insectologist of prize bug, Ranier dodged away from the vegetable booth and went after the professor. It was not until he had crossed the No Man's Land of the square that Ranier discovered the park monument was no Haitian national hero but the Angel Gabriel, he had to look sideways at one slab that had remained standing in the granite celestial's lee. He couldn't have spied it from the square.

There was the headstone—

HIER RUHET IN GOTT
OBERST JOACHIM OTTO

Gest. 3 Januar 1922

ICH HATTE EINST
EIN SCHONES VATERLAND

There was the familiar pattern of opened grave, mound of steaming clods, broken longbox, something which had once been human spraddled in the trampled grass at graveside. Something which had once been human, but had never been a Colonel Joachim Otto.

Ranier only had time to recognize the Imperial German Navy in the cobwebby sea-cap arranged at a jaunt across the skull's left eye. He muttered, "Captain Friederich!" and hastily shifted his attention to the shadow of Professor Schlitz stealing off into fog. Moving without sound, Ranier trailed across the graveyard after his quarry. No time to wonder what had become of Kavanaugh and his party. No chance to worry about the night that crouched like a waiting, watching animal behind his back, or guess the meaning of the insectologist's presence in this vandalized cemetery. Another minute and the thin man would be in that hedge.

Ranier inhaled the word, "Now!"

The professor was about five feet from the bushy backwall, and Ranier some twenty paces behind the professor's unsuspecting coattails.

Ranier shouted, "Put them up, Schlitz! I've got you covered!"

The man whirled, throwing up frightened hands. He whinnied: "Oh my! Dr. Ranier—!"

Dog-legged, bristling, Ranier walked at him slowly, menacing with empty gun. "One move and I'll blow your head off! Caught with the goods, by Judas! I saw you sneak around from behind that monument where the grave is dug—"

He couldn't see the face under the sun helmet, but he could

see the eyes. The thin man squeaked, "No, no! It was like that when I got here!"

Eighteen paces from the man. Ranier took another step at him, slow-motion, vigilant for a break. "What's the game, then? How'd you get here from Morne Cuyamel after you cut Carpetsi's throat?"

"I didn't!" Professor Schlitz squealed. "I didn't kill the Italian."

Fifteen paces from the man, fixing him with unswerving eyes. "You didn't kill him, eh? Your eye-glasses. You shouldn't left them under the body like that."

He could see the man writhe, lifting one foot and then the other like someone cornered and in a hurry to go somewhere. "Eye-glasses? Eye-glasses?" shrill as a piccolo on a sour key.

"You killed him," Ranier's words were slow as his next step forward, "because you heard him tell me, back there in the Marine cemetery, he was going to spill the works. So you waited for him out there on the road at Morne Cuyamel and when he—"

The thin body squirmed, "But I—why—I *lost* my glasses in that Marine graveyard. Yes, yes! Dropped them in the grass. Mr. Coolidge bumped into me on the path and in the darkness I dropped them."

"Keep up those hands, you!"

"Don't shoot!" the other gasped. "I didn't kill Mr. Carpetsi. Good God! You're making a mistake. I was hiding out on the road, crouched by the stone wail, when Carpetsi ran by. I'd been going to run away, but I was too frightened to move. A little while later I heard Mr. Coolidge call out. He'd found the Italian's body."

"Oh, sure. Suicide. Nobody did it. Nobody's doing any of this. Same as that body that dug itself up back there in the grass."

Hitching closer, Ranier had to stretch his lips in an ugly grin. Some motes of eerie moonlight drifted under the brim of that tourist sun helmet, illumining a false-face underneath; a professorial parody, bilious green, dripping perspiration. What struck Ranier funny was thought of his own face, bluffing above a scotched gun.

"I didn't do it," the false-face was chattering. "Then I saw you driving away with Carpetsi. Mr. Kavanaugh and the others were taking the dead *gendarme's* car. I heard them say they were going to look for me, and I didn't know what to do. Then I remembered about you—"

"About me! "Ranier halted his advance.

"How you clung to the spare tire of our car on the way to the hospital. So I ran out of the bushes where I was hiding, and caught the spare tire of the *gendarme's* car. Mr. Kavanaugh drove straight to this village. To this cemetery."

"You came up here with Kavanaugh?"

"They didn't see me," the false-face panted. "I dropped off in the market place, there. When they left the car and ran into the cemetery, here, I crept around by the church. I heard them shouting, then they ran back to the car and drove away, leaving me behind. I ran into the graveyard to see what was here."

"How long ago did they leave?"

"It couldn't have been half an hour. I tell you," excitement overcame fear in the thin man's windpipe, releasing his voice in a sudden blurt, "—I tell you, I've found out something. Something important. I should have run all the way to the hospital to tell you, but I feared I would never find the road, and then I thought—"

His blurting tapered into a strangely, wolf-like howl.

Nine paces from the man, facing him squarely and limping toward him, Ranier was caught completely by surprise when it happened. Caught by surprise, and, for a piece of a second, stunned to stone by the change that leapt across Professor Schlitz's face. Jekyll never altered to Hyde as swiftly as did the professor. The features under the foolish sun helmet screwed in a terrible paroxysm. Eyes crossed. Cheeks went out of shape. Lips flattened back and upper teeth popped out like sprouted fangs.

In that background of moonlight, fog and cemetery it would

have chilled the veins of a witch. Uttering that half-throttled howl, the thin man flung out his hands and plunged straight at Ranier, charging from a standstill like a dummy thrown from a springboard. Ranier had only time to think, "Schizophrenia! Dual personality!" and fling the gun.

The weapon missed; sailed crashing into the hedge. Missed because the charging man lost his footing, tripped, fell. Hands reaching for Ranier, he stumbled and went down, his tongue flapped out, a plate of artificial teeth jarred from his mouth. Sprawled in front of Ranier, his fingers just touching the toes of Ranier's frozen shoes. Shuddered violently, and then, as if the paroxysm had worn itself out, relaxed face-down in the grass, fainted away.

Empty-handed, staring, John Ranier could have fainted away himself. His eyes swivelled and swerved, shooting glances around that sleeping burial ground as if to see a thousand enemies there. Save for himself and the man at his feet there was no one in sight. Ants crawled on his skin as he glared at the spot where Professor Schlitz had been standing at bay. Five feet beyond the place where the professor had stood was the brambly black-green wall of hedge, fence-high, thick as a small dyke, a thorny if porous barricade against the forest's intrusion. Too high to jump, too dense for a cat to get through, it would have demanded sealing. But no one had gone over that wall. And no one could be hiding in the thin wisps of vapour straggling and uncoiling through moonshine.

John Ranier, shifting his glare to the unconscious body at his shoes, could have been no more thunderstruck if the granite Gabriel five graves distant in the gloom had flapped his stone wings and cracked the cemetery silence with a blast on his immortal horn. No more appalled if the unearthed residue of Captain Friederich had swooped to a stand beside that open grave, croaked, "I don't belong here!" and stalked off, creaking, through the mist!

"Professor!" Ranier gasped.

From the body in the grass came no answer. But a tomato-colored juice was spreading across the flattened shoulders. Ranier saw it had been no manic-depressive violence which had scrambled the man's features and inspired his reasonless rush. His snap diagnosis had been wrong.

Professor Schlitz had gone livid with pain, and his charge had been impelled by a blow from behind. Facing Ranier, standing there with his hands in the air, Professor Schlitz had been stabbed in the back!

CHAPTER XX

TO LAY A GHOST

THE INSECTOLOGIST WAS not heavy. Clutching the man's grasshopper frame in his arms, Ranier raced across the cemetery, speeding over the flat white marble slabs as Eliza might have sped across the ice. The skull of a German sea captain grinned as he went by, and the Angel Gabriel watched his departure with a lofty frown. The market place, a blur of empty vegetable bins. The alley of sleeping doorways. The Model T parked before the discontented cow.

Ranier deposited his burden on seat cushions, previously stained by Italian blood, then slammed the rear door, sprang to crank the engine. A witness to his actions would have guessed them to be the irrational maneuvers of a madman. Flinging into the driver's seat, he played with the gas lever, reviving the motor until the car shook on motionless wheels. Blue smoke bulged from the rear as he slowed the motor to a drone, then switched off the ignition, lights out. Shading his pocket torch under his hand, he climbed from front to back seat; fumbled hospital bandage, cotton, bottle of merthiolate from his pocket; set to work in the close gloom. A minute sufficed to stem the bleeding. Another to bandage the wound. He stooped to catch the man's snuffly breathing. That was all right. The savant from Upsala would live.

Opening and closing the tin door, Ranier's fingers made no sound. Two silent leaps to skirt the front fender, and he was disengaging the crank. Iron felt good in his fingers. He weighed

Ranier stumbled out of the boneyard, carrying Schlitz

the solid bar in his fist, grinning at the darkness, daring its next move. Once, in the old ambulance-riding days, he'd stitched the rhinoceros skull of a taxi driver cracked by a similar weapon. Crank in fist, he began to run.

"Damnation!"

The sound broke loose as he reached alley's end, jolting him to a stockstill. Somewhere in the vicinity of that night-drugged, mountain-lost village a horse was running. Hell-bent for leather. Explosion of hoofbeats spattering out in the dark *Rat-a-pat! Rat-a-pat! Rat-a-pat! Rat-a-pat!* He hadn't expected that answer to his hoaxed departure, and he listened to galloping hoofs in raw dumbfoundment. Startling the nocturnal silence, the echoes might have issued from Sleepy Hollow. Any minute now and the Headless Horseman should go by.

But the hoofbeats were drifting away; fading off through the night—Ranier traced the direction with an oath! They went off somewhere behind the cemetery.

Ranier peered from the alley-mouth, wary of some ruse. Then, at a break-neck gallop of his own, he crossed the moon-shadowed marketplace; but instead of entering the graveyard as before, he ran around the front of the church, sprinting into the shadow of a buttressed wall, following a wing of old masonry that threatened to crumble under the ray of his flashlight.

A brass plate on an ancient door said God and the bishop were home, but he couldn't stop now to call on either of them.

Chasing the flashlight's ray, he discovered a monkish foot-path that rambled behind the church, and this brought him to the rear of the neighboring cemetery.

Here he could follow the outside wall of the hedge, clawing through entanglements of plantain, berry and gourd vine which crammed the narrow isle between hedge and forest. Moonlight couldn't get in there, but a horse had. A mile off in the night the hoofbeats were melting away, but the prints were left behind, a design of horseshoes stamped in the soft loam. Ranier spotted them with his pocket torch; sent the white circle playing up and down the hedge; swore. There was the gun he'd thrown at the professor. Sergeant O'Grady's automatic, imbedded in the bushy wall like a raisin in a sponge cake. Which meant the professor, when hit, had been standing on the cemetery side of the hedge at this point. And on this side a horse had stood, trod the leaf-mold, curvetted, galloped off through trees.

Dunced, open-mouthed in bewilderment, Ranier glared down at printed horse-shoes there, while his memory somer-saulted back through fog to a waterside café, a dank room jaun-diced in lamplight, tourists at table, a taffy-haired man sitting back to an open window, stabbed in the spine. Ten feet from that window Haarman had been, there'd been tracks. Man-tracks—

Now, deep in the mountain forest, echoing from what sounded like a ridge, hoofbeats were expiring away. But even a horse couldn't reach five feet through a hedge of briar to stab an insectologist in the back!

WHEN RANIER reached the car, revived it with the crank, slammed into the driver's seat and kicked the gears, he was winded by something more than running. Professor Schlitz squawked to life as the wheels struck the uphill grade; in the rear-view mirror Ranier could see eyeballs, white-circled and frantic, glowing in the back-seat dark as if a current in the sockets had been turned on. Ranier pulled his mouth sideways, keeping his own eyes on the road.

"Have a good sleep?"

His passenger struggled to bounce upright; opened his mouth; closed his mouth; clapped a horrified hand to the lower part of an ashy face; began to paw wildly at the cushions.

"I've—I've losh my teef!"

"In the graveyard," Ranier shouted. Another time and he could have chuckled. "Sorry. I didn't have time to look for them."

"Wha—wha happened?"

"You caught a knife back there in the cemetery. Remember?"

"Haaaaa—" Professor Schlitz grabbed his bandaged shoulder as if he feared somebody might steal it, exhaling in pain.

Ranier shouted above engine-roar, "Don't move that left arm any more than you can help. It's not fatal. Fleshy part of the shoulder; went through clean without severing any muscle. Just a slice under the skin, and tell me if it starts bleeding. You're a damn sight luckier than Angelo."

"I'm dying." White-rimmed eyeballs revolved in the man's contorted face. "Who did it, Doctor? *Who?*"

"The Devil!" Ranier grinned at the windshield. "I heard his hoofs."

"Hoofs?"

"Running away."

"Thash it!" the insectologist leaned forward, clinging to the front seat. Under the simian concavity of his upper lip the man's toothless gums, pink in the gloom, yawped at Ranier's clipped ear. "Thash wha I was going to tell you about in the graveyard. I remember! Yesh! Hoofs! It was after Mr. Kavanaugh and his Aspasia and Misher Coolidge had driven away—p'raps fifeen minutes after."

His hot-potatoed words spluttered out above the thousand-tongued rattle of the car. "I'd been shtanding there wondering wha to do, right beside thash awful open grave, and shuddenly I was sure I heard a horsh walking behind the hedge. You know how a horsh walks? Yesh, I was sure! Nexsh minute I thought I heard a car shtop in the village, but I couldn't shee anything, so I shtarted for the hedge again. Great heavensh! I thought it was a *horsh!*"

"It was," Ranier snarled. "A horse hiding back there, and it stabbed you through the hedge. Make anything of that?"

"No!"

"So do I. Anyway, I did see the tracks. After I lugged you back to the car, it cut and ran."

"Where?" the professor gasped.

"How far can *you* see in this black fog?"

"I can't shee anything," the professor, chinned hooked over Ranier's shoulder, was staring at the vacuum ahead of the windshield as if all the spectres of Tophet were concealed at the next turn. "Where are we?"

"On the dirt road leaving Bois Legone somewhere in Haiti. Can you pull yourself together and quit breathing in my ear long enough to answer a couple of questions?"

"Yesh," the man breathed in his ear. Breath that rose to a howling gale as the car missed a tree, swayed through clouds of brown puddle-water, hit a corrugated stretch of straightaway. "Why? Why did I ever leave Upshala and come on this gashly Haitian cruise?"

"Funny," Ranier shouted. "That was one of the questions."

"I'll never take another shabbatical year! Never! To think I wash going to Arizhona to shtudy the *Cimex lectularius!*

Inshtead I come to Haiti to shtudy the grave worm! The grave worm!" Professor Schlitz repeated in the Low C of a mouldy pipe organ. "The grave worm of Haiti is—"

RANIER WAS willing to dispense with the subject, pertinent as it was in that locality. Certainly the professor had come to a grave-worm-hunter's Paradise. Ranier cried hastily, "All right. All right. Then have you got any idea who tried to dent your spinal column back in that deserted village? Know anyone who might want to kill you?"

"I feel as if shomeone had," the insectologist wailed. "My God, aren't there already enough corpshes in thish miserable country? Who could want to kill *me?*"

"Mr. Coolidge, Mr. Kavanaugh, his Aspasia as you call her, Mr. Brown, Monsieur Marcelline, Dr. Eberhardt or his adopted niece or that Senegambian house boy with the radio eyes. Or Hyacinth Lucien, or half a million voodooed Haitians," Ranier ticked the possibilities hoarsely off his tongue. "Right now it looks as if your *bête noir* was a horse. I might want to kill you myself," he concluded bitingly, "if you don't come through with the truth."

At least it served to get that mouth out of his ear. Professor Schlitz flopped back on the rear cushions with a terrified snort. Twinged his shoulder. Caterwauled. Yelped as the car rocked around a curve, "Troof? I'll tell the troof! I schwear I will! What do you want to know?"

"Why you pulled a fade-away at Morne Cuyamel," Ranier called back at the shrinking man. "How you got to this neck of the woods, Colonel Otto's grave, by yourself."

"I told you. I told you the troof. I came on the back of Misher Kavanaugh's automobile. He blamed me for Carpetsi's murder—I heard him shay I did it. Because my glashes were under the body. I don't know how they got under the body. I didn't kill the Italian. I never killed anything exshept a few *Stylopyga orientalis* and *Zeuzera pyrina* and *Stagmomantis Carolina* speshimens and—"

"Naturally. Wanting to hide from Kavanaugh, you hooked a ride on his car."

"But I couldn't shtay behind! Not on thash road by that mission housh! Besides, I thought on the shpare tire—he'd never shink to look for me so closhe behind, and when he drove away—owwow—!"

"Keep off your left arm. What then?"

"There I hung," the insectologist described with a graphic groan. "What could I do? They didn't shee me. All the way up thash dreadful road, thinking every moment would be my lasht, the way Misher Kavanaugh drove. Like you're driving now! Oh my God—there'sh a shkull!"

He was leaning over Ranier's shoulder again, blowing in his ear, pointing a finger of dread at the windshield, at something discovered by the car light in the creamed night ahead. Ranier hadn't forgotten that semaphore-armed sign post with its gewgaw decoration. Apprehension filled him as he saw it now. It confirmed a suspicion that he had, thirty minutes ago, chased a gunman to this road-fork in the mountains, and maybe what had happened afterwards in Bois Legone wasn't his imagination. So the mush-mouthed hunter of *Stagmomantis Carolina* and grave worms, squawking over his shoulder, was real! Just when he'd decided the whole thing was a midsummer night's dream.

SIGN POST and skull streaked by. Car and professor screeched at the strain as Ranier took the fork, top speed, wrenched the front wheels out of a shimmy, missed a jay-walking pig, and raced up the graded gravel. On through the night. *Port-au-Prince.* 105 *Km.* Well, the girl had said it was on this main road, and it wouldn't be long now.

Ranier shouted at the man behind him. "If that's your story, stick to it. You drove with Kavanaugh to Bois Legone. Then?"

"I told you how it wash. They didn't shee me, and Misher Kavanaugh drove shtraight to that village back there and parked in the marketplace. I wash terribly frightened. There washn't a soul in schight, and I wash afraid they'd shoot me. But Misher

Kavanaugh and Misher Coolidge and thash woman, they climbed out and ran right into the shemetery."

"What'd you do?"

"I jumped off the car and ran and hid by the schurch. I could shee them, but they couldn't shee me."

"What'd they do?"

"They shtood," the professor swallowed a gurgle, "—they shtood looking at thash awful open grave—just like all those others we shaw. Misher Kavanaugh shaid, 'By God, itch Captain Friederish's body here at the Kraut colonel'sh grave. Itch the girl'sh Dutch uncle!' He began to shwear, and Misher Coolidge looked schared and began to shwear. Mish May shtarted in shreaming and shwearing and cursing at Misher Kavanaugh—'Itch your fault! Itch your fault!'—calling him names. Never have I heard sush language from a lady! Never! I tell you, sh'sh a terrible woman! Yesh! Misher Kavanaugh just went black in the face. He told her to shut up or he'd give her shomething to bellyache about, and when she continued shreaming, he struck the woman in the nose and knocked her into the grave. To thing I've been ten days on shipboard wish sush terrible—"

"Go on! He knocked her into the grave—"

Professor Schlitz pulled an elbow across his boneless upper lip. "But thash all. Only when Mish May climbed out of the hole, all wet sand and weeping, she had shomething in her hand. She shaid she found it down there. Misher Kavanaugh snatched it away from her. I heard him shay to Misher Coolidge, 'Well, thish proves he was here, all right'!"

"What?" Ranier, half listening, his attention bent on a zigzag treacherously fogged, pulled up sharply. His hand lept from the wheel to snare his passenger's lapel. Dragging the man unceremoniously up and over, planting him upright in the seat at his side, he cross-questioned him fiercely, "Kavanaugh said that? Who was he referring to?"

"I don't know—owow! My shoulder. If I only had my teef—!"

"Never mind," Ranier yanked his companion's lapel, "the teeth. Try to remember!"

He released his hold just in time to grab the wheel for a precarious grade crossing. Railway metals swimming up off the road; *rumpety-bump!;* an alarm bell affixed to the warning, *Chemin-de-Fer,* whizzing by the window with a vaguely-heard dinging that was snuffed out astern before it was there, a tocsin as futile in this fog-swamped, drum-periled night as a banged dishpan in a hurricane at sea. Would a train be coming across Purgatory? As if locomotives were the danger in this chaos!

"Who'd Kavanaugh mean by *he?*"

But the professor, addled by pain and fright, didn't know. "Thash all Misher Kavanaugh shaid. And Misher Coolidge shaid, 'Didn't I tell you, Dave? Don't that prove I'm on the level?' Then Misher Kavanaugh shaid Misher Coolidge better be on the level and so had everybody else, or he'd soon put them sixsh feet under it. He waved his gun at Misher Coolidge while he shaid it, and then he shtarted running for the car. 'We got to catch up, and catch up quick!' he yelled. They all ran to the car and jumped in, and Misher Kavanaugh drove away like mad, leaving me there alone. For a while I was too shcared to move. Then I crept out into the shemetery, and thash when I though I hard a horsh, and you came. Where," the thin man appealed, "is thish awful thing going to end? Murderers! Corpshes! Stabs—!"

HAILSTONES SHOWERING up under the fenders drowned out the professor's concluding jeremiad. Ranier swore at an oily curve; banking through mist like an airplane. Trees swished by and, surprisingly, a steamroller somebody had brought from America and left to rust of loneliness in roadside weeds. He strained his throat above the crackle of newly-tarred highway, twisting his mouth sidewise to shout.

"What'd you say it was the blonde found in the grave that touched off Kavanaugh?"

The insectologist, who'd been crooning moans and petting his bandaged shoulder, stiffened violently upright, flung hand to mouth, palming a startled gasp. "Why—I didn't shay! Why—of coursh! Thash the important thing—the very thing I wash going to tell you just as I wash shtabbed! Mish May, in that grave back there—she found a hat!"

Rainer's attempt to take an S-curve with one hand and catch his companion's throat with the other almost capsized the car. Wheels and chassis screeched; Ranier was yelling, *"A hat? What kind of a hat?"* and Professor Schlitz's eyes were round gas globes in the dusk under his sun helmet, his mouth yammering between blown cheeks:

"A man'sh hat! All squashed and shtepped on, too! A Panama!"

Ranier cried across the steering wheel, "He's the one Kavanaugh meant, you fool! He must've been at Colonel Otto's grave before you got there. I knew all along that smooth Haitian never went for the police! That Panama belongs to *Marcelline!*"

"Yesh!" the professor wailed. "Marshelline—!" His mouth collapsed on a howl. Tarred gravel slashing the underside of the fenders made a hailstorm rataplan as Ranier, barking oaths, jammed on the brakes. Smoke poured from the emergency, gagging the air with a pungence of calcined grease. The Model T slid, vibrating; jerked convulsively; stopped in mid-career and choked silent, as if appalled.

Directly in the path of the headlamp, a man's legs were outsprawled, shoes carelessly exposed on the road. The body, doubled as if broken, was almost concealed in the rushes of a shallow ditch that drained the road's edge, and a great yellow tree, its vast girth protruding from the forest's wall, towered like a shade from Erebus summoned to stand sentinel over the dead man.

Ranier knew the body to be lifeless by the pigeon-toed posture of the shoes, even before his own pigeon-toed shoes reached the road. He limped past the headlamp for a better look. There was no use walking quietly. Two miles over the mountain they must have heard those tires eating up the tar, and now his footfalls made a peanut-brittle crunching loud enough to wake the dead. But the body in the weeds didn't waken. When Ranier halted, regretting his curiosity, there was only that otherworld hint of man, the noiseless smoulder of the fog, and the presence of the tree. The body had been skewered. Skewered by the splintered end of a bamboo pole, a sliver of which had gone through the ribs and punched out under the shoulder blades. Blue fists had a death-grip on the pike where it entered the chest, and the force which had driven that jab had broken the long pole at a dozen of its joints; shivered the light stiff wood so that it looked as if it had been struck by lightning.

Then, backing inadvertantly from this grim-reaped harvest, Ranier walked against the tree, grazed his scalp on iron, whirled to direct his flashlight up the column of bark. At the height of a tall man's head, driven to the hilt, a knife had been stabbed into the tree. White cord fluttered from the iron handle. As if a frog or some other trademark had been dangled there to sign the job. Ranier's flashlight, hunting some token in the roadside weeds, found nothing but tracks. On the shoulder of the road, close to the mud-splashed body, a trail of horse-shoes hoof-stamped in warm tar!

There was a gargled exclamation from Professor Schlitz.

"Shpeared! Shpeared like a bug! He was shtanding by the road, and shomebody went by like one of those horshmen in the *Lives of the Bengal Lancers.* Shpeared him on the pike; then left the knife in the tree as a warn—why, heavensh! Itch—"

Ranier steadied the flashlight's occult circle on the dead man's face. Speaking of the Devil!

"—Itch Marshelline!"

Ranier nodded. "Come on, we've got to get out of here."

"Whuh-where are we going?"

"Captain Friederich's mausoleum! Last stop! To lay a ghost!"

CHAPTER XXI

UNHOLY GROUND

THE MAUSOLEUM LOOKED naked through the creamy scud.

HIER RUHET IN GOTT
HAUPTMANN VICTOR FRIEDERICH
Gest. 3 Janur 1922
ICH HATTE EINST
EIN SCHONES VATERLAND

Approaching that black-lettered legend cut in stolid German capitals on the marble door, it came to Ranier that this might be his last stop, for a fact. The little white house was still. Too still. With the fog-drift smoking around its base, moonlight slanting across the peaked roof and falling in mile-long shafts down the cliff at its back, the little house gave the impression of a tomb afloat in space. On that lonely corner of the mountain it had come detached from its lugubrious surroundings, been set adrift. Ankle-deep in mist, Ranier wondered if he were on solid ground.

His shoes made no sound on the turf. Around him the graveyard, its one side fenced by the monolithic boles of Caribbean pine, its terrain littered by tumbled memorials, faded plaques and a flock of angels brooding over mounds, slept as a graveyard should. Or as a graveyard shouldn't, on a night in Haiti when all rules were reversed, the towns playing dead and the cemeteries playing Going to Jerusalem.

Skin twitching, acutely conscious that something had gone

wrong in a place where nothing should be right, Ranier halted, listened. Had that bullet-scratch on the ear made him deaf? In this silence, the turn of a leaf would have made a report. It couldn't be possible this half acre on a summit under the moon had been left out of the game. Nervously, he eyed the mausoleum. If the little white house saw him coming it gave no sign.

He was sorry, now, he'd left Professor Schlitz in the car parked at the entrance-way urns; he could have welcomed even that companionship. Something should be here that wasn't. This graveyard was dead. All at once Ranier knew why.

Those drum-beats which had followed him for the past six hours had stopped. Weren't coming. As if the pulse of Haiti had quit. Nerved to that ceaseless repetend, Ranier's senses had become adjusted to the tension, and now, released from strain, his nerves went to pieces as if too suddenly deprived of drugs.

He ran. Charged at the little white house with bursting lungs and fists clenched, forcing climax by assault. The silent door was waiting three inches ajar, a gouge in the marble where a crowbar might have pried the casement. Any minute now and something would come out of that door. Green hands. A knife-blade. Bullets. Ranier laughed as he strove to widen the breach, swing the massive barrier. There was a gush of stale air mixed from mold, old earth and mortar. A screech from hinges atrophied by disuse.

Then he was standing in the damp solitude of a tomb, jelled in a twilight that might have been left there since the third of January, 1922, eyes riveted at what lay on the floor.

What lay on the floor were an overturned coffin, an axe-split coffin lid, and about two hundred dry, disjointed human bones. There were, too, on the floor a mess of footprints and about a million beetles and something Ranier didn't notice until later. Right then he saw nothing but those two hundred odd human bones.

They weren't bones to Ranier, but fragments. Two hundred

jumbled fragments of a puzzle he wanted more than anything in his life to solve.

HUMERUS. TIBIA. Pelvis. Clavicle.

Long afterwards he was to wonder how he did it. Long afterwards—the memory sending a draught down his neck—he was to wonder how, in that cold-walled vault in a seance of blue-windowed moonshine, a thousand creeps in the silence close around him, graveyard at his back, mice-feet in his hair, his mind harried by the ghosts of mass-murder and unknown killers and vanished dead—how he could pit himself against that jigsaw of bones and bettles to reconstruct a man.

"Radius. Femur. Ulna. Scapula—" Naming the pieces as they came to hand. On his knees; panting; fingers flying over that scrap heap of human kindling in necrologic dexterity, sorting, collecting, fitting, matching. Rummaging for an elusive metacarpus. Picking the heap for a handy patella. Wishbone here. Shins there. Now the cuboid—

The great Vesalius, himself, would not have worked faster. Ranier's fingers ached and his eyes burned. Knuckles. Vertebrae. Now he needed the seventh cervicle. Harder to find than Adam's missing rib. The bones, straw-colored, marrowless, made a faint dry tattling as he sorted them in the gloom, and their problem was further involved with particles of cloth that turned to dust at the touch, snarls of faded wool yarn that might have been a sweater, scraps of leather, in the macaroni heap of the ribs a few tarnished brass buttons. Like a box of dominoes mixed with an old lady's sewing basket, then scattered across the floor.

Some of the bones had been snapped underheel; stepped on and splintered like that bamboo jousting pole through Monsieur Marcelline. It was a job to repair a fractured fibula with that picture in mind. Marcelline, dead on the Port-au-Prince road—what had his Panama been doing in that grave at Bois Legone? How came Marcelline to these backwoods when, presumably, he'd gone with Mr. Brown for police help down the coast?

Where did that leave Brown? Had the dumpling-faced tourist in plus fours met with some crimson come-uppance, too?

Faces, bodies, incidents, scenes raced in merry-go-round circles through Ranier's head while dried bones raced through his fingers. The merry-go-round whirled in fog through Nowhere, and its riders were living and dead. Some rode in half-seen second hand Fords and one, headless, unidentified, on a horse. Some dropped by the wayside, and others disappeared in the murk, and the brass ring was an answer you snatched at, thought you had, and missed.

On this cloudy carousel a web-footed man named Haarman was stabbed (why?) and his body vanished. A Haitian *gendarme* appeared, shot through the head. A dance-hall Italian had his jugular hacked on a pair of glasses which belonged to a pundit of insectology, himself the victim of a knife. Murder, an unknown killer drunk with blood and success, impaled a fourth victim on a bamboo pole. You got on the merry-go-round; that was one way of getting off. Faster and faster went the ride. Graveyards flew by. You hung on, leering at emptied coffins, bodies propped on headstones they didn't own. Hanging on with you was an Irishman, diamond-eyed, snarly, socking his blonde woman friend, pistolling a listener with a pointed finger, accusing you over a gun. (That killer, firing from an automobile, had had a gun!) Near-by was a goo-goo eyed Daisy, romping about in terror, assuring her Irish escort the fault was his. A man named Coolidge of mighty muscles and mangled nerves stood on the merry-go-round with muddied feet, grimacing, somehow in the show. They got on and off, like the man named Brown, and for a while you couldn't see them, but they might be there.

The ride started in a waterfront café run by a Negro who mixed voodoo cocktails, and went off into unmapped space. In an outer circle of night nameless shadows moved; shapes cadaverous as the undernourished and grinning Holbein figures of Plague and Death pictured in old medical book wood-cuts. The shadowy presence of Resurrection Men tip-toeing on the outskirts with barrow and shovel. A faceless physician wearing pink rubber gloves and an invisible cloak, hiding behind a fog-bank, a possible Knox in cahoots with Burkes and Hares.

Centered in the merry-go-round was a hospital where a frightened girl waited between closed doors with secrets in her eyes. You didn't trust her any more than you trusted any woman, but you feared for her safety. Her companions were dead left-overs from the War, and her uncle, a ship's captain dead fourteen years had evacuated his mausoleum in a land where corpses learned to walk, and the walls around her were closing in. The walls closed in as the speed of the merry-go-round shrank its dimensions. The night with its outer band, its shadowy perils closed in. The people on the carousel, all that were left, Coolidge, Brown, the blonde, Kavanaugh (their whereabouts uncertain) closed in. A mob of black men silenced their drums to advance. The faceless doctor was there. A grave-worm expert called frantically for help but made no sound through bare gums; and a strange body, compost of German sailor, *zombie* and murdered tourist menaced the girl, muttering, "Adolph Perl! I am Adolph Perl!"; and the only way you could save her was by solving a jigsaw puzzle made of human joints, but the joints were scattered, scattered—

RANIER JERKED his chin from his chest in panic. Lord, what a dream! Whole nightmare in forty winks. He couldn't pass out now from that *aguardiente.* Scared out of exhaustion, he went at the bone pile in redoubled fury, cursing a seventeen-second nap where every watch-tick counted. On the edge of breakdown it was hard to know where hallucination ended and reality began. When the night, itself, was a fog. Reality a tomb in moonlight on the corner of a cemetery.

"Now the twelfth thoracic. First lumbar. Coccyx—"

Talking aloud to concentrate. Grabbing, joining, arranging with feverish haste that sepulchral design. Putting two and two together for an answer that wouldn't make four. Piece by piece he assembled the human spine. Tacked on the ribs. Joined shoulder blades, arms, fingers; then pelvis, thighs, thin white legs, bony feet.

It was almost done. A place for everything and everything in its place. Marionette ready for its strings. Or, in that moony tomb-light, a beheaded spectre drawn by swift chalk-strokes there on the floor, wanting only one final touch for identification. The head.

Queerly, in haste to accomplish the more difficult pattern, leaving the easy for the last, Ranier had ignored the skull. Come to think of it now, with the scrap heap straightened, the corners left to the beetles—he wheeled and glared in dismay—it wasn't there. All that fearsome artistry for nothing? Cursing, he went to his knees, clawed through splinters of coffin lid for that last jigsaw-fragment. It wasn't in the corners or under the chopped wood. A horrifying thought assailed him as his hands ransacked and couldn't find. Had the corpse, once gracing that framework, been minus a head when entombed? Sweat came through his collar.

"That would mean Dr. Eberhardt—uh!"

He found the skull gratefully. Behind the upsided coffin, wedged against the wall. Returned the stare it gave him with its cavernous eyes looking up at his flashlight. Then, staring, Ranier experienced a numbness of the face. That skull had been cracked, at some long-past date, like an Easter egg. The occipital bone fractured at a time when it wasn't a death's-head. Blunt instrument, fall, heavy blow from behind—it was written as if by a fine black pen in shaky hand across the base of the hollow gray globe; but it wasn't that, Nor was it the fact that this death's-head occupied an address registered for another.

It was something about that grin. Something freezy and unsociable in that white-jawed skull-smile that sent what his Scotch ancestors would have termed a "cauld grue" through Ranier's being. His down-reaching hand started back as if those bony jaws had snapped. But they didn't snap. He looked in spite of himself. That skull was holding something between its teeth.

Locked in that merry grimace was a piece of faded broadcloth, as if it might be biting a handkerchief to stifle uncontrollable laughter from within. Jutting tonguelike from a corner of those jaws, a rag of shiny yellow material, such as a bulldog might tear from an oilskin raincoat. And chewed between the white teeth, looped out through the molars, lustrous, iridescent, unbelievable even in the Aladdin's Lamp of his flashlight—a string of pearls!

Pearly teeth in that skull! Ranier's hand shook so in the act of picking the thing up that its lower jaw dropped loose. Bites of cloth fell to the floor. Pearls scattered, rolled like marbles around his shoes, as if a jewel box had spilled.

"Pearls!"

IT WASN'T an oyster! It was a skull! A skull dropping chewed white pearls from its teeth! Petrified, confounded, Ranier glared at the skull in his hand; could not have been more thunderstruck had it opened its jaws and delivered Hamlet's soliloquy. His reflexes strained for release, as if he were standing with a live bomb. He must rid his fingers of the laughing thing, drop it, throw it. Then he saw, although it had been waiting before him all this time, his unfinished diagram on the floor. Summoning a final effort of will, he went to one knee; set the skull to its owner's bony shoulders, and reeled back, panting. The skeleton was restored.

A shadow fell across the mausoleum door. The terror-bugged eyes of Professor Schlitz looked in. The thin man pointed at the skeleton.

"Who'sh *there?*"

Eyes on the skeleton, Ranier blurted, "Holy—!"

The response, of course, was "Holy Who?"

But the insectologist failed to give it. Somewhere in the night outside the sepulchre a succession of sharp gunshots broke the silence like blows on glass. The shots were far away. They were followed up by an undertone baying, a distant many-voiced clamor as of a myriad hounds suddenly sighting a trapped fox.

The shots repeated, *crackety-crack-crack-crack!* and the baying grew.

"Look!" Professor Schlitz screamed.

Ranier leaped out into moonlight to see.

Through holes in the cloud-roof of a valley now visible below this cemetery height, at a lower and distant level in the night, a red smudge was glowing, a flush of fever developing through far-off haze. Sparks darting behind, and bringing to view, a fringe of miniature trees; and bedlam as one might hear it from a cloud high above an opened grating of Hades.

The drums were thudding again!

And on a ribbon of blue-black road perhaps a mile below the cemetery, seen where it emerged from fog and followed a cliff-edge into obscurity again, a horseman was riding. Midget in perspective, he broke out of vapour, raced through a drift of moonlight on a downhill gallop. No horseman such as Ranier had seen before! More like the creation of a scared child's imagination. For that figure bent in saddle seemed a faceless blob-smear of yellow, a shapeless spook composed of something that gave off fish-scale flashes of moonshine, formless as a watery shadow blown through wind.

"It's the hospital on fire! He's heading there! We've got to save the girl—!"

CHAPTER XXII

SIEGE AT THE HOSPITAL

THE PIKE'S PEAK HANDICAP. The Italian Grand National. Oldfield's coast-to-coast grind. Campbell at Daytona. Galliéni's immortal taxi-dash to save Paris. All the Indianapolis heats, the hill-climbs, road tests, historic drives and record races of motordom were nothing, Ranier knew, to the drive he started then. Sixty miles an hour in a twelve-year-old Model T implies a steep downhill grade and the fastest ride in the world. Add the hazards of fog, unmarked curves, cliff-rims innocent of guard rails, uncertainties of moonlight and night, and a road that twists and winds in the quick-wrench convolutions of jiu-jitsu through a mountain maze of Caribbean forest, tropic jungle, canyon, and coal-mine invisibility, and you have something more than a joyride.

Ranier had it. There were times when, the steering gear almost torn from his hands, he marveled that the chassis didn't rip from the wheels and jump the curve. Moments when the wheels soared over razorback bumps and his head cracked the roof. Bump, swerve, screech and bang on an unpaved stretch. Slewing a hairpin downhill turn as if cracked on the end of an invisible whip. *Slam-bam* on the grade crossing. *Ziff-ziff-ziff* the trees went by. The fog cut to whistling mist-ribbons. The night streaming past like soup. *Swish!* a curve. *Zip!* an underpass. *Rrrrrrt!* the narrow span of a mountain bridge. *Hmmmmmm* on a downhill chute.

The car spurted and tipped on two wheels. Bounced and

shook and jumped like a goat. Pieces broke away and were left behind, the right front fender shying off like a wing shot from a plane. Floorboards came loose under the clutch and things dropped from the dashboard and disappeared. The radiator cap went. The tires, any moment, would explode, the engine drop through, the car burst into a cloud of machinery, nuts and bolts.

Ranier took his chances without looking. Of that wild down-the-mountain spin, the road itself, he could afterwards remember nothing. He drove like a drunkard, leaving accidents to fate. The road was a vague streak fleeing under the headlamp; there was a steering wheel fastened to his hands; an impression on the eardrums of flying downhill. If he guided the mile-a-minute course it was with seventh-sense instinct and the corners of his eyes. His mind wasn't in it, but in a burning hospital where a girl might be trapped in a snare of mystery and fire. His face watched through the windshield, but his eyes were glued for a horseman somewhere in the dark ahead, his attention nailed to a rosy smudge in blackness back of beyond.

The smudge moved around in the sky as the road dodged. On the cliff-edge where they'd spied the horseman it seemed leftward and below. An S-curve later it had moved to the right. At the last it was fixed dead ahead, a crimson mirage above red-stained forest-tops, blushing clouds toiling upward against night, fattening, merging, hanging in a pall. The red light spread in a widening haze. Where the clouds blushed deepest, gold sparks went up in spirals and scrolls, curling and whirling about like the rollercoaster skyline of an amusement park. On the wind a hint of wood-smoke, on the eardrums a sound as of nearing battle, an undertone long-roll pandemonium like a sustained cheering, but too low-pitched for applause.

"It's the voodoo mob! They're attacking Dr. Eberhardt's hospital. If *she's* there—!"

Ranier didn't know he was crying out, for he'd forgotten there was anyone to listen. Professor Schlitz had long since given up trying to call attention to himself, his risked life and the speedometer. Bouncing on broken cushion-springs beside Ranier, he lounged in complete lackadaisy, thin legs outstretched, sun helmet rolling around his shoes, back slumped, face relaxed. What more could happen to an insectologist after a night of larking about graveyards with mummies, bones and back-stabbings? He'd lost his glasses and his teeth. Having abandoned hope for life, he retired into the superb detachment of some auto-race mechanic bored with the hazards of the hundredth lap; fainted.

HE DID not see what Ranier saw. That sudden swerve around a hill of darkness into unnatural light. A last quarter-mile stretch of road leaping visible in fire-glow. Trees red and black standing up in the night; the fog dispersed; landscape around; the sloped silhouette of a ridge ahead, and scarves of blue-scarlet flame leaping up from behind the ridge, their racket drowned by a Baalish tumult of shouts, poundings, gunshots, drum-thunder.

He did not see what Ranier saw on that otherwise deserted stretch of road between the curve and the ridge. A yellow, shapeless figure that might be a man, dismounting from a roan horse, grabbing the reins, leading the horse off the road into a forest in a tangent toward the flame-lit ridge. Ranier saw those road hindquarters melt in the underbrush, and set his teeth. But the wheels under him could go no faster. Bolts clattered to the ground as he yanked the emergency at the roadside where the horseman had been. Professor Schlitz went under the dashboard, and the car shocked up short in a nest of ilex scrub. Ranier left them there.

He was following a path, a horse-tracked bridle trail that ambled through forest toward the crimson-lit ridge. The path ambled, but John Ranier didn't. Body stooped, he ran Indian fashion, powerfully, sullenly, spurred by scorched wind in his face, the roar of close battle in his eardrums.

He caught his man at the top of the rise where one could glimpse the burning hospital and the mob. The man was tying his horse to a trailside sapling. His excited hands botched the knot, and his head was turned toward the fire carnival on the slope below. Seen at close range, he was not a spectre, but a lumpish figure in a yellow oilskin raincoat that fell to his shoetops, his face and head almost hidden by the whaleboat brim of a shiny yellow sou'wester.

Ranier hit him from behind like a panther. Caught him in a headlock, throwing him helpless to his knees as a cowboy bulldogs a steer.

"*Donnerwetter!*" the voice exploded under Ranier's arm. "Who does this to Dr. Eberhardt!"

"Eberhardt!" Ranier wrenched the man in an arm-lock. "Where have *you* been all night?"

"Been? Been? *Gott in Himmel!* where do you think I have been? Asleep in some bed? Sitting with holded hands? Then you do not know anything about quintuplets!"

"QUINTUPLETS!"

It was, of all that red phantasmagoria of demonism, death and madness, the strangest moment, the craziest impossibility of all. That word! Dropped like a spoonful of milk into that witch's goulash of mayhem and murder. Against that fog-and-firelight background where the shadows ran flitterjibbet through the mutilated shapes of tropical trees, and the tang of hot woodsmoke invaded a basic perfume of orchids and vegetal decay. That word, on a four o'clock dreary with vanished dead and obligatto terror, above the battle yells of black men, the crackle of gunfire, the bedlam of jungle drums. *Quintuplets!*

An uncontrollable feeling of laughter came over John Ranier. Staring at a quaint little man in a yellow sou'wester and swaddly oilskins—the figure off a cod-liver oil bottle, for all the world—he saw a face as German as a cooken with funny-paper walrus moustaches and apples for cheeks and innocent confoundment in round blue eyes. And around that figure the vision conjured by the little man's word—a string of babies, five in a row, black mites as like as five peas in a pod. Babes in *that* wood! It made the sweat come out on his forehead and his stomach ache.

"You've been all night—to a delivery!"

The gnome was bewildered. "Why not? Why not? The woman's husband came for me at seven forty-five. Of course I told Polypheme to take the car. So I must go in this husband's buggy. Fifteen miles north in the mountains, and I was not prepared. I had expected next week, diagnosed twins, not a litter! *Herr Gott!* Five of them. Nothing ready. I must boil water. Wash linen."

His voice rose, annoyed, pettish. He'd mislaid his present surroundings and become the absent-minded country doctor impatient with the annoyances of his practise, irritable after a sleepless all-night call.

"These ignorant Negroes. Quintuplets! At this time! Am I a laundress? A dishwasher? All that I must do. I am busy! I am a scientist, not a baby doctor! But, *ja,* I must leave my laboratory in the midst of a vital discovery and play stork for five little—!"

It was remarkable. So remarkable that Ranier, who wanted to reach that storm-swept hospital more than anything else in the world, could only stand with his mouth open, wordless, the sweat of fright on his face and hysterical laughter under his belt. It was the little yellow gnome who woke up first. Staggered back on the path as if realizing for the first time he'd never seen Ranier before. Became indignant, recalling he'd been attacked. Then frightened, his beaver eyes catching firelight, reminding him of his hospital.

"Himmelkreuzdonnerwetter! Aber, my hospital! My laboratory! What is the meaning of this mob down there! Who are *you—?"*

Then Ranier could break into action, grab, point, shout. "The girl. I left Laïs Engles in there! Quick! We've got to get her out before they—!"

"Laïs!" Dr. Eberhardt screamed. *"Mein Gott—!"*

Ranier was running. Dragging the gnome in oilskins at his heels. Helter-skelter through dense undergrowth, down-slope, racing for the blazing villa around which fog and smoke tumbled in turmoil and black figures danced ring-around-the-rosy like fiends around a bonfire in the Pit. The farther side of the villa was in darkness, but the near wing, as they drew closer, went up like tinder. A Vesuvius of gold flame jumped skyward. Surrounding grounds came to light under a blizzard of sparks, and Negroes were swarming everywhere, running, jumping, shadows flickering in and out through the blacker boles of trees.

"They've fired the hospital! It is the work of those *bocors,* those witch-doctors! They have incited the natives!" the cod-liver oil gnome behind Ranier was raging now. "To ruin my work! To capture Fräulein Engles. They will kill her! Sacrifice her! *Gott, Gott!* See, Shooting—!"

"No—look!" Ranier cried out as he ran. "It's not the mob's gunfire. They're armed with knives. It's in that upper window!"

IN THE window at the villa's front, overlooking the open gallery in the shadow of the big sablier tree above the driveway. The laboratory window! It's light was out, but another light was there. On and off, on and off, stabbing electric-blue spurts that jabbed out over the sill, flashing and gone with staccato explosions that spanked one-two-three above a bolero of pounded drums, an oratorio of howls, and crashings that sounded like axes on wood.

Axes on wood! Ox-bowing out toward the highway, the forest path gave momentary glimpse of the hospital verandah where the mob was packed in mass-meeting fury. Flung stones smashed through the verandah screen, banging the inner wall, and dark shapes were bunched at the front door like firemen, fighting to chop an entry. But they weren't firemen. Ranier could distinguish their screams; see the flash of axe-heads at work; hear the punishing blows above the roar behind them and the *spank-spank-spank* from that upper window.

"She's up there! The girl and Polypheme with a rifle!" His throat prayed, "God! Hold on! Hold on!"

The little man screamed, "The door cannot last. If those voodoo priests get their hands on a white girl—!"

The cry put wings to Ranier's feet. Yanking the other's arm, he jerked him into a thicket; fought, dragged, pulled him through dense-grown palms, shaping a course for the hospital's rear. Bronze smoke lolled around the incendiary wing, and in this acrid smother they broke from the jungle's wall, unseen by coal-skinned firebugs dodging in the haze.

The rear grounds where outbuildings and a barn were in shadow, seemed left to a squad of torch-bearers, arson-bent. Dancing savages doing an adagio to a roundelay of meaningless squalls, the glow from their flaming pine-knots putting a crimson polish to ebon muscles, gleaming on curved banana knives, shining on egg-shell eyes and mouths of piano-key teeth.

Ranier shouted, his voice masked under the din. "Window of the emergency room! In back!"

He'd be a long time grateful for his foresight in bolting all those shutters; a long time grateful for the memory of that one window which had no hurricane blinds or glass. The black torch-bearers, charging the barn, gave the chance for an open dash to that wing which was screened by poinsettias. Ranier yelled at the gnome, and they made it. Smashing mosquito-wire with a fist, he boosted the little doctor over the sill; followed with a violence that left him breathless, dizzy in the inner dark.

The room, fitful with running wall-shadows and red reflections, trembled to the pounding of the villa's front; a rumpus of voices coming up the hall. The small man in sou'wester and oilskins started for the corridor door—the door that in a long ago dream had been slammed in passing by a dead man with a webbed foot. Ranier cried, "Dr. Eberhardt! Wait!" and fled around the shadowy operating table, fingers stretched toward a bottle-laden shelf.

Whang! The door was slammed again. Slammed open, this time, bursting inward to catch Dr. Eberhardt in the face, knock him kicking to the floor. Smoke rushed in from the corridor. And a coffee-browned Haitian pyromaniac, a Samson of a man with a stevedore's torso, vast flat feet, a torch in one Statue of Liberty fist and a banana-knife the size of a headsman's scimitar in the other. Torch uplifted, he paused on the threshold, glared at two white faces in agreeable surprise. Then he got another surprise.

CHAPTER XXIII

MIDNIGHT

CAUGHT AT THE medicine cabinet behind the operating table, Ranier had spun at the intrusion of this ogre, not unarmed.

The black man had no time to comprehend the bottle in John Ranier's hand. Like a flash Ranier threw. Squarely and truly at the giant's ace-of-spades nose. Smash! a tiny bomb-burst of shivered glass. A small bright explosion. Vitriol.

It brought the muscle-monument down plunging, squalling, blinded, thrashing with paws to face against the operating table, spinning in a carom against the medicine cabinet. There was a bull-in-China-shop collision as the dark Samson fell. A cascade of bottle-glass, powders and volatile fluids burying the colossus in a chemical bath. The machete was lost under the pile-up before Ranier had a chance to grab; and a howl from Dr. Eberhardt announced the arrival of a second adversary in the corridor door.

Ranier met the challenge with a projectile of carbolic. There was a scorched shriek in answer; the burnt face departed the doorway; a new crop arrived. Ranier screamed, "Let 'em have it! Let 'em have it!" thrusting bottles into the little doctor's hands. Flinging iodine from an uncorked jug, he charged the corridor, shouting, boring through a thresh of wildmen that fought like circus carnivores panicked in a runway. The jam fell back, battle yells changing to peals of anguish as poison bottles burst on mouths of teeth and eyes bleared with scalding chemical.

Shattering the emptied jug on a wooly topknot, Ranier

kicked, slugged and bit a path for the hall, and the gnome in oilskins was a following vengeance, scattering antiseptics on malingerers in the wake. Jubilant screams received them at the corridor's turn; became frantic howls at the touch of acid. But the dark crush storming through the chopped front doors kept coming, shoved forward by those behind. From wall to wall the hall at stairway's foot was packed with Haitian rabble, black-skinned, brown, lavender, high yellow; a subway-like riot of tar-brushed faces going Uptown under a display of machetes, pitchforks, clubs, *cocomacaque* bludgeons, butcher knives.

That hall was hot. Somewhere a furnace was going under forced draught. The steady monotone of flames shook the building with a menacing chant. Heat breathed through the sidewall opposite the staircase, surcharging the riot-rocked air with an autumnal woodsmoke. Upstairs the pump gun was chattering to a multisonous hubbub as of crockery breaking, wood being kindled; and through that upper smashing of breakage and gunnery and the lower bombilation of the fire and the stormed hall, there threaded the jungle-tone of *Rada* drums and the roar of the crowd outside—wolf-howls, jackal screams, outbursts of song, mad shouts. The rifle cracked small in that hullaballoo, but its sound filled Ranier with a hope that powered his punished body with a reserve charge of dynamite.

"Hold on! Hold on, upstairs! We're coming—!"

A madman fighting madmen to reach the stairway. Punching, tackling, driving a wedge through a sea of torches, teeth, African baseball bats, giant razor blades. Somehow he reached the post. Somehow, the little doctor at heel, he was half-way up the stairs.

A dagger, missing both of them, lodged quivering in wallpaper beside Ranier's head. Black hands reached over the bannisters, pinning Dr. Eberhardt's oilskins to the steps with a pitchfork.

"Go on! Go on!" the yellow gnome screamed. "*Himmel!* do not wait for me!"

Ranier tore the man loose with an arm-sweep, the raincoat ripping on pitchfork tines. Reminded of a skull with a bit of oilskin in its teeth, he laughed savagely, boosting the little man up the steps ahead of him, four at a time. Turning to fling a venomous pint of ammonia at a ragged Cacao. Pursuing his climb with yells and a blood-thirsty sickle. Laughing fury at something he could see to combat, something he could hit with fists, something he could revenge on.

The black man fell downstairs, caterwauling, but his twin loomed wraith-like in the smoked murk at the stairhead, beckoning them up with a butcher-knife, daring their ascent. Ranier wiped the grin from that smoky countenance with nitric acid. The enemy came down in a tumbling acrobatic, head under arm, knees to belly, bouncing by like a Roman chariot wheel with outthrust blade. Ranier spurred the descent, kicking lustily; had all his limbs at the stair-top. He yelled when he saw the balcony unpopulated, the laboratory door closed on the upper gloom. Yelled and attacked the panels with frantic fists, pounding, crying the girl's name.

"Open up! Let us in! For God's sake—!"

He was beating on the door, and a Cape Cod little figure crouched at the balcony rail pouring driblets of liquid fire on fiend-faces raging below. Tan smoke piled up the stairway; embers geysered from tossing pine-knots; in the demoniac bedlam, torchlight on his cheeks, whiskers as if fire, red coals for eyes, Dr. Eberhardt made a small Mephisto measuring out penalties on mutineers in a hell-well. Ranier tore his throat to be heard.

"Laïs! Miss Engles! It's Ranier and Dr. Eberhardt! For God's sake, Laïs, if you're in there—!"

"M'sieu—!"

IT WAS Polypheme. More goatish. More overwhelmed by the sombrero. Polypheme, gray as terror, who plucked back a bolt, turned a key, opened the door. Behind his electric-bulb eyes and crowlike shadow, the room was a cavern. Light flashed with sound in this blackness, filling the room with a thundercrack and a bluish, instantaneous flash that showed John Ranier the girl.

She was standing by the window, pressed close to the wall beside the upright frame. Shooting at an angle and a little downward at enemies somewhere below the gallery under the fire-reddened foliage of the sablier tree. She had changed to a nurse's costume; a play of flickering crimson colored the smoke-haze in the window, illumined her profile, found bright gleams in looped hair under the nurse's cap. Her face, too, might have been starched. She fired again, giving Ranier a gun-flash glimpse of her white shadow-figure, tense marble face. But she looked calm, soldierly. Firing, ejecting the shell, drawing aim, firing; handling the Winchester with the workmanship of a man.

"Laïs—!" Ranier plunged through the door.

"Laïs! *Liebes Fräulein! Ach, du lieber Gott in Himmel!*" the undersized gnome in yellow romped forward with open arms. "*Aber*, you are safe. We are in time—!"

Ranier slammed the door against assault mounting the stairs; fought to fasten lock and bolt. He could hear the girl crying, *"Unkle Doktor! Unkle Doktor! Wir warten schon den ganzen die Nacht!* Oh, I thought you would never, never come! It is terrible! They broke in the contagion ward. I saw them kill the patients—terrible things have happened. Oh, God, where have you been—?"

"Been? Been?" It was the querulous voice Ranier had heard on that path in the forest. "Didn't you see my message? Where do you think I would go and stay all the night? That black Maman Celestine did not have twins, but five. I must wash. Scrub floors. Borrow a horse to get back. As if quintuplets are not enough, I am seized by this ruffian on the path—"

Ranier shouted, "John Ranier. Ship's doctor. S.S. *Cacique*, Atlantic-Caribbean Line." At the girl, "Have you seen those people—Brown, Kavanaugh, the big lug, the woman—?"

She cried, "No one! I have been trapped up here since—"

"People? People?" Dr. Eberhardt's voice rose shrill, that of a peevish child quarreling over a doll in an earthquake. "A ship's doctor! People! Laïs, why did you not get my message? You know I always leave one on the table, here, when I—"

There was a ping like a violin string snapping in the darkness; glass smashed on the wall to Ranier's right, releasing an aromatic smell. Polypheme, hiding in a corner, howled; and the Winchester flashed *bang-bang-bang!* in the girl's hands.

She cried, "Keep back, *Unkle Doktor!* Do not come near the window! They are throwing knives, rocks—!"

"My laboratory!" the small physician came back into the situation with a yell. In the gun-flash Ranier saw him standing hands to forehead, wild-eyed. "My experiment! *Himmel herr Gott!* it is ruined. My cultures! And my papers, my writings, my documents, my records—!"

He was on the floor, pawing desperately in rubbish and blowing papers. Ranier shouted, "Records?" and the wailed reply was, "*Ja, ja, ja,* of all my life work, my case histories, the births, the deaths—!" and Ranier almost forgot to hold the door. Objects broke to pieces all around him, but pieces fitted a puzzle on his mind. Another answer! Death records!

He stood as if something had hit him; then something did. A stone from the window. A despairing cry from the girl:

"They come up the gallery! Dear God! they are climbing the tree!"

A CRASH on the door behind him threw him to his knees. Wood quivered under a triphammer pounding, and a long sliver splintered out of the panels, admitting a thin axe-blade and a ribbon of scarlet light. The window! The door! No place for slackers. Somehow he pummeled Polypheme out of hiding; made the terrified little Negro understand about the desk. Wrenching at weight, they shoved the desk against the cracking portal while the girl sniped from the window, Dr. Eberhardt wailed, missiles whined into the laboratory with the velocity of hornets, banging and bouncing on floor and shelves, shattering glass.

"The chemicals!" Ranier dodged to Dr. Eberhardt's side. "Quick, quick! Before they break in! Which bottles—"

"These shelves, these above the laboratory sink. But the potent ones were in the emergency room. A little acid here. *Gott in der Höhe!* Give it to the ungrateful, ignorant, witch-burning devil's—!"

Here, there the little man raced, pillaging cabinets and cupboards, heaping ammunition on the center table. Precious little, and they'd need it from the sound. Ranier's heart sickened when he heard the girl cry after a shot, "The rifle—all the cartridges are gone!"

Promptly the door burst to pieces. Ranier swept Laïs Engles into a corner; yelled, "Dr. Eberhardt, take the window!" spun to peg a bottle at a face coming in from the hall balcony. Breaking glass, a screech from the windowsill told him Dr. Eberhardt had simultaneously scored. From then on he was busy with his own sector of defense, fighting to hold the door.

They came, fled, reappeared. Attacked and counter-attacked. Ebony devil-masks, tar-barrel torsos framed against torchglare in the jagged door-jambes. Not the educated Haitian of the cities, but the mountaineers, peasants, huggermugger mobsters who can be summoned for any vandalism or riot—this crowd the black equivalent of European book-burners or American lynch gangs, without so far back to go. Like barbarians they charged; superstition-maddened, drum-maddened, primitives with the darkness of the Ivory Coast and Dahomey in their veins; souls untamed by four generations in coats and pants, undomesticated by life in the Caribbean jungles.

They'd kept their gods, Damballa, Papa Legba, Gbeji-nibu, Ayida-Wedo. Kept them behind a thin lip-service of Christianity—as white men keep their dark gods—hidden in grass-roofed outhouses, secret temples, tucked in the blacker corners of their hearts. Kept them for just such a night as this when white men stabbed their brothers with invisible knives in waterfront cafés, when the dead left their graves to walk in cerements of fog.

"Damballa! Vini 'gider nous!"—"Papa Legba, connais moon par out"—"Damballa Oueddo! Lé-lé sang!"

Brayed from thick chocolate throats those invocations put an icicle up Ranier's spine. Damballa, guide us! Legba, know your worshippers! Damballa, this is the hour for blood!

Drums roaring, throats roaring, fire roaring behind them, they charged the doorway, battled to get over the barricade. John Ranier drove them back. Drove them, scorched and yowling, back from the desk with throws of astringent liquid, jets of watery flame. Crouching at the table in mid room, he uncorked the bottles with his teeth; hurled the contents as if the desk were an Argonne parapet, the bottles hand grenades. Behind him Laïs Engles sobbed over an empty gun; Polypheme was under the sink; Dr. Eberhardt bouncing in frenzy between table and window to hold his side of the fort.

The room shook to the crackle of glass, clang of thrown knives, snap of sticks, smash of crockery. There was a time while the overhead dimness was thicker with missiles than a remembered twilight over Belleau Wood. Sappers might have been under the floor. Smoke, turgid with the smell of burning varnish and fried wood, clouded the hall balcony, swirled in through the door. Puffs of chemical in colored tint and stifling acid fumes choked the doorframe. Another charge was coming.

"Damballa! Damballa Oueddo!"

Ranier met the assault with liquid fire. Showered the breach with uncorked bottles of flame. Nitric acid. Deadly sulphuric. Household ammonia. Try a drink of that! Here's an eye-opener! Something to remember us by!

A shower of hydrochloric cleared the doorway. Not the first time in history the primitive warrior was stopped by a judicious use of chemistry. But it couldn't last. The charge was coming again. Those assorted vials of concentrated pain were giving out. Heat burned the air to bronze. The floor was blistering, becoming untenable. A cry from Dr. Eberhardt's whiskers flung Ranier around to see the tree beyond the window monkey-jammed;

Negroes shinning up the trunk, lizarding out on the gallery-touching limbs, hanging in the bright foliage like clusters of monstrous fruit.

He scoured the doorway with a throw of carbolic; pressed a last bottle into Laïs Engles' hand. A Negro had thumped down on the outside gallery, trotted to the window, put one leg and a shining steel machete over the sill. Scowling, he drove Dr. Eberhardt aside with a vengeful slash, swung in the other leg, dropped lightly into the room. His scowl watched Dr. Eberhardt and his teeth grinned.

His silhouette blocked the window, and his Congo presence filled the room with a lion-like breathing and a fetor of black grease. A dented top hat was tilted Ted Lewis fashion over his brows; around his naked shoulders a circlet of pig's-hoofs dangled; ragged pink trousers were belted by a dead snake from which hung an apron of gourd-rattles. Knife aloft, sweaty sinews glistening, he stood with his nostrils opening and shutting like gills while his rocking-horse eyeballs measured the scene as if it were a feast.

STARING AT this dreary master of ceremonies, Ranier couldn't believe Dr. Eberhardt's cry:

"Hyacinth Lucien! *Aber*, you *Schweinhund*, I will see you killed for this. When the police find out you are not a bar tender, but a dirty *hougan* priest, a *bocor—!*"

The black man rumbled, *"Pas capab'! Gendarmes* too late. You bad witch-doctor, *chauché, de culte des morts.* Dig *zombies;* raise dead. We know." His scowl saw Ranier; deepened to a thunder-cloud. Saw Laïs Engles and beamed delight. "You witch-doctor, too. Talk with *zombie. Zombie* friend of *mademoiselle!*"

Running thumb across knife-blade, he crouched for the spring. John Ranier swung the girl behind him in sick suspense. The black man's feet were noiseless on the floor. Ranier broke from fascination to meet him half way. His fist started from his shoe-tops; flush on the point he caught that grinning jaw. He didn't miss because he couldn't. All the pent desperation, all the power in his being, the last ounce of dynamite went into the blow, as if that shining black jaw were the focal point of the whole night's evil.

Crack! It should have felled an ox. It did not so much as alter the black man's facial expression. The jaw never turned. Ranier felt as if he had punched an anvil. The Negro was on him; the knife a guillotine poised to whack. It was coming down—

It stopped!

Stopped as if that upraised arm had jammed at the shoulder socket. A convulsion scribbled the minstrel face under the top hat. Eyes jerked sideways as if fish hooks had caught them. Breath gushed through the teeth, blubbering the black rubber lips. *Ffffffaaaaaaa!*

A backward leap for the window. Somersault over the sill. Dive off the gallery rail, crash in shrubbery below, scream to curdle the night. In a vertigo of astonishment, John Ranier was gaping at the vacuum where the champion had stood. Knife and executioner were gone!

Laïs Engles screamed, "Frogs!"

A bullfrog, making a green streak out of shadow, landed bellywhacker on a mat of firelight where those black feet had fled. The frog was followed by another. A third. Two more. Ranier saw the floor was alive with green mites. Bouncing and flipflopping, squat-tag over the heating boards, looking up at him with the bulged, indignant eyes of United States Senators routed from a Lilliputian election hall. An amphibian stampede escaping that aquarium smashed on the laboratory table.

A sentence went through his mind; Marcelline's alto words in a café setting nine hours or nine thousand years ago? "I give you my words, messieurs, if you dropped a live bullfrog through the skylight of our government buildings, every soldier in the place would jump out of the windows—"

Frogs! It went with "Quintuplets!" With Haarman's webbed foot, Professor Schlitz's spectacles, that cracked skull with a string of pearls in its teeth. He captured and held up one of the slippery creatures by a Jumbo leg. Black faces looking in through the window screeched and vanished as if exorcised. Ranier spun to see dark savages mounting the doorway barricade. The leader gestured a meat-axe. He spied the thing in Ranier's clutch.

"Waaaaah!"

RANIER TIGHTENED his fingers, and the frog shot from his squeeze like a cake of wet green soap. The frog lit on the balcony; the balcony was cleared by magic. Dr. Eberhardt sailed a greenback out of the window. Chorused terror, a wild stampede in the branches of the sablier tree—

To his last day Ranier knew he would remember that escape from that abominable laboratory; that frog-fusillade across the smoking upper balcony; that charge behind a barrage of croaking swamp-mites. They carried the broken tank to the stairhead; Ranier threw. Fat frogs and lank. Frogs that went like green arrows through the smoke, sailed like speckled bats in the stifling haze. In the cinnamon smudge below an Ethiopian riot milled, clawed and fought to get through the front door and evacuate the hall. Where hydrochloric acid had failed, where bayonets would have failed and the Charge of the Light Brigade been barbecued, a plague of green amphibians turned the tide.

Ranier would always remember that. Old Testament deliverance in 1936. Himself, at the stairhead, pelting those black backs with bullfrogs. Dr. Eberhardt yanking greenbacks from the pockets of his yellow rainslicker and ten-word German oaths from his throat, hurling both with raging accuracy at terrified Negro skulls. Doctors gone back to witchcraft! Medicine failing, resorting to a remedy in Voodoo!

And he would always remember Laïs Engles flying down the stairway in her nurse's costume, fierce-eyed, hair a loose golden shawl, chin up to the last, racing to snatch a gray tabby from the smoke below, hugging the cat in her arms. And the sight of Polypheme, the house boy, lavender with fear, slipping on a frog that was spread like a banana peel on the bottom step and floundering on greased-heels across the hall. Like a roller-skater he hit the side wall, head on, grabbing for equilibrium.

The night must disgorge another horror before they could get out of there. For the house boy's grabbing hand caught a knob, and the knob yanked open a cupboard door. That closet in the wall! There had been a moment engraved on Ranier's memory when an Angelo Carpetsi hooked high-waisted suspenders on that same door in the wall, fetching to light an umbrella and sun helmet which might have been (and wasn't) Dr. Eberhardt.

What spilled from the cupboard this time—the door springing open like a jack-in-a-box at Polypheme's touch—was something that might have been (and at one time was) Mr. Haarman.

He had not been waiting for a street car. Not in that baking hotbox, with one shoe in his pocket and his webbed foot bare; his eyes two staring zeros, mouth agape; hands stiff at his side and palms outward, the right palm showing a scar in remembrance of an Indian at Para, Brazil.

Ranier shouted, "Haarman!" and he came out of the cubicle, bowing. He bowed too far. Bowed off balance and toppled, mouth baked open, eyes front, throwing affectionate arms around Polypheme's neck to drag the squalling house boy to the floor.

It cleared the last superstitious Haitian from the verandah outside and the last Haitian superstition from John Ranier's head.

The girl was crying, "He was alive, *Unkle Doktor!* Only dying when they brought him to the hospital tonight. You remember the *Kronprinz Albrecht,* the plague, the funerals? It is the mate who died—Adolph Perl—!"

Outside the mob was a fleeing elephant herd; a dragon-tongue of fire burst from the cupboard doer. In that blast of incandescence Dr. Eberhardt bawled: "Adolph Perl! *Ja,* it is! How? *How?*"

Matchflares of fire were exploding around the little man's rooted feet; Ranier saw in alarm that his own trouser-cuffs were smoking. He screamed, "I'll tell you how!" and kicked. Kicked out with his lame foot and gave that taffy-haired dead body a boot that made his bad foot ache!

CHAPTER XXIV

EN ROUTE

FIVE A.M.

Port-au-Prince—69 Km, said the sign.

Flat miles of coastal highway Ranier had not seen before. The road smooth as glimpses of obsidian gulf. The Model T settling into a rhythmic hum. The grayness thinning ahead where presently the city would be seen. The night charred black behind where a conflagration, long visible in the sky, had burned to carbon. Behind him in the car—Laïs Engles, Dr. Eberhardt, and Professor Schlitz....

It couldn't have happened. None of it could have happened. At the *Gendarmerie* in the fishing village five miles back the *Gardes* had not noticed a tall white man, a stout woman with blonde hair, and a big man all mud going by since four o'clock in any car. *Non,* they had seen no fat American in short pants driving for Port-au-Prince. *Oui,* this was the only road, and cars go by with much frequence, but then there had been the fog. A fire? *Oui,* they had seen red sky and heard drumming on the mountain, "But such things are common in Haiti, monsieur, and on a night such as last—"

Besides, the telephone line to the west had not answered. Doubtless, Caco bandits had cut the wire. But yes, monsieur could telephone Port-au-Prince from here. Monsieur and his party were in distress? A pity they did not have time for breakfast, a jug of *clairin,* perhaps a glass of *aguardiente.*

Ranier had only had time for the *aguardiente* and two cryptic long-distance phone calls to the capital. One to the All America Cable office. One to general headquarters of the *Garde d'Haiti.*

It couldn't have happened, but here was Polypheme at the steering wheel beside him; a pale girl in nurse's costume and a little walrus in Cape Cod oilskins and an insectologist without his glasses in the back seat. Ranier had waited for calm while Dr. Eberhardt re-bandaged the professor's wound and hysteria died. In the gray light he could see his passengers, haggard, bewildered, sitting in limp exhaustion; the doctor's beaver eye had not been off him for a minute. The girl's quiet sobbing had stopped long ago. Hugging the cat, she watched him too.

RANIER TURNED to face the back seat, and was saying: "To begin with—I was there in Hyacinth Lucien's Café when this tourist came in. I suppose," narrowly, "you know the place, Doctor?"

"*Aber,* that swine will never run it again with his black neck broken from that jump like we saw!"

"He's out of it now," Ranier banished him grimly, "but Hyacinth had nothing to do with what happened there. He merely used that stabbing in his bar as propaganda to incite a race riot and burn your hospital. Probably been laying for you a long time for cutting into his witch-doctoring racket. Getting back to the café—this tourist Haarman walked in and saw me a little tight. That must've been about quarter to seven last evening."

"Tight?" the old German snorted.

"Means a few drinks. Enough to put me on edge," Ranier described, "and at the same time make me wonder if what happened afterwards wasn't my imagination. Haarman ordered me out, and, when I didn't go, took a punch at me, getting me unawares. I went off the verandah and hit my head. Woke up wandering in a daze some minutes later, and saw Haarman sitting at my table inside.

"Haarman looked queer, then, but he'd always been deathly pale on the ship, and I figured he was one of those dipsomaniacs

who think they can beat up the world when they're liquored up. He'd been drinking my *aguardiente,* I saw, and I suppose he'd had plenty before he came ashore." Ranier turned his glance on the insectologist. "He was oiled on shipboard yesterday afternoon, wasn't he, Professor?"

"In the ship's bar before dinner," the thin one remembered. "We were all there talking of the motor drive. He wash drinking heavily then."

"I'll bet. Who," Ranier narrowed his eyes at the wan face under the sun helmet, "bought him those drinks?"

"Carpetsi, moshtly. I bought him one." The man's toothless

mouth puckered as if he might cry. "He'd ashked me to join the drive and I felt obligated. Obligated! Oh, my! I don't know why he ashked me. No, I don't."

Ranier said, "I do," grimly. "But we'll come to that. Well, Haarman was walking on his heels when he came to Hyacinth's café. The rest of you were to meet him there, is that right?"

"Yesh. He went there a half hour ahead of ush."

"Or, maybe, he was *sent* on ahead. I've an idea he got there early for reasons other than his own. Perhaps to see if the coast was clear. At any rate, he didn't like my company, and he wasn't diplomatic about asking me to leave. From the look in his eyes, I've a hunch he may have been doped. I could see his face in the back-bar mirror, and he seemed to pass out. Then some time after seven o'clock," Ranier directed his words to Dr. Eberhardt, "about the time you got your R.F.D. call, I should judge, this tourist party from the ship showed up at the café. I was a trifle woozy, myself, by that time—from that knock on the head, I guess—but these tourists walked in and ordered a round of drinks with Haarman. Professor Schlitz can check me if I'm wrong."

The professor groaned an affirmative to this, and Ranier waited for the wheels to take a curve before going on.

"From the alcove I could watch this bunch at table in the middle of the room. They'd all come down from New York together on the cruise, except Marcelline, who'd boarded ship at Cape Haitian. This Marcelline sat at the bar-end of the table; the others ranged along the side. A Mr. Brown from Ohio; the professor, here; an Italian named Carpetsi, now dead; a Mr. Coolidge.

"On the opposite side, a blonde Broadway relic, and her Irish boy friend, Mr. Kavanaugh. Our Mr. Haarman was at the far end of the table, sitting with his back to an open window and about ten feet from the sill. Dense fog outside, and he was pretty fogged, himself, by then. He'd cooked his own goose by drinking that *aguardiente.* So there's the set-up; the victim anaesthetized, the café a good quiet place to put him on the spot, and the fog just suited their scheme."

Professor Schlitz cried, "*Their* scheme? Who'sh?"

RANIER LEANED over the back of his seat to fire a cigarette, watching three faces in the match glare.

"The ones who maneuvered Haarman to that out of the way café," he shook out the match, "to kill him. The ones in that little tourist party who were in the know. Maybe most of them—maybe only a couple of them—I'm not sure which ones, but it won't be long before I find out.

"Anyway, this innocent little jaunt across Haiti by motor was to have been something more than a jaunt, and not so innocent. The original plan, the scheme behind this motor trip, was Haarman's. Kavanaugh claims he was driving to Port-au-Prince on business and wanted company. Whether Haarman and his crowd attached themselves to an innocent party remains to be seen. But the big idea was Haarman's game. He had helpers. They double-crossed him."

Ranier pointed his cigarette at the insectologist.

"This underground game of Haarman's calls for a gang. I knew there was more than one on the job from the first. You can't stab a man at table and nobody see it happen, sitting at close quarters like that. Prepared with alcohol, Haarman didn't know it when the knife went in; never made a squeak. But someone at your table had to know it. Someone must've seen it. Someone was holding out. Well, Carpetsi, for example, saw it. He was in on the scheme, one of the gang. He was going to squeal, later. That's why his throat was cut."

"The Italian boy," Laïs Engles cried.

"One of the gang," Ranier snapped. "There *was* a gang when the thing started. A gang that left New York together and sailed to Haiti, playing tourists on a Caribbean cruise. A gang headed by Haarman, who came to Haiti after something Haarman knew about. As I say, Haarman was double-crossed; knifed by one of his pals. You're lucky, Professor. I think the knife was originally intended for you."

The insectologist grabbed himself by the throat.

"Me?"

"I can only guess on this point. You were invited on the so-called motor tour as a fall guy. A blind. A dupe to make the drive look innocent. Besides, this scheme called for a stooge, somebody to be wounded to give the gang a chance to call on Dr. Eberhardt's hospital. Wait—" he apprehended an explosion of German from the gnome-face under the sou'wester. "I'll explain that when I come to it. The point is Professor Schlitz was picked—maybe I'm wrong—to be this accident-victim. It would look quite natural. Party of American tourists driving cross-country to see Haiti at night. A white man mysteriously injured in a waterfront dive. Rush to the nearest doctor. The gang, I believe, had planned this accident for Professor Schlitz. But something went wrong. Haarman, himself, got the works."

Ranier exhaled smoke. Then he continued:

"Why? I can only speculate again. Suppose that devil, Hyacinth, recognized Haarman when the crowd came into the café? Suppose Hyacinth recognized Haarman's scarred hand when he served him a drink, and Haarman's gang realized it? Or just suppose it was opportunity for a fast double-cross—Haarman was soused, sitting with his back to a window, fog handy—a good chance to knock him off and grab his major share of the profits—"

Ranier drew a sharp lungful of cigarette smoke; expelled it through his teeth. "I think that's it. They wanted his share. Anyhow, this scheme that mushroomed out of Haarman's brain turned into a toadstool and killed him. His gang was tougher than he was. *He* was stabbed."

THE SPEEDING car hit a jolt in the road, and Dr. Eberhardt, bounced, exploded. "But all this is impossible! *Donnerwetter!* Impossible! How could this man you call Haarman be in that café last evening? How can he have a gang, as you say, and come on your ship from New York? How can he be alive in the first place? When he is one Adolph Perl! When he is a man who came to Haiti in 1922 and died of a plague, and I, myself, saw him in his coffin fourteen—"

Professor Schlitz shrilled, "Then he *wash* a living dead man—"

Ranier shouted above voices, wind and tires, "He was a living dead man, perhaps, but not the kind you think. A living dead man from the minute he trusted a gang with his dirty work, and put his back to that window in the café last night. This is what happened.

"Everybody at the table was chattering about the fog, the proposed motor drive. Marcelline, the guide—he wasn't a guide, by the way, but one of the gang—Marcelline went out to see about the Winton he'd hired. About ten minutes later he came back into the room. During that time, Haarman was stabbed."

"But I wash at the table," the insectologist gasped. "Nobody at the table made a move."

"No."

"Then how—"

Ranier made a red circle with his cigarette. "I'm a fool or I'd have guessed it at the time. Only I wasn't looking when it happened, and when Haarman did get my attention, I was seeing a reflection in the mirror behind that bar, so the angle there didn't give me a clue. You," he pointed the cigarette at the thin man, "didn't see it because your attention was probably snared in another direction. Afterwards I saw tracks outside the café, but they stopped six feet from the window. Haarman was stabbed through that window just the same."

"But if he sat ten feet from the sill on the inshide—?"

"A long reach," Ranier shook his head. "But so has bamboo. Ever see these Haitians cutting down ripe cocoanuts? Then recall that splintered pole we found in Marcelline's ribs."

"Good God!"

"Good weapon. Stiff bamboo. Knife lashed to the tip. A quick jab; exit knife through window curtained with fog; enter murderer through door talking about the weather. He occupies the conversation, holding attention to his end of the table with a discourse on voodoo. No one is more astonished to see Haarman unwell. In the ensuing hue and cry, he spies a face at the window. Maybe it was his conscience, but I doubt if Marcelline had any."

"Marshelline!" Not many hours before, the professor had mashed the name through his gums on a similar cry. "Marshelline shtabbed Misher Haarman?"

"His tracks outside. Who else left the café and went around by that window? Remember that thicket of bamboo out there? Afterwards he chucks the pole, hides the knife in the Winton—not the only tools he's stowed in that 'hired' car—and comes back into the room; no blood on *his* shirt. Two birds killed with one stone. The gang has cut Haarman out of his share of the spoils, and they've got their accident-victim. Now the secret machinery is under way, they've ditched its inventor, and they're going to run the machine for themselves. First stop: Dr. Eberhardt's hospital."

CHAPTER XXV

RANIER'S EXPLANATION

A ROAD SIGN whizzed by the window. Ranier craned his head to read it in the coming daylight. *Port-au-Prince—53 Km.*

He picked up the story harshly, "But before the machine gets out of the café, there's a cog in the gears. That's me. They didn't know how much I'd seen, and they had to let me walk out and work on Haarman—they couldn't kill me with the professor and Hyacinth Lucien looking on. Professor Schlitz was another cog—what to do with him? Well, they took him along to get him later—he could add to the confusion at the hospital, and that's what they wanted. Confusion. They got it when Miss Engles recognized Haarman. I don't suppose they counted on the girl being there."

Dr. Eberhardt hunched forward from the back seat. "Am I going mad? Still you talk about this man Haarman as if he had been alive! I tell you, he was a German sailor named Adolph Perl, who died—"

"Fourteen years ago. 1922. And was buried in a graveyard three miles down the road west of your hospital," Ranier nodded wearily. "Miss Engles identified him, too. By the scar on his hand, by the webbed foot she'd seen when he was a sailor on her uncle's war expedition up the Amazon. That was a cog in *my* machinery, when I heard that. I thought Miss Engles was lying."

He shifted his eyes to the white dimness of her face. For the past ten miles she hadn't stirred; had sat white and strained, cat in arms, her eyes unswerving on him as he talked. An expressionless headshake refused a cigarette. He told her huskily:

"And *you* were an unexpected wrench in this gang's machinery. I don't suppose they'd been told about that little girl who was on your uncle's secret expedition for Germany. If they were, you were probably described as a little girl because people forget children grow up. More likely the supposition was you'd been sent back to Germany long ago. You were a cog in the gears," Ranier gestured, "but not too dangerous a cog. This gang could use your story, as a matter of fact, to advantage. Make it seem like Haarman's a *zombie.* Cloak their machinery under a mask of voodoo magic.

"It was all right, after all, because it scared the hell out of everybody, myself included, and the gang was plenty anxious to get rid of me when I turned up in the hospital. They had to work fast in that hospital."

"I do not understand. *Nein!* Why should anybody come to my hospital," Dr. Eberhardt panted. "Who are they? Why?"

"Haarman, stabbed in the back, dying, was used as an entrée. An excuse to get in. I think," Ranier guessed, "the idea was to get you, Dr. Eberhardt, busy in the emergency room. Keep you downstairs. The gang had been told about the layout of the hospital. Haarman knew the rooms; knew your desk was in the upstairs laboratory—"

"*Heilige Gott!* But he was Adolph Perl, I tell you!"

"He was dying, all right, in your emergency room last night. But Dr. Eberhardt was unexpectedly out on a call. The ones who killed Haarman didn't care. Remember, Professor, who carried Haarman into the hospital?"

"Brown and Carpetshi carried him in. Kavanaugh and hish blonde woman and I followed after." The thin man rinsed sweat from his forehead; leaned back groaning. "We put him on the operating table."

"Leaving Coolidge and Marcelline outside in that Winton. And while the rest of you were inside, and I was around in back looking through the window, the laboratory upstairs was wrecked.

"Can you guess who shinned up the gallery and did the job? Well, I wouldn't put it past Coolidge, but we don't know yet. Marcelline was in it, that's certain. The lab wasn't just smashed up, either, but left as a set-up to make it look like the work of Haitian vandals. Dissected hands over that Bunson flame. Frog left on that spike as a voodoo sign. That's why Miss Engles didn't find her message from Dr. Eberhardt. One of those rats found it, saw the doctor was out, stole the note. But I didn't know what this gang was after until that battle with the mob hours afterward. Dr. Eberhardt's records, that's what they were after. Dr. Eberhardt's *death records.*"

"Himmel herr Gott!" the little physician choked dramatically. "What for?"

Ranier lifted himself on an elbow to growl, "Haarman wasn't able to tell his crew of criminals where Adolph Perl was supposed to've been buried. That's what they had to know. They wanted to find the grave that belonged to Adolph Perl. And they knew you'd kept a record of it somewhere in your files."

"Perl's grave? Perl's grave? A dead man comes back to life and has to have my files robbed to find his own grave—?"

"I tell you, Coolidge *or* Marcelline, or both of them, ransacked your desk, wrecked the lab, stole the death records and got back to the car parked in the driveway. Down in the emergency room Miss Engles kept ringing for you. You didn't come. She ran upstairs to find out why you didn't answer; she saw the mess in the laboratory and screamed."

THE GIRL said to the gnome in German, her voice low, toneless, "I thought you had been abducted by the natives. I thought you had been killed."

Dr. Eberhardt panted, "I do not understand any of this. Shades of Kaiser Wilhelm! What does it mean?"

"Curiously enough," Ranier told him, giving him a hard stare, "the shades of Kaiser Wilhelm were in your hospital last evening, doctor. In those death records, too; the ones stolen from your files. Of course, when the girl screamed upstairs and I dashed around to the front, Coolidge and Marcelline were there sitting in the car. They followed me into the hospital and played amazement at sight of that upstairs room. Meanwhile Haarman died on the operating table downstairs. Hemorrhage. The gang inherited his profits; had the death records in their possession; the machine was running smoothly except for my reappearance.

"Everything conspired to their advantage, though. Miss Engles was terrified, telling her astounding story about Haarman. Your absence, Dr. Eberhardt, played up the mystery. The fog outside made it perfect because it would keep the natives indoors with their heads under their pillows. Kavanaugh sent Coolidge, Brown and Marcelline back to the village to bring the police. Then he started a murder investigation on the Haarman stabbing.

"By that time I was certain one of the tourists killed Haarman, but I didn't know who and there seemed to be no motive. The mystery of the laboratory appeared to make it a voodoo job, though. And Miss Engles' story had me down. We got up to the laboratory; Kavanaugh accused *me* of Haarman's murder. A door banged downstairs. The Irishman went down, came back, said Haarman's dead body had walked off. Well, we knew where the body walked off to—into that cupboard in the hall. But who put it there? I'd think Kavanaugh put it there—to further scramble the mystery and make us believe Haarman a *zombie*—but he was upstairs when that door banged. Unless—"

Fingers in his hair, Ranier stiffened up; glared at Laïs Engles. "By George! That cat!"

"Meine Katze?"

"She was downstairs in that room. *She* could have brushed the door. Or wind could have slammed it. Then Kavanaugh, running downstairs to see, could have hidden the body, and rushed back saying it was gone. So the *zombie* angle is established and we're addled out of our wits, providing it *was* a trick played by Kavanaugh. We don't know yet. We don't know."

Ranier glared at countryside passing the window, fields of millet, thatch-roofed huts, thick-leafed banana plantain gray in early light. Fog was lifting on the Gulf of Gonaives and soon there would be some sky. He waited for the tires to screech on a long flat curve; smoking impatiently. His listeners in the back seat were coming out of shadow like negatives forming on a film.

"We do know," he went on sternly, "what happened after that. Polypheme, driving back from the village to tell us Hyacinth was rounding up a mob, saw a dead body sitting by an open grave in the cemetery by that road. Adolph Perl's grave, as it turned out. The boys with the death records had located Perl's headstone. Who disinterred that coffin??

"We know Brown, Marcelline and Coolidge never reached the village *Gendarmerie.* Coolidge said Marcelline wrecked the Winton in the fog. Did he? Did he ditch the car to get rid of Coolidge and Brown, and open that grave by himself? Or did Coolidge help him with the shoveling, and Brown, too. Or was Brown, innocent, left dead in the jungle somewhere?

"I'm sure of one thing. There were pickaxes, spades and ropes under the seats of that Winton, and *Monsieur* Marcelline worked on that grave. And then, with everything running like hot oil, the machinery blew all to pieces. Smashed up right there in the light of those shaded lanterns in the fog. It was Adolph Perl's headstone, all right.

"But a little old lady in taffeta and bonnet was in his coffin!"

"Was ist das? Was ist das?" Dr. Eberhardt's puffed eyes blazed at Ranier, cheeks swelled, purpled. "You try to say an old lady was at the grave of Adolph Perl instead of—! *Who put her there?"*

Ranier shook his head.

"Nobody put her there. She was there."

"Aber, nein! I, myself, buried her—*ja,* with Polypheme's help, in a little cemetery the other side, at the east, of my hospital! Fräulein Laïs will tell you—"

"She did tell me," Ranier ground out. "She did say that, Dr. Eberhardt, *and so did your death records!* So did the headstone over the grave. When we found an old woman's body at that grave marked for Adolph Perl—I thought she'd been transferred. But she wasn't transferred. She was there last night when those ghouls exhumed that coffin. They didn't expect to find her in that coffin under Perl's headstone. You bet they didn't! And it smashed this secret machinery of theirs, this dirty underground machinery they'd stolen from Haarman—smashed it to hell!

"I'd like to've seen their faces, I tell you! If Haarman had been alive to engineer the thing, himself, he'd have dropped dead. We thought we were crazy when we saw the old woman's body at Perl's headstone, but those rats who dug her out from under must've had twice the shock."

RANIER'S VOICE cracked in excitement, crying at his stunned audience. "And if you think those grave-diggers had a shock, if you think *I* had a shock—I'm sorry, Miss Engles, it was horrible for you!—think of the blow it handed the rest of the gang, the ones who'd stayed there with us in the hospital, expecting everything was running smoothly and on schedule. What did *they* think? Carpetsi, for instance. Well, *he* thought he'd been double-crossed by this double-crossing mob. He thought his jackal pals who'd done that bit of digging had pulled a fast one, tricked up the grave with this old lady's corpse, hidden the body that should have been there, and pulled a sneak with the spoils. If Kavanaugh is in on this racket, that's what he thought, too. The Italian was all for chasing after Coolidge and Marcelline and Brown, right then. But his idea was wrong. His gang hadn't double-crossed him. They'd found Old Gramma Sou there in the first place.

"Now the machinery was off the track, if you understand me. Way off! Those grave-diggers didn't know what to do. They had to work fast, too. Marcelline probably clawed through the death records and found the location of the old lady's grave.

"That Haitian was clever. Fearing his own countrymen,

knowing the Haitian Penal Code strictly forbids tampering with graves—knowing, too, the superstitious fear of his people—he leaves a frog tied to the exhumed body, enough to scare the police galley west. That's why he'd appropriated a jar of frogs from the laboratory. Good protection.

"The next step is to dig up Old Gramma Sou's grave—maybe the prize they're looking for is there, since she's (for reasons they can't fathom) *here.* Can you follow this, Miss Engles?"

The girl whispered, "I think so, but I do not understand."

"Let's follow the grave-diggers. Marcelline was one of them, if Coolidge and Brown were the others, I don't know. They raced, unseen in the fog, to the old lady's grave. Don't think they didn't work fast. If that soil hadn't been dry sand underneath we'd have caught up with them in a hurry. But what happens? Under the old lady's stone they find the body of the U.S. Marine. The machinery of their plan is wrecked again. Nothing for it, but they've got to open the grave of that Marine. Foiled again. A celluloid collar. The missionary in the grave of the Marine. So on to the grave of the missionary."

"Then they did not," Laïs Engles breathed, "move the bodies from one cemetery to another?"

"Angelo Carpetsi thought that was what they were doing. So did I, at first. God knows what the rest of this gang thought. There are two gangs working now, see? The ghouls, racing from cemetery to cemetery, following that list in the death records—that list who were buried fourteen years ago on that night of the plague. And there was that half of the gang which was pursuing the work of the ghouls, didn't know what was happening, couldn't figure the game any more than you and I were able to figure it."

Ranier paused for breath, then went on.

"Do you recall what happened at Adolph Perl's supposed grave? Coolidge turned up. Was he one of the grave-diggers, or did Marcelline really ditch that Winton and drive on, alone, in another car? Coolidge said the Winton was wrecked and he didn't know where Brown and Marcelline were. But what did he tell Kavanaugh when they walked off in the fog by themselves? Did he tell Kavanaugh to wait around a while, then hit for the old lady's cemetery and keep stalling on the mystery angle? Anyway, that's what happened, wasn't it? We beat it to the grave of Old Gramma Sou; saw the Marine; beat it to the grave of the Marine; found the missionary—exactly as those diggers ahead of us had. But I hit on something at the Marine's grave," Ranier made a white fist and considered the knuckles grimly. "I hit on something on that grave under the big tree where the missionary's bones were in that soldier's coffin—"

He paused for breath, mopping a glaze from his grimed face. Smoke hurt in his throat, and his tongue, dried, was reluctant to go on. A stiff glass of *aguardiente* would have been venison at this point—why had he ever left that café in the first place?

He resumed thickly: "That grave under the tree wasn't sand. It was wet earth loam, easy digging, a compost of leaf-mold, damp and absorbent soil. So there was little left of the coffin; not much left of the bones; hardly more than that clerical collar. See the point, Dr. Eberhardt? Those other bodies, buried in dry sand at an altitude generally dry, had—had almost mummified. Like those mummies you see in Mexico—at Guanawato, bodies turned to leather by atmospheric condition. But in that compost under the big tree, the leaf-droppings of a thousand-year-old forest giant—decay, yes. There was the proof. The missionary had been buried in the Marine's grave *from the first.* The Marine in the old lady's. The old lady in that one marked for Adolph Perl.

"Then while I was staggered with that discovery, more mystified than ever, we heard shots on Morne Cuyamel at the missionary's mismarked headstone. The ghouls, of course, had exhumed the body of Colonel Otto. And their wrecked machine hit another snag. A *gendarme,* driving by the mission house, saw them at work. They shot first." Ranier sighed.

"**MURDER HAS** a way of developing like cancer. After you've killed once, I suppose, another homicide or two makes little difference to the hangman. That secret machine Haarman had set in motion was fueled on a murder at its inception. Those grave-robbers were desperate. They shot the Haitian *Garde* with a U.S. service automatic they'd found on the buried Marine; planted it in the fist of your Colonel Otto; dumped the *gendarme* into the grave and lit out for Bois Legone—"

He punched out his cigarette on window-glass, pale with a suggestion of day. "I'd like to know why nobody in the vicinity roused at that shooting. Loud in that fog as stones banged under water. Doesn't anybody live in that Morne Cuyamel mission house?"

Dr. Eberhardt grunted, "The Reverend Waldo Claphouse. *Aber*, he is down with *dhangi* fever. The natives would not dare put their head out of doors near a cemetery. On a night of fog—"

"It was thick on that Morne Cuyamel road, all right. Thick enough for another murder. Angelo Carpetsi's. Convinced he was being double-crossed, the Italian gave me a whisper, told me he was going to talk. Somebody overheard him, and from then on he was marked for a tonsillectomy."

"On my eye-glashes!" Professor Schlitz gagged. "The glashes I losht when I fell down in that Marine graveyard. Hish throat—my glashes—!"

"Somebody," explained Ranier, "picked 'em up. Piece broken from a lens. Good gag to leave behind. But it took a blade to cut a throat that might be talkative. If Angelo hadn't lost his nerve and tried to run away, if he'd stayed with me, there, he might not be a handful of ashes back in that hospital. But that Morne Cuyamel stage-set was too much for a Carpetsi. Took a cue from the professor's exit, and tried to exit himself. He did. Miss Engles says," he looked across his cigarette at Dr. Eberhardt, "she saw Mr. Coolidge start off in the fog after Professor Schlitz."

The girl said tightly, "That is what I saw."

Ranier speculated, "But couldn't he have changed direction without being seen? Everybody was staring at the graveyard. Couldn't he have sneaked a wide circle, steering clear of the car lights, and caught up, say, with Carpetsi? Perhaps it was Coolidge who picked up those pince-nez of yours, Professor. Left them under the body to frame you. But he used a razor-blade."

"You mean to shay—you mean Misher Coolidge cut—?"

"Jugular vein and carotid artery." He was staring at a little splash of sunlight, crimson over his head, that had come through the windshield.

He heard the insectologist protesting weakly, "But Misher Coolidge was Misher Carpetshi's friend. On the boat they—they were thick as fleas."

He suggested dryly, "Thicker, perhaps. But, Professor, you ought to know about fleas. If Coolidge didn't cut the Little Angel's throat, who did? Did you? No," he waved off a gum-spluttered denial hurriedly, "you wouldn't leave your spectacles, I imagine. That was a dumb attempt to throw suspicion on you. However, at the time I didn't know. Still don't. Maybe somebody else did it, somebody who was behind us all the time we were behind the grave-digging crew.

"We weren't far behind those ghouls, either, at Morne Cuyamel. Sand or not, all this shoveling had slowed them. I think I'd have overhauled them if I'd gone straight to Bois Legone, but Coolidge was still alive, there was a chance to sew him up and a doctor can't let a man die. Miss Engles and I," he told Dr. Eberhardt, "rushed this Italian back to your hospital. I've an idea our gangster friends weren't sorry to see us go. They weren't sorry Professor Schlitz was gone, either. We were a problem, and this scheme of theirs, haywire as it was, was driving them crazy. Three murders, now, and still no prize in sight.

"So Coolidge, Kavanaugh and Miss Daisy May set out for Bois Legone to find out what capers had been cut at Colonel Otto's tombstone. Incidentally, Professor Schlitz attached himself to their car—the car that murdered *gendarme* had driven up in. They find the grave at Bois Legone is vandalized; Captain Friederich's body, there, where the colonel's should've been—"

LAÏS ENGLES put her face in her hands.

A hoarse roar from Dr. Eberhardt, "You—you are crazy! I do not believe a word of this, *nein!* Fräulein Engles' uncle, the captain of that ship, we put him in a mausoleum high on the mountain. A mausoleum built by a French planter who was lost at sea before he could use it. I bought it, myself, when I first came to Haiti, and I gave it to Fräulein Engles for her—"

"Just the same," John Ranier said evenly, "Captain Friederich's body was in Bois Legone at Colonel Otto's grave."

"I shaw it," Professor Schlitz put in, drearily. "It wash there, all right. Wish a shea cap on itch head."

"Meanwhile," Ranier pursued, "the grave-digging detachment, scotched again, have gone up the mountain to that last cemetery. Kavanaugh, Coolidge and Miss May follow. What happened from there on is in the dark; all I can do is guess by the evidence, I know the workings of the machinery, not the engineers. I think Kavanaugh and party caught up, there, with the grave-diggers. If Kavanaugh wasn't one of the gang—he's dead. The blonde is dead, too. Or if Coolidge isn't in the gang, *he's* dead. I'm not worried about Mr. Coolidge, though. Carpetsi was his cabin-mate, his pal. Birds of a feather.

"Anyway they're up with the grave-crew. Can that be Brown and Marcelline? We haven't seen a sign of Mr. Brown all night. Who helped Marcelline shovel? At all events, Marcelline was sent as an emissary on horseback. My guess is, the Haitian guide had been leading the chase in the Winton which was never wrecked at all. But he returned to Bois Legone on a horse he'd picked up somewhere—cattle walk all over these damned roads. Why? *To pick up a hat he lost by accident while digging that Bois Legone job.* Fatal for the gang if that hat was found. For Marcelline, anyway. He wanted that Panama.

"And somebody else was dispatched on an errand. Given a gun and the dead *gendarme's* car. The errand being to stop *me* from any investigation I might be making on the sly. This gunman caught me on the road near the hospital."

"You were shot?" Laïs Engles gasped through her hands.

"Shot at. The fellow missed. I suppose I'll never know who it was." He described the chase through the fog. "Of course he took the fork going toward Port-au-Prince, to join his gang at the cemetery on the mountaintop. I went to Bois Legone, wrong choice. Lucky for Professor Schlitz, though. Marcelline, coming on a back trail, had reached Bois Legone and sneaked up on horseback behind a hedge that bordered the cemetery. And he stabbed the professor through the hedge, just as the professor was going to tell me about seeing that Panama hat. Stabbed him right in front of me. I didn't see how, in the fog. But the same weapon he'd used on Haarman, remember. Thinking he might need such a weapon, Marcelline had cut himself another pole and lashed his knife to the tip. The hedge spoiled his aim."

"My shoulder!" the insectologist, his wound suddenly remembered, exhaled a loud groan. Then straightened up to gasp, "In that case—who was the rider who killed Marshelline?"

"Marcelline," Ranier said through his teeth. "Hoist on his own petard, by God! Talk about justice. Racing back up the mountain, he came out on the main road for better speed, spurred to rejoin the gang. Horse hit that roadside ditch, full speed. Marcelline was thrown. Pole hit that big tree, jamming the knife up to the hilt. Other end, splintered, went through the Haitian like a lance. Score one for fate. And we're getting," Ranier promised, "to the end of that trail."

It was almost light in the sedan. He could see their faces; the girl's expression masking a fear that had never left it since a moment, there, in the hospital when he'd unlaced a dead man's shoe; the insectologist's, greenish, somehow like that of a magnified mantis on its stalk-thin neck; the purpled cheeks, marble eyes, sea-cow moustaches of Dr. Eberhardt in a mutiny of disbelief—he could see their faces, and he could see his own reflection, ugly with soot, black quills on his chin, hammocks under his eyes, blood on his ear, tousled, beaten, haggard, looking back at him from the rear window. The lips snarled back, showing teeth, and he was saying:

"Those curs found what they wanted in Captain Friederich's mausoleum. It had to be there. Their underground machinery was off the track, but it was following a certain course, and they finally guessed the reason. So did the gangsters following the grave-digging crew. So did I, as I told you, at that grave under the big tree. Listen, Dr. Eberhardt. Your death records were wrong."

"Whaaat!"

"That night you buried those six plague victims. January the third. 1922. Fourteen years ago. Those coffins lined up in the hall. You turned out the lights so the natives wouldn't see what you were doing. You sealed the coffins. Polypheme helped you carry them out to the car. Miss Engles told me you wrote the names in pencil on the roughboxes. You were working fast, in the dark, putting those bodies down from cemetery to cemetery—"

"Ja, ja! I buried them myself, I tell you. I—"

"You were one ahead each time on the list," Ranier said slowly. "Think. There was Adolph Perl, number one. The old lady, number two. The Marine, Sergeant O'Grady, as three. Missionary, four. Colonel Otto, five. Captain Friederich, six. But you jumbled them in your haste, understand? You buried the old lady first. Number three in *her* plot. Number four at number three's. Colonel Otto at number four's. Captain Friederich at Colonel Otto's. And in Captain Friederich's mausoleum you put—"

"The coffin—*the coffin that had Adolph Perl's body in it!"* Dr. Eberhardt shouted.

"No," Ranier said.

THERE WAS a long, stunned pause.

"What is that you say?"

Slow ribbons of smoke drifted from Ranier's nostrils as he said, "Dr. Eberhardt, do you remember what happened that night fourteen years ago when you laid out those people who died of that plague?"

A flush of exasperation, anger, bafflement crimsoned the plump face under the yellow sou'wester.

"You do not make sense. Nothing tonight makes sense. Am I going mad? Do I hear this? Just now you tell me Adolph Perl—number one coffin—is put by mistake in the mausoleum of Captain Friederich—number six—*aber,* then you tell me—"

"I asked you if you recalled what happened that night you buried those people. Something disappeared, Miss Engles told me."

"A suitcase!" the red face blurted. "A suitcase of valuable—a dispatch case owned by the German Government which I have returned to Berlin if Adolph Perl, the mate, should die. It was stolen. It was stolen by a sailor—"

"The sailor, Hans Blücher," Laïs Engles helped him in a breathless tone.

Ranier said roughly, "This Blücher ran out of the door. Perl went after him to bring him back. Perl came back alone, crawled up on the operating table, saying he was dying, he'd contracted the plague."

"That is so," the girl whispered.

"He asked Dr. Eberhardt to lay him in the hall so that he might die beside his officers. Dr. Eberhardt went out to the barn to fetch the coffins. You, Miss Engles, ran upstairs, hid for a while—"

The little doctor roared, "What? What is this about?"

"The body of Adolph Perl was not in that coffin in the mausoleum."

Laïs Engles sobbed, "But it was! It was! I saw it there when the lid was nailed on—saw his hand—the scar—"

Ranier leaned across the seat, eyes squinted, stern. "Dr. Eberhardt! You know what was in that suitcase owned by the *Wilhelmstrasse.* The case that secret mission intended for the Chilean diplomats in exchange for Chilean help—to buy explosives from Valparaiso. What was it?"

"Documents," the old man muttered. "Papers from the Kaiser."

"That's not all!" Rainer's tone was iron.

"*Nein,*" came the thick-throated whisper. "Also there were jewels. The neutral powers would not take paper money. Germany had no gold. There were jewels in the suitcase, heirlooms, the last hopeless donation of a beaten people. Four million marks worth of jewels."

"Four million marks," Ranier said harshly, "equalled one million dollars. There were a million dollars worth of jewels, gems wrapped in packets of oilskin, in Adolph Perl's coffin, but Adolph Perl's body wasn't. The body in that coffin was that of a smaller man, thinner, a scar painted on his hand—I'd guess with iodine from your laboratory—a body exchanged in the dark while the little girl was upstairs and you were out in the barn with Polypheme. That body had four million marks worth of jewelry stuffed up its sleeves, its trouser-legs, under its sweater—Adolph Perl's clothing, incidentally—to make it look heavier and give it weight. I suppose it was too dark with the lights out to see the face, but you should've examined it more closely, there in the hall, Dr. Eberhardt. More closely, before nailing on the lid. That body had been smashed on the back of the head. I saw the fractured skull. It had *this* in its teeth."

With numb fingers he fumbled from his pocket a handful of pearls, a string of bitten cherry-sized globules that rolled about on his palm and shone skim-milk blue in the morning light.

"In the skull—" Dr. Eberhardt choked. "In its teeth—!"

"A man suffocating might bite his own arm," Ranier said huskily. "Hans Blücher woke up in that coffin. Hans Blücher was entombed alive."

CHAPTER XXVI

END OF THE TRAIL

IT SPOILED AN orange sunrise that flamed with tropic flamboyance down the eastern *mornes,* painting a panorama of crinkly green-brown mountains, blazing blue gulf, the Jim Crow roofs of Port-au-Prince like litter on a beach, the tall masts of the wireless station incongruous on a skyline as luminous, exotic and gaudy as a macaw.

Haiti yawned by on a mule, going to market. Highways into town were clogged by circus parades of oxen, burros, dogs, goat-carts, trick bicycle riders, minstrels in bright costumes, jugglers balancing great baskets of fruit on cannon-ball heads, pickaninnies, turbanned crones, parrots and Nubians; cackling, mooing and shouting to create an impression of activity in a republic of sloth, a celebration to Morning after Night.

Ranier silently cursed slow traffic, his eye on the sprawled confusion of the waterfront where the Swastika-painted stacks of a great German touring liner overshadowed the town, placidly smoking in preparation for departure. She was, Ranier recognized, the ship which had moaned its way down the gulf last evening when the fog began. Other than a tangle of small fishing vessels, the only ship in port.

His own hooker wasn't due till noon, but he took the Model T from Polypheme and didn't spare the horse-power, racing for the municipal pier. Grim-jawed, tense, he drove; shifting his eyes but twice from those three black-and-white funnels, when he turned his head to answer two questions.

Laïs Engles asked in an odd, stiff voice, "Then—then Mr. Haarman *was Adolph Perl?*"

"Yes. The webbed foot settled it in my mind. Too rare an abnormality for coincidence. I had to assume he was the mate on your uncle's schooner; then figure out who it was you saw in that coffin, instead. Had to be the other sailor, of course. Blücher, panic-stricken in that quarantined hospital, would naturally try to run for it. Natural enough for Adolph Perl to've gone after him, but it wasn't so natural for Perl to come back, the place a death-house as it was. No, he must've come back for something more than patriotism in a cause long since lost.

"We'll never know the truth of it, but Adolph Perl caught Blücher from behind, cracked him with a gun-butt probably, and my guess is he tucked Blücher into that cupboard, that same cupboard in the hall where he himself was stuffed fourteen years later. Then he played the big dying scene for Dr. Eberhardt, faking the symptoms and pulling a phony death-rattle. And Dr. Eberhardt took it for granted the man was dead."

"Herr Gott!" the old physician blurted. "How could I make such a mistake?"

"I can see how," Ranier's tone was without censure. "An epidemic bursting out on you like that, late at night, excitement, one death after another—and anybody'd be up in the air. You gave Adolph Perl a hasty once-over, maybe hurriedly felt for a pulse, in the darkness and all his acting deceived you.

"Besides, if that mauve death was as contagious as you say, you'd instinctively be pretty leary of close contact. Anyway, he wasn't dead, and when you hurried away to build him a coffin, as he knew you'd do, he got busy. The little girl had run somewhere to hide, the lights were out, it was a cinch to change clothes with the body in the cupboard, paint that artificial scar, smear up the face. A long chance of course, but a million dollars is a long shot anywhere. And it worked. Adolph Perl emptied that suitcase, stuffed the packets of jewelry into the clothes he'd put on Blücher, and fled.

"A perfect scheme in its way. German agents would be looking for Blücher, not Perl. He couldn't have passed a suitcase loaded with four million marks worth of jewelry through the customs, either. So he'd buried his treasure; all he had to do was hide out till the uproar blew over, then come back to Haiti with a batch of grave-diggers, exhume the loot and smuggle it back to Germany. What I can't understand is why he waited fourteen years."

Dr. Eberhardt mopped a stricken forehead. *"Himmel!* To think that man, Blücher, was only unconscious when I nailed up the coffin. I was excited that night. Worn out. I feel as if I had murdered—"

"Not you," Ranier corrected, kindly. "Haarman—Perl—killed him."

"The *arachnid!"* the professor condemned learnedly. "The dirty *solpugid!"*

Laïs Engles breathed fiercely, "They must all be punished! Do you think we will catch them at the pier?" and Ranier turned his head the second time to smile at her thinly and answer by a shoulder-lift.

THEN, WITH the ship's iron hull towering up alongside like a long dark cliff against the sun, midgets gazing down from a lofty fo'c'sle head, officers bright trifles on the bridge, tugs fussing under her nose, sailors standing by the lines—all the hustle, bustle and dock-halloo of sailing time, Ranier was certain he'd backed the wrong hunch.

Customs police met him at the pier gates with negative headshakes. *Gendarmes* greeted him with shrugs and empty hands. A line official accompanied the car down the long jetty to the gangway where tourist passengers were straggling up the roped incline, and a white-and-gold purser, passenger-list in hand, was examining the papers of a party anxious for cabin-space.

An ultramarine sky heated overhead, and the crowded pier, cramped between ship's hull and walls of a warehouse, was baking. Ranier fried in perspiration and impatience, waiting a word with this Nazi-moustached ship's purser who was tied up with red tape at the gangway's foot. The purser tried to speak bad French, and his prospective passengers were trying to speak bad German. Ranier gave the group a quick scrutiny.

The man of the party, French and elderly, stoop-shouldered in dark cutaway, pointed Vandyke beard and green sun glasses, was excitedly hunting for mislaid visas and demanding to know if German pursers thought Frenchmen were stowaways. The German was fussy about details. There were three women in the Frenchman's party, standing by in gloomy silence, all dressed in the sombre black of deep mourning, heavily veiled in tragedy, and the Frenchman wore the black arm-band of bereavement on his sleeve; but the ship's purser was a stickler for rules. Nobody could have escaped his eagle eye to stow away on board, tragic or no.

No, he finally found time to answer Ranier's question, there were no other new passengers embarking. Those who were going aboard were German tourists who had come on the cruise. *Ja*, all the tour people were now aboard, and so soon as he could straighten out difficulty with this Frenchman and his party, the only newcomers so far, the liner would sail.

"Man and three women," Ranier shook his head glumly at Dr. Eberhardt, waiting in the shadow of the godowns. "Only ones going aboard from here. Guess I've missed the turn. But there are other ports in Haiti, and the *Garde d'Haiti*, this morning, is watching every one."

"Cable pour m'sieu." A line official touched his arm.

Ranier ripped open the envelope, read sullenly, handed the missive to Professor Schlitz. The cable read:

> *Man Answering Your Description, Scar, Webbed foot, Sentenced Stale Prison Auburn, N.V. August 1922, Second Degree Murder Conviction, Killing in Utica, Under Name Gustaf Tropmann. Released Auburn January 1936.*

"There's your spider for you, Professor. Another murder, soon as he could reach New York from Haiti. Auburn Prison. So that's why he was delayed. Explains his pallor on the cruise, too. I took a long chance and wirelessed a friend of mine in the New York police. At first I thought he was a consumptive, remember? I—"

He choked on a smoking oath.

Watching him, Laïs Engles gasped, "What is the matter?"

He'd been going to ask the professor to recall how, on pointing out Haarman's pallor to Kavanaugh, the Irishman had stopped him on the syllable "con." Had Kavanaugh known Haarman to be a convict?

JOHN RANIER never voiced that speculation, or answered the girl's query. Brushing his three companions aside, he leapt away from the sheet-iron wharf-wall where they had been standing; went threshing across the pier like a small whirlwind, elbows going like pistons, boots kicking a path. Stevedores, porters, darkey dock wallopers struggled to make elbow-room. People saw the steely eyes, the purposeful jaws and ugly pallor of this man battling to reach the gangway, and trampled to get out of range. Somewhere sailors were yelling, the khaki *gendarmes* were running from the customs gate. Clamor broke loose in the sunshine.

The ship's purser, in voluable argument at the gangway's foot did not notice Ranier's approach, but the Frenchman with the parted Vandyke and smoked glasses saw him coming, whirled in spry alarm, cried out to the three veiled women.

Ranier punched with everything he had, uppercutting the man's neat beard a blow that tore it loose by the roots. *Crack!* Van Dyke and sun glasses went flying.

Everything whirligigged around him as his finger's found the man's throat and they locked together. He could hear himself squalling, "Kavanaugh! Kavanaugh!" while white faces shouted and boiled around them, police whistles shrilled, Germans bellowed down from the ship's upper decks, riot churned on the pier.

Kavanaugh's complexion was goose-color save where adhesive had peeled the skin from his jaws. His eyes squeezed shut and his tongue poked blue from his teeth. John Ranier would have choked him to death, gripping like a bulldog, if it hadn't thundered. Not exactly thunder. A gun jabbed under his arm went *Bonk!* The bullet scorched cloth under his armpit; hit the unmasked Irishman in the liver.

Kavanaugh died against him, and he had to fling the body off, leaping around just in time to catch a revolver by the barrel and deflect a second bullet into planking at his feet. Black cloth and a woman's funeral veil ripped in his clawing right hand; then he was waltzing furiously with a lady in black, an astonishing lady who breathed hoarse profanity on an odor of strong tobacco at his face, and kicked his shins like a soccer player.

With a violent wrench he wrested the gun from this enemy's grip; drove a knee into a corseted midriff; the astonishing widow went down, skirts tearing to the hip, exposing golf stockings and plus fours. Ranier removed hat and veil with a soccer-kick of his own, and Mr. Brown looked up at him with a dislocated grin and poping unconscious eyes.

Gendarmes were chasing a second black figure down the jetty. Afterwards he wondered whether she fainted or tripped on stretched hawser; but he saw her veil tear loose as she fell; saw that half-second glimpse of blowzy peroxide hair, shrieking baby-mouth, horrified goo-goo eyes; saw her plunge in a roil of pink underwear and skirts down between ship and pier.

An oily geyser spouted up the ship's side.

Somewhere Professor Schlitz was screaming, "Mish May! Mish May!"

Somewhere Laïs Engles screamed, "Look out!"

Another gun was banging; people were running past him, running from that third black figure in funeral weeds which was standing against a sheet-iron warehouse wall and firing indiscriminately at everything.

"Come and get it!"—*(Bang!)* "Come on, you dingy lugs, and get it!"—*(Bang-bang!)* "First guy that touches me is it!"—*(Bang-bang-bang!)*

It was strange. Strange to stand there frozen at that deserted gangway, staring at that black figure against the bright wall as if at the personification of death come to take him in broad daylight. A sort of magic had cleared the pier. In a twinkling the crowd had gone, the *douane* become deserted, the faces vanished from tier on tier of deck-rails in the ship's wall behind him. People were crouched behind cotton bales, salt bags, mounds of luggage, loading trucks, and he was left in the open like the Last Man, a dead Irishman and an unconscious fat man between himself and Death. Death waiting there in the sunshine, grotesque and clownish in appropriate mourning costume, black skirts, black veils, a tub-shaped black hat dowdily over the forehead. Death aiming an automatic pistol in one hairy big-knuckled hand.

"SO IT'S you?" Death was addressing him in a buttery chuckle. "Gummed the works for us after all, didn't you, doc? Well, I missed you last night in the fog, but I ain't gonna miss you this time."

A big paw cleared the veils before the eyes, and the Coolidge face looked humorous in its masquerade; eyes like merry carbuncles, jaws grinning a gorilla display of gold-plated teeth. The countenance of a Mack Truck decked in the feminine elegance of a Parisienne funeral-hearse, First Class. He winked at John Ranier over the levelled gun, his expression mischievous.

"I'm sorry," he said amiably, "because I kind of liked you, Doc." He paused to wipe suds from the corners of his lips. Said plaintively, "You hadn't oughta upset me just now when I'm a mass of nerves."

Ranier had a feeling of everything in suspended animation. His arm hung volitionless. There was a gun in that hand, but it would take a thousand years to aim and fire, and the gesture would mean suicide. Facing Mr. Coolidge in yellow sunlight, Mr. Coolidge like some huge urchin having fun in his aunt's bustle—facing that gold-toothed grin and hair-trigger gun, Ranier felt heavily depressed.

Everything, now, was over. Something inside him had finished.

Tomorrow he would be a bum ship's doctor dealing seasick pills and tomato juice to American tourists on an endless cruise. Tomorrow he'd be on his way from bar to bar, *aguardiente* to *aguardiente*, a little duller, a little grayer.

Funny, wasn't it? All night expended in an effort to prove there were no such phenomena as the "living" dead? He perceived he'd been chasing the wrong man. *He* was the *zombie*—

He said wryly, "I'm sorry, Mr. Coolidge, because I kind of liked you, too." Deliberately he raised the gun.

The revolver was heavy and his hand was slow. He could see his shabby cuff climbing past the lower buttons of his tunic. Years went by. When his wrist came even with the fourth button, the big man opposite him fired. Ranier heard the explosion, but he never saw the flash. Laïs Engles' scream was simultaneous with gun-roar, her movement fast as a shadow blown by wind. Like a shadow she was there, flying from obscurity near the gangway behind him to throw her arms about Ranier and bring him to his knees at the moment of Coolidge's shot.

Instantly the whole pier seemed to blow up. Fire flashed and banged from the liner's bridge, from the foredeck, from portholes under the deserted railings. Spurts of flame from behind bales and crates near the cargo booms, from luggage-stacks on the jetty, from doors in the *douane.* A blizzard of bullets raked across the pier, beating against the sheet-iron warehouse wall. Germans are invariably good marskmen, and the *Garde d'Haiti* once took second place with their Olympic Games rifle team.

When the smoke finally cleared, the sheet-iron wall looked like a sieve.

Mr. Coolidge was a mass of nerves.

John Ranier sat on the gangway holding a slim girl in nurse's costume in his arms, cursing a scarlet blotch spreading under her crumpled collar.

THE GONG was going *damn-damn-damn-damn* to voice his

thoughts, and the ambulance, hitting fifty, seemed to crawl. Somehow he drove Dr. Eberhardt, Professor Philemon Schlitz and a scared Negro interne to the front end of the swaying white compartment; then, outwardly cool, worked deftly with calm hands over the unconscious girl. By pretending this was Philadelphia, a traffic accident, he could ignore the white pain on her face and steady his touch.

"I've stopped the hemorrhage, Dr. Eberhardt. She's going to be okay."

"Gott sei dank!" the old man was wringing his dry sou'wester in dripping hands. "She will not—she will not die?"

Ranier gave him an upturned grin. "Not her. Bullets don't stop her kind. Bullets are for those rats back there on the pier."

Professor Schlitz burst out with: "But how did you recognishe them when you did? How did you know it was Misher Kavanaugh and—"

"The Mick put over his disguise all right," Ranier said. "Probably learned the art of make-up in prison shows at Auburn. They must've had those costumes in their luggage. But you can't change a habit overnight, even if you can change your face. Kavanaugh gave himself away. I recognized him when I saw him pull that habitual cocked-finger gesture of his at the ship's purser."

"The *Schweinhund!*" Dr. Eberhardt swore. "Dogs! They shot my little girl—my poor little girl—!"

John Ranier snarled, "Cheer yourself on this, Doctor. Think how those rats must've felt when they found Captain Friederich's mausoleum already opened when they got there—opened when the first gang of grave-robbers arrived. Hijacked, see?"

"What is that you say? What is that?" the old physician took his eyes from the unconscious girl; yelled.

"I say Marcelline and Brown, the grave-digging crew, found the tomb already opened when they got there from Bois Legone. Somebody'd beat them to it." Ranier lifted his voice above the ambulance gong. "Somebody'd been there ahead of them and rifled the coffin. Some job to explain to Kavanaugh, Coolidge and the blonde, when they arrived on the scene and wanted their share. I'll bet there was a row. But Kavanaugh and his gang never got those jewels at all."

"How do you know?" Professor Schlitz was half out of his leather seat. "How do you know those crooks didn't get the—"

"Because they didn't have the loot at the pier," Ranier told him. "I telephoned ahead to the *Garde d'Haiti* and told them to examine every last piece of baggage going aboard that German liner. That's what the argument was about at the gangway. But the pier officials didn't find the stuff at the customs gate, and told me so when we arrived at the pier. I thought I'd missed my guess. But—"

"But who got the jewels?" Dr. Eberhardt burst out. "Who robbed the mausoleum first?"

"A nice question," Ranier mocked a frown. "Kavanaugh, Coolidge and the dame didn't get them, and the grave-digging crew didn't get them. Must be someone else, then. Someone who guessed where they'd be from the way that game of Going to Jerusalem was progressing. Someone say, who didn't go from Morne Cuyamel to Bois Legone, but cut Bois Legone from the itinerary and jumped straight to that last cemetery on the list. Someone, say, who rode as far as the fork in the highway on the back of Kavanaugh's car, dropped off at the road fork and, maybe, picked up a stray horse. Then beat the grave-diggers to the mountain top, broke into the tomb with a shovel or pick such as might be left lying around; smashed the coffin and got the goods.

"YOU," RANIER switched the pronoun, "then circled back to Bois Legone; ducked the horse somewhere, and waited around in that graveyard, knowing I'd turn up and *you'd* have an alibi story as well as protection. Marcelline was sent back to get his Panama, but he was also sent back to get *you* and when—"

The thin man's leap did not take Ranier by surprise. Truly

and with ferocity he drove his fist to the man's boneless mouth, reducing Professor Schlitz to a heap on the ambulance floor.

John Ranier had never, in his surgical career, had so astounded an audience or worked so miraculous an operation. A gastroenterostomy that produced from under the prone man's vest an amazing viscera of precious stones, strings of amethyst, pearl necklaces, a diamond tiara, loops of azure light and vermillion brilliance, a handful of sapphires and a chain of topaz. Diadems, lockets, bracelets, brooches. Opals and three emeralds and moonstones. A tumor under the belt produced a flow of jade. Rubies were blood.

The ambulance was stopping under a vine-cooled arch, and Ranier saw the calm white facade of a quiet hospital. The professor could tell a pair of *gendarmes* leaning in the entry about his operation.

John Ranier straightened up to dump a million dollars worth of jewelry into Dr. Eberhardt's stunned lap. He was thinking of Wilde's comment on the price of everything and the value of nothing. Which was true in some cases, but not in the case of four million marks worth of jewels which the German government would pay plenty for; and not in this ambulance case.

He saw Laïs Engles was conscious, smiling gamely at him through white pain. He took her hand in his.

"You'll be all right," he promised gently, smiling down. "I'll have that piece of lead out of you before you know it, and I'm going to take care of you, myself. I've just done a million dollar job, and I'm appointing myself Dr. Eberhardt's new assistant. We'll start work rebuilding his hospital as soon as you're on your feet."

John Ranier knew he was grinning foolishly, unprofessionally, but he couldn't stop it. He'd found something worth doing, something he wanted to do. There was no such thing as a *zombie,* after all.

SERIES 7 INCLUDES:

* BRAND * TUTTLE * BECHDOLT *
HORN * MCCULLEY * ROSCOE *
* HALL & FLINT *
* BEYER * MCCALL *
* MONTGOMERY *

THE BEST FICTION FROM THE FRANK A. MUNSEY LINE

1. **GENIUS JONES** by Lester Dent
2. **WHEN TIGERS ARE HUNTING: THE COMPLETE ADVENTURES OF CORDIE, SOLDIER OF FORTUNE, VOLUME 1** by W. Wirt
3. **THE SWORDSMAN OF MARS** by Otis Adelbert Kline
4. **THE SHERLOCK OF SAGELAND: THE COMPLETE TALES OF SHERIFF HENRY, VOLUME 1** by W.C. Tuttle
5. **GONE NORTH** by Charles Alden Seltzer
6. **THE MASKED MASTER MIND** by George F. Worts
7. **BALATA** by Fred MacIsaac
8. **BRETWALDA** by Philip Ketchum
9. **DRAFT OF ETERNITY** by Victor Rousseau
10. **FOUR CORNERS, VOLUME 1** by Theodore Roscoe
11. **CHAMPION OF LOST CAUSES** by Max Brand
12. **THE SCARLET BLADE: THE RAKEHELLY ADVENTURES OF CLEVE AND D'ENTREVILLE, VOLUME 1** by Murray R. Montgomery
13. **DOAN AND CARSTAIRS: THEIR COMPLETE CASES** by Norbert Davis
14. **THE KING WHO CAME BACK** by Fred MacIsaac
15. **BLOOD RITUAL: THE ADVENTURES OF SCARLET AND BRADSHAW, VOLUME 1** by Theodore Roscoe
16. **THE CITY OF STOLEN LIVES: THE ADVENTURES OF PETER THE BRAZEN, VOLUME 1** by Loring Brent
17. **THE RADIO GUN-RUNNERS** by Ralph Milne Farley
18. **SABOTAGE** by Cleve F. Adams
19. **THE COMPLETE CABALISTIC CASES OF SEMI DUAL, THE OCCULT DETECTOR, VOLUME 2: 1912–13** by J.U. Giesy and Junius B. Smith
20. **SOUTH OF FIFTY-THREE** by Jack Bechdolt
21. **TARZAN AND THE JEWELS OF OPAR** by Edgar Rice Burroughs
22. **CLOVELLY** by Max Brand
23. **WAR LORD OF MANY SWORDSMEN: THE ADVENTURES OF NORCOSS, VOLUME 1** by W. Wirt
24. **ALIAS THE NIGHT WIND** by Varick Vanardy

25. **THE BLUE FIRE PEARL: THE COMPLETE ADVENTURES OF SINGAPORE SAMMY, VOLUME 1** by George F. Worts
26. **THE MOON POOL & THE CONQUEST OF THE MOON POOL** by Abraham Merritt
27. **THE GUN-BRAND** by James B. Hendryx
28. **JAN OF THE JUNGLE** by Otis Adelbert Kline
29. **MINIONS OF THE MOON** by William Grey Beyer
30. **DRINK WE DEEP** by Arthur Leo Zagat
31. **THE VENGEANCE OF THE WAH FU TONG: THE COMPLETE CASES OF JIGGER MASTERS, VOLUME 1** by Anthony M. Rud
32. **THE RUBY OF SURATAN SINGH: THE ADVENTURES OF SCARLET AND BRADSHAW, VOLUME 2** by Theodore Roscoe
33. **THE SHERIFF OF TONTO TOWN: THE COMPLETE TALES OF SHERIFF HENRY, VOLUME 2** by W.C. Tuttle
34. **THE DARKNESS AT WINDON MANOR** by Max Brand
35. **THE FLYING LEGION** by George Allan England
36. **THE GOLDEN CAT: THE ADVENTURES OF PETER THE BRAZEN, VOLUME 3** by Loring Brent
37. **THE RADIO MENACE** by Ralph Milne Farley
38. **THE APES OF DEVIL'S ISLAND** by John Cunningham
39. **THE OPPOSING VENUS: THE COMPLETE CABALISTIC CASES OF SEMI DUAL, THE OCCULT DETECTOR** by J.U. Giesy and Junius B. Smith
40. **THE EXPLOITS OF BEAU QUICKSILVER** by Florence M. Pettee
41. **ERIC OF THE STRONG HEART** by Victor Rousseau
42. **MURDER ON THE HIGH SEAS AND THE DIAMOND BULLET: THE COMPLETE CASES OF GILLIAN HAZELTINE** by George F. Worts
43. **THE WOMAN OF THE PYRAMID AND OTHER TALES: THE PERLEY POORE SHEEHAN OMNIBUS, VOLUME 1** by Perley Poore Sheehan
44. **A COLUMBUS OF SPACE AND THE MOON METAL: THE GARRETT P. SERVISS OMNIBUS, VOLUME 1** by Garrett P. Serviss
45. **THE BLACK TIDE: THE COMPLETE ADVENTURES OF BELLOW BILL WILLIAMS, VOLUME 1** by Ralph R. Perry
46. **THE NINE RED GODS DECIDE: THE COMPLETE ADVENTURES OF CORDIE, SOLDIER OF FORTUNE, VOLUME 2** by W. Wirt
47. **A GRAVE MUST BE DEEP!** by Theodore Roscoe

48. **THE AMERICAN** by Max Brand
49. **THE COMPLETE ADVENTURES OF KOYALA, VOLUME 1** by John Charles Beecham
50. **THE CULT MURDERS** by Alan Forsyth
51. **THE COMPLETE CASES OF THE MONGOOSE** by Johnston McCulley
52. **THE GIRL AND THE PEOPLE OF THE GOLDEN ATOM** by Ray Cummings
53. **THE GRAY DRAGON: THE ADVENTURES OF PETER THE BRAZEN, VOLUME 2** by Loring Brent
54. **THE GOLDEN CITY** by Ralph Milne Farley
55. **THE HOUSE OF INVISIBLE BONDAGE: THE COMPLETE CABALISTIC CASES OF SEMI DUAL, THE OCCULT DETECTOR** by J.U. Giesy and Junius B. Smith
56. **THE SCRAP OF LACE: THE COMPLETE CASES OF MADAME STOREY, VOLUME 1** by Hulbert Footner
57. **TOWER OF DEATH: THE ADVENTURES OF SCARLET AND BRADSHAW, VOLUME 3** by Theodore Roscoe
58. **THE DEVIL-TREE OF EL DORADO** by Frank Aubrey
59. **THE FIREBRAND: THE COMPLETE ADVENTURES OF TIZZO, VOLUME 1** by Max Brand
60. **MARCHING SANDS AND THE CARAVAN OF THE DEAD: THE HAROLD LAMB OMNIBUS** by Harold Lamb
61. **KINGDOM COME** by Martin McCall
62. **HENRY RIDES THE DANGER TRAIL: THE COMPLETE TALES OF SHERIFF HENRY, VOLUME 3** by W.C. Tuttle
63. **Z IS FOR ZOMBIE** by Theodore Roscoe
64. **THE BAIT AND THE TRAP: THE COMPLETE ADVENTURES OF TIZZO, VOLUME 2** by Max Brand
65. **MINIONS OF MARS** by William Gray Beyer
66. **SWORDS IN EXILE: THE RAKEHELLY ADVENTURES OF CLEVE AND D'ENTREVILLE, VOLUME 2** by Murray R. Montgomery
67. **MEN WITH NO MASTER: THE COMPLETE ADVENTURES OF ROBIN THE BOMBARDIER** by Roy de S. Horn
68. **THE TORCH** by Jack Bechdolt
69. **KING OF CHAOS AND OTHER ADVENTURES: THE JOHNSTON MCCULLEY OMNIBUS** by Johnston McCulley
70. **THE BLIND SPOT** by Austin Hall & Homer Eon Flint

www.ingramcontent.com/pod-product-compliance
Lightning Source LLC
Chambersburg PA
CBHW032212030726
47494CB00020B/985

* 9 7 8 1 6 1 8 2 7 4 4 7 2 *